JANET MARY TOMSON

THE JANUS FACE

Complete and Unabridged

ULVERSCROFT
Leicester

First published in Great Britain in 2000 by
Robert Hale Limited
London

First Large Print Edition
published 2001
by arrangement with
Robert Hale Limited
London

The moral right of the author has been asserted

British Library CIP Data

Tomson, Janet Mary
  The Janus face.—Large print ed.—
  Ulverscroft large print series: romance
  1. Inheritance and succession—Ireland—Fiction
  2. Ireland—History—18th century—Fiction
  3. Love stories
  4. Large type books
  I. Title
  823.9'14 [F]

  ISBN 0–7089–4438–8

Published by
F. A. Thorpe (Publishing)
Anstey, Leicestershire

Set by Words & Graphics Ltd.
Anstey, Leicestershire
Printed and bound in Great Britain by
T. J. International Ltd., Padstow, Cornwall

This book is printed on acid-free paper

The captain always made love twice, once to his wife and once to his mistress. He did so in that order because, he claimed, once his hunger was assuaged, the prospect of sleeping with his wife would not have aroused him whereas the thought of bedding his beautiful, sensual mistress at any time of the night or day, never failed to do so . . .

1

When I was eighteen my family moved from Dublin. My stepfather was rich and we never wanted for anything, at least not in the material sense. Sir Julius Richborowe owned land throughout Ireland and occasionally during my childhood he would take my mother and me, and my stepsister Clarissa to pay visits to his estates in County Meath or Kildare or Waterford. There we would spend a few, heavily chaperoned weeks getting to know a strange household and exploring the countryside.

Wherever we went I loved the great green emptiness, the mists and magic of new places, but always my pleasure was tempered by the icy watchfulness of my stepfather's tenants. Subservient, obsequious, I could still feel their hostility. They reminded me of Papa's hounds, grudgingly obedient yet always in their eyes you could see a hot, simmering anger. Like the dogs, if Papa was not there to whip them into obedience, I fancied that the tenants might fly at us and tear us to pieces.

Warmly wrapped in my English cloth, or cocooned in furs, or sporting lace-trimmed satin in summer, I wondered why the peasants did not buy new clothes, or move from the dark, poky middens they called home, that offered nothing in the way of comfort.

'Why do Papa's tenants not like us?' I asked my mother when I was quite small.

'Of course they like us. They respect Papa. They owe everything to him for he is their landlord. You must not say such wicked things.' Mama looked frightened and I stored away this curious piece of information along with those other, accumulated, puzzling questions that no one seemed willing to answer.

In contrast to his other visits, whenever Sir Julius travelled to County Cork he always left us behind. For this reason I was amazed when Mama announced that within the week we would be moving to Kilcreggan, his huge estate just outside of Cork itself.

'Why?' I asked, sensing that there was something that she was not telling me. We didn't talk about Cork, in the same way that we didn't talk about Papa's moods, his absences or the occasional black eyes that Mama sustained when he came home.

'Papa has business there. He may be away for some time and he wants us with him.'

I snorted my derision and Mama looked

pained. 'Karenza, please,' she begged. 'Don't cross Papa.'

I didn't say any more, but usually when Mama was pregnant, as she was again, she did not travel well which was presumably one reason why Sir Julius normally left us behind. So far none of her pregnancies had produced live children although she was hopeful that this time it would be different. Mostly I suspected that my stepfather travelled alone because he had no wish to spend more time in our company than he could avoid. This alone made the proposed visit to Kilcreggan mysterious.

These are not the sort of things you realize when you are a child. Such knowledge comes only gradually, a chance remark often made with the intention to hurt, or some snatch of conversation you were not meant to hear. It was in such a way that I learned about my father, my real father that is, Richard Ashburn.

In Dublin we had a fine house on Sackville Street, built in the latest style for, as I said, Sir Julius Richborowe, my stepfather, was truly wealthy. It was constructed of the best Dublin granite, several bays in width, with a large basement for the servants, tall sash windows, ornate iron grilles and high ceilings. No expense had been spared. Skilled imported craftsmen had moulded the elegant, sweeping staircase while the door handles and window catches gleamed opulently in the light from the German chandelier, my stepfather's talking point. English cabinet-makers furnished the house, and French and German porcelain graced the marble chimney pieces. Only the best damasks and calamancos covered the chairs and settles and *chaises-longues*.

Until now all of this had meant very little to me but soon I would be of an age to be present at the concerts and soirées that Sir Julius put on for the cream of Dublin Society. In the past when he was entertaining, I sometimes watched from the upstairs landing and witnessed the grudging admiration, overheard the fulsome praise for his good taste and I began to see the house in a new light. I heard him tell visitors that even the king himself had no better decoration.

In the first-floor sitting-room with its Florentine mirrors, gilded clocks and rugs from China, I would sometimes sit and look down across the broad avenue of trees known as Gardiner's Mall and on towards the Liffey. From our house, the river was not quite visible, but in my mind's eye I would imagine myself drifting down towards the open sea and on to some adventure with Barbary corsairs or Spanish grandees, or in truth, any escape that would free me from Sir Julius. This was one of his many complaints about me, that I had an unhealthy imagination, that I was too often idle and that I could only meet with a bad end. He made it his mission to beat my failings out of me.

By contrast, with Clarissa he was indulgent, seemingly blind to her physical imperfections, for in my view she was short and stubby and her cheeks had a permanently inflated look which made her sharp, piggy eyes seem even smaller. I saw, too, that he encouraged her in her spiteful treatment of the servants, her rudeness to my mother, not to mention the lies that she told about me: '*Papa, Karenza went out today, even though you forbad her to do so. She went to ride her pony.*' Perhaps it was because I was bright and healthy, not to mention that I was another man's child, that he hated me so. This was another thing that Mama and I did not discuss.

Not far away, forming a natural bulwark where our elegant neighbourhood gave way to the peasant hovels which in turn led to the gaols and hospitals and lunatic asylums of the old town, were the stables. Here, we kept a carriage and two fine, English-bred greys, plus Sir Julius's big bay hunter, Lisburn. The stables also housed my beloved pony, Shamrock.

Mama, who had herself grown up in the country had early on requested that I learn to ride and to our surprise, her husband had agreed. With hindsight I suspect that he hoped I might break my neck and relieve him of the burden, but in this, as in all else, I disappointed him, for though I say it myself, I am a fine horsewoman.

Thus, although I was supposed never to venture out alone, whenever I had the chance I escaped to the stables and if Abel Carter, our groom, was there then I could usually wheedle him into escorting me out to ride in the park. Abel had been with Mama's family since before I was born. He was utterly reliable and even she trusted him to look after me.

A few days after Mama announced the move to Kilcreggan, I paid one of my visits to the livery yard. It had been raining but the sun suddenly came out and I knew that like me, Shamrock would be in need of exercise. Sir Julius was away visiting Kilkenny and now that she was in the third month of her pregnancy, Mama spent much time in her chamber. Clarissa had gone to stay with friends, people of good breeding whom her father encouraged her to cultivate. Although the family also had a girl of my age, I was never invited which suited me well.

Usually when I reach the stable-yard, I poke my head in through the door of one of the stalls to check who is there, but for some reason on this morning I didn't. As I walked round towards the main door I heard Abel's voice, low and slow and conversational. The sound made me hesitate for a moment, wondering if it would be impolite to interrupt, then I remembered that a new stable lad was due to start that day. Before I actually reached the main door, however, I caught Abel's words.

' 'Course, the master married Missus for the land. When the old master died his estate was confiscated, but as his widow, the mistress was still entitled to a third. It was this that Sir Julius had his eye on. He was granted the rest of the estate by the king, but greedy like, he wanted it all. The other land to the north and west he simply took because it belonged to Catholics and they had no choice but to let him have it.' He gave a little grunt, adding, 'I know whenever he visits Kilcreggan he sleeps with a loaded pistol under his pillow. He can never sleep safe in his bed because one of these days the locals will surely get their revenge.'

In the silence I heard one of the horses

pawing the ground then Abel chiding him for wearing out his shoes. A moment later he took up his tale. 'First of all he tried to frighten Mistress off with tales of what might happen to her, but she had no reason to fear her Irish neighbours. When that failed he offered to buy her out and when she refused he did the only other thing he could and married her. That was the worst day's work she ever did, marrying him.'

My heart began to thump, partly from the revelations but also because I was afraid they might discover me. I couldn't decide whether to walk on in as if I hadn't heard, or to attempt a retreat and risk being noticed. Before I could do either, the other voice asked, 'What happened to the old master then?'

Abel sniffed. 'The captain? Well, he was a man and a half, I can tell you. Sadly he killed a fellow officer and was court-martialled. Some chance remark the man made over a woman.' He gave a little chuckle. 'What a man.'

People talk about stepping back in time and hearing Abel's tale, I felt as if I had suddenly gone back into history and was about to meet the father I had never known. I was caught up in the pain of his noble death, defending the honour of a lady. Anger against

8

my mother spilled over. How could she have betrayed his memory by marrying Sir Julius Richborowe?

I willed Abel to continue and tell the unseen listener what my father had been like. When he finished I would make myself known, introduce myself to the new boy as the daughter of the hero they had just been discussing.

I heard Abel pick up a broom and start to sweep the stalls. His conversation came in rhythmic bursts between each stroke of the brush.

'Captain Ashburn was found guilty of murder. On the night before the execution they offered him anything he wanted. 'An hour with my wife to say goodbye', he said, then, laughing in that boyish way he had, he added: 'Then a bottle of the best aquavit, a pipe of ripe tobacco and the company of my Orla until dawn'.'

'Orla?'

'Orla Kilbryde. His mistress.'

His mistress? My cheeks flamed with shock, the shock of my father's adultery, the shame of his betrayal. Holding my breath I began to creep backwards, step by stealthy step, my breath choking me, but I could still hear what was being said.

Abel's voice again, tinged with what?

9

Affection? Respect? He said, 'It must have been one of those God-given miracles. I don't know what else you'd call it. The master had been wed for two years and he had been with Orla nearly as long without any sign of a child and then that last night, the very last night before they killed him, both women fell.'

'You mean . . . ?'

'Aye, they both gave birth. What do you make of that?'

I didn't stay around to hear. It couldn't be true. It was malicious gossip, said to discredit my father. Abel was in the pay of Sir Julius and Sir Julius hated my papa. He would not allow his name to be mentioned in our house. It could not be true. But Abel hadn't sounded malicious. There was genuine affection in his voice, even admiration, and Mama always swore that he was a true servant.

I forgot about Shamrock, took little heed as to where I was heading. In any case I didn't care, anything, anywhere would do. A huge tidal wave of knowledge hurtled in my wake, intent on sucking me under, sweeping away the fragile footholds that until now had been my history.

I began to run, skittering ever faster until my lungs were bursting and I was forced to stop and take heed of my surroundings. This was a part of the city I did not know. Worse, it was a quarter haunted by unnamed dangers, hazards darkly hinted at, perils real, yet as insubstantial as the ghosts and evil spirits conjured up by our nursemaids Eibhlin and Aisleen to frighten Clarissa and me on stormy nights.

Gasping for breath I took in the unfamiliar terraces of gaudy brick houses that shut out the light, seeming to block my escape. Here was an alien architecture of curved gables and meaner streets, a place where foreigners lived, Dutchmen, French refugees, weavers and spinners with their fiercely partisan apprentices.

Fearfully I shrank into myself, fighting the urge to run from the invisible eyes watching my presence. I tried to think of nothing other than the route home, turning south and heading in the direction of the river.

In spite of my fears no one seemed to take any notice of me and as I approached Ormonde Quay, the way became increasingly crowded. An air of anticipation buzzed around the assembly, unspoken but almost tangible. I thought that I would walk along the quay and then take a turn back up to Sackville Street when I reached the bridge, but the approach soon became impassable. I tried to push my way forward but my path was dictated by the swaying of the crowd.

Little by little I edged closer.

From behind me a spearhead of watchmen began to force their way through, pushing the bystanders to left and right. Somehow I became caught up in their advance until suddenly the way was cleared and I found myself face to face with the reason for their intervention.

A vivid picture claimed my mind as I was swallowed up once more in the tales told to us by Eibhlin and Aisleen, Aisleen, her eyes flashing with the pleasure of our fear.

'Sure and tis a terrible thing to behold. Ye've never seen so much blood as when the Liberty Boys and the Butchers' Boys meet. Carnage it is, pure carnage.'

In my mind's eye I had seen it often enough for did she not tell the tale whenever she could, in all its grisly detail, of how the Liberty Boys, the fiercely Protestant apprentices, fought the mostly Catholic Butchers' Boys from the Ormonde Market? The skirmishes might last for days, closing the bridge until they eventually burned themselves out. In the meantime, if the Butchers' Boys were not cutting the tendons of the Liberty Boys' legs, then the Liberty Boys took revenge by hanging their opponents up with their own meat hooks where they swung and swayed, suspended by the skin of their jaws.

It was a horrible image. In the past, it had kept me awake. Now, as I surveyed the scene before me the awful vision became a reality as, like some huge, pendulous fruit, bodies rotated in the breeze. Vomit rose in my throat and I spewed and heaved where I stood, the light flashing from white to black as my head spun out of control.

'Quick, catch her.'

I was dimly aware of arms supporting me, leading me away.

'There's nothing to be afraid of. Let me help you, I'm a physician.' The voice came from a great distance and I tried hard to concentrate on what it was saying, to focus on the source of the sound. Hazily, a face formed before me, youngish, roundish. I grasped for the man as a lifeline out of the nightmare.

'Cut them down,' I begged. 'Their faces. Their poor faces.' At the thought of the vicious hooks I heaved again, gasping at the bruising emptiness of my stomach.

'Don't you be fretting now. It's only the Trinity Boys. There's no harm done. They're only hanging from their belts.'

I could hardly take the words in, hardly believe that what I had seen was a high-spirited prank played by the apprentices on that third group of tearaways, the students from Trinity College.

My rescuer held on to my arm and I took several deep breaths to calm myself.

'Where are you going?' he asked.

'Sackville Street. I must get home.'

He hesitated as if undecided what to do, then he said, 'Well, you go straight home now. I would come with you only there are a few cut heads back yonder and I ought to go and help.'

I nodded, partly reluctant to leave him yet anxious to get away from the throng. I turned to thank him but already he was nowhere to be seen, swallowed up by the meandering crowd. In a daze I drifted on, feeling alone and vulnerable again. Somehow I fought my way free of the mêlée and once I was sure I was clear of the crowd I stopped to get my bearings.

For a while I stood gazing out at the river traffic although I wasn't really seeing it. It was still difficult to breathe but gradually the rhythmic lapping of the oarsmen and the gentle tug of wind-filled sails on the water began to calm my heart.

Near the water's edge, work had started on clearing the site for a new custom house and among the rubble a ragged man and a dirty, barefoot woman were squabbling in Gaelic. The men labouring on the site stopped to watch the entertainment. The ragged man raised his hand to hit the woman and in response she kicked him on the shin, screaming abuse as she ran off, accompanied by a chorus of cheers from the labourers.

For a brief moment I was distracted but soon the thoughts were back, thoughts of the apprentice boys, of the physician whose name I did not know and, unwelcome as flood water, memories of Abel's conversation.

Scalding jealousy of the woman called Orla Kilbryde began to overwhelm me, distorting, tearing down the image of the father I had so carefully nursed all these years. And the child? Could there really be someone else out there who bore the name of Ashburn, perhaps doing so proudly, not like me, having to use the name of a man I hated — Karenza Richborowe — not a real person at all?

I became aware of the curious stares of bystanders. Young girls of good breeding do not go out alone and never down to the hustling cesspit of the Liffey. For a moment I was undecided as to what to do. The water glistened with a peculiarly brown tinge and the carcass of a dead dog floated by. My throat closed against the stench and I quickly turned away.

In our smart house on Sackville Street, everything was clean and sweet smelling, but as I stumbled my way back up the hill towards the place I called home, I knew that beneath the fine exteriors and the expensive fittings, the same filth lurked.

* * *

'What was my father like?'

I had been rehearsing the question ever since I got back to the house but I did not ask it until Mama descended from her afternoon rest to take tea. As she walked into the room the mantel clock struck four, a gentle, tinkling sound that seemed at odds with my turmoil. Although Mama had been resting for over an hour I thought that she looked drawn and listless. This made my task the more difficult for I was sure that I was going to upset her.

Outside, the sun of the morning had been short lived and a steady drizzle sapped the light. Keeping my back to her I began to light the candles, the flames flickering under my tense fingers. The heat from the hearth did little to stop my sudden trembling.

I tried to sound unconcerned, as if I was merely evincing a mild curiosity, but inside, my heart pumped as if an unseen hand was squeezing it like some half-deflated bladder.

Mama looked around quickly as if she feared to be overheard. Papa was not due back until the following day but he had a

16

habit of turning up unexpectedly as if hoping to catch her out in some misdeed. Invariably he criticized whatever he found.

As she sank wearily into a chair, I said, 'I want to know about him.' She did not respond so I added, 'Where did you live, when you were married to him?'

'Why are you asking this? Who have you been talking to?' She sounded increasingly distressed and I thought she might burst into tears. Her face had gone quite white and a sheen of cold sweat glistened on her nose.

'No one. I don't know what you mean.'

I watched as she worked her fingers, squeezing the ribbons on her bodice into a ball in much the same way as the unseen hand kneaded my heart. Drawing in her breath, she announced, 'Your father died before you were born. He left us in dire straits. I was alone, a foreigner in this country.'

I waited a respectful time before asking, 'Where did you live?'

'In County Cork. Your father was there with his regiment.'

Could it have been at Kilcreggan? Was this why Sir Julius never took us there? I could hardly contain my questions.

Calming herself, Mama began to explain,

not about my father but about the circumstances of the time. At her bosom the ribbon
was now a crumpled mess.

She said, 'After the Troubles, many young
Englishmen who had done military service in
Ireland were given property. The government
owed them wages and it was cheaper to pay
them in land. They were mostly second sons
like your papa, adventurers who knew how to
look after themselves and how to keep the
natives in order.' She paused and I thought
about Sir Julius's tenants and the way he kept
them in their place. I wondered if my father's
men had looked at him with such loathing.

Mama seemed to gain a little courage. She
said, 'We were wed in England but your
father insisted that I come here to join him. I
didn't want to leave my family but what else
could I do? Where we went to live it was a
god-forsaken place, not at all suitable for an
Englishwoman. I told him I wanted to go
home.' I watched her drift away from me into
the memory of those times.

'So what did you do?'

She made a visible effort to continue.
'Much of the land was hard to work and lots
of the young soldiers sold up, but they could
only pass their property on to other men like
themselves. I tried to persuade your father to
do the same but instead, he bought out his

18

neighbours and acquired even more land. He seemed to believe that he could make a success of it. He was quite determined to stay.' She faltered. 'Then . . . '

I kept very still, not wanting her to stop. After an eternity, she added, 'Then he got into trouble with his regiment.'

'What did he do?'

Her voice strangely flat, she announced, 'He challenged one of his fellow officers to a duel and killed the man. As your father was the one who issued the challenge he was charged with murder.'

'What was it they quarrelled about?'

'I don't know.'

I knew that she was lying but I didn't have the courage to confront her with what I had heard. Instead, I asked, 'What happened next?'

'After his . . . death, most of the estate was taken back by the government. The king granted it to Sir Julius. His Majesty holds Papa in high regard.'

As always she was trying to show my stepfather in a good light but I ignored the remark, asking, 'What about the rest of the land?'

'That was mine.'

'What happened to it?' I knew the answer but I wanted to hear it from her.

'Papa — your papa that is, had been friendly with the local people. Some people said he was soft with them but I think it was for his sake, in his memory, that they helped me as much as they could.' A wistful smile touched her lips as she murmured, 'Everybody thought that he was a hero.'

I caught a glimpse of the raw longing she was fighting to deny, saw in her face the loss of things past. I felt sure then that she had loved my father. She tilted her head slightly as if listening to an unseen questioner, then she said, 'Well, of course, they looked after their own interests first and foremost but they were still kind to me.'

'Why did you not stay on?' I didn't mean it to but it came out like an accusation. I would have stayed. If somebody left me land, I would work it and manage it and make myself independent so that I would never be beholden to a man in the way that Mama is dependent upon Sir Julius. Had she stuck it out then I would have helped her and one day I would be the one to inherit the property. The possibilities seemed endless. I felt angry with her for depriving me of my birthright.

Mama sighed. 'At first I thought perhaps I would stay. I heard rumours that there was trouble brewing but everything seemed calm in our neighbourhood. In the meantime, Sir

Julius had taken over the rest of the estate. He was so kind. He was concerned about me, being a solitary Englishwoman. He would not hear of me staying on alone.'

My hatred for him surfaced. 'Why did you marry him?'

She shrugged, her expression begging me not to voice my feelings. 'He was a widower with a young daughter; I was alone with a baby. It seemed the . . . sensible thing to do.'

'Was it?'

She looked away from me. 'It was the right thing to do. I'm sure I did what was best for all of us.'

'Did you love my father?' The very words threatened to unleash my feelings. I was afraid of her answer so I added, 'What about his family? Do I have aunts and uncles and cousins?' To myself I wondered: does she know about his betrayal? Does she know about the other child?

She was a long time considering my question. Just when I thought she wasn't going to answer, she said, 'He had an elder brother who inherited the Ashburn lands in England, in a place called Wiltshire.' She hesitated. 'The family never saw eye to eye with your papa. He was always something of a rebel. After we wed he never took me back there.'

21

Calmer now, more under control, I repeated, 'Did you love him?'

I could hear the excuses in her voice, the unspoken plea that I should not judge her. 'Richard was devilish handsome, brave, the sort of man to steal any young girl's heart, but he was wild. He was always chasing after something he couldn't achieve.' There was a catch in her voice as she added, 'If he had not died I think, sooner or later, I would have left him and returned to England.'

The thought shocked me. In my ideal world, women did not leave their husbands, especially handsome, dashing ones like my father, although I acknowledged that it would be different if they were greedy bullies like Sir Julius Richborowe.

I tried to imagine what my life would have been like if my father hadn't died. And what would have happened if Mama had left him? Presumably we would have lived with her parents in England. I have been to visit them several times. They are people of quality and I know that as their only grandchild, they would have made a fuss of me. As it is, I haven't seen them for years.

But what of my father? If he had lived, would I have come to Ireland to visit him? Rash, wild — he must surely have been the most exciting man. I know that he and I would have got on well. I saw myself riding out with him galloping our horses across the untamed expanse of his estate. Perhaps I would have chosen to leave Mama and come to live with him. By now I could have kept his table, run his household.

I felt sucked in by an almost exquisite longing but then I remembered Orla, his mistress. With Mama gone would he not have chosen to live with her? And with her child — my half-sister — or brother?

The questions came tumbling but I could not ask them. In any case, my moment's reverie had given Mama her chance and quickly she rang the bell, ordering hot chocolate to be brought up. As Maraid, our parlour maid, came in, Mama said to me, 'Don't let's stand around gossiping. We have a lot to do. We are leaving in three days and you must think about what to take with you. Take everything you need because we may be gone for some time.'

I wanted to grasp the nettle, and ask her if Kilcreggan was where she had lived before, with my father, but she was giving Maraid orders to draw the heavy drapes, to put away her sewing silks and to stoke up the fire. I knew then that I had missed my chance and that the conversation was definitely at an end.

2

I think God must have been angry when he created Ireland. Oh, he started off well enough, moulding the thickly wooded mountains and lush pasturelands that face across the Irish Sea, but as his journey carried him further south and west, something must have happened to upset him.

Maybe he ran short of material. As I surveyed the rocks and bogs that grew more frequent on our journey towards County Cork, it seemed to me that the Creator had grown increasingly mean, sprinkling the soil ever more thinly so that only the sparsest of grass, the most stunted of trees, managed to find a foothold. In a moment of anger, He must have positively hurled the huge boulders up from the ocean as if possessed by some great rage.

Perhaps He was angry with the men who came here, trying to carve a living from the barren wastes. On the one hand He gave them an abundance of fish to eat and peat for their fires, but on the other He denied them soil rich enough to prosper. Perhaps the old, heathen Irish fared well enough with their cattle and their wandering ways, but for those others like my father who tried to farm the land, there could be little comfort. No wonder Ireland is such a troubled place.

This was one of many thoughts that kept me occupied as we set out on the journey to Kilcreggan. Mama, Clarissa and I travelled in the carriage, while Papa rode ahead on Lisburn, his hunter. Once we left the confines of Dublin, the already inadequate roads descended into little more than ill-defined tracks. Although it was raining I thought that Papa was the lucky one. I would rather be wet and mounted than dry and jolted like butter in a churn.

Trailing behind, two sturdy Irish ponies pulled sleds on which some of our household goods were strapped while two other pack horses stumbled under the weight of yet more domestic essentials. Abel Carter followed the carriage, riding Shamrock.

Inside, Mama endured the rocketing with stoical silence while Clarissa whined and whimpered until I could have scratched her pudgy cheeks. I was in two minds as to whether to suggest that Abel should ride inside so that I could escape to the peace of Shamrock's broad back. At the thought of Clarissa's outraged expression if I were to suggest that a groom came to join her, I

25

couldn't help but smile.

Our journey took two days. Since our conversation of that afternoon in Sackville Street, Mama had not referred to Kilcreggan but it was never out of my thoughts.

'Have you ever been there?' I asked Clarissa. She was two years older than me and I wondered if she had any memory of the place. Perhaps she had been born somewhere nearby. Perhaps this was where her mother had died soon after giving birth. Poor woman, the prospect of Sir Julius and this disgruntled offspring must have been too much for her.

'How much further?' Clarissa ignored my question.

'Not far.' Mama looked very pale. All this jolting could not be good for her. I felt a rush of anger with Sir Julius for subjecting her to this. He paid lip service to wanting an heir but did little to ensure my mother's wellbeing.

But then I remembered where we were going. This was surely where my father had lived and died and I had been born — or was it? There was so much that I did not know.

We stopped briefly to eat the meats and bread that the servants had packed for us. We all drank wine to warm us. Sir Julius did not bother to dismount but stood by the carriage, helping himself to food through the window which could be raised up and down with the aid of a leather strap.

'Drink up quickly now. You can eat as you travel.' He shoved a great lump of mutton into his mouth, leaving gobs of fat on his greying and usually immaculate whiskers. The gauntlets he wore had gems embedded in the soft leather and over his stylish riding cape he wrapped himself in a second, silver-skinned cloak made from the fur of martens. By contrast, the men leading the ponies, with their bare hands and inadequate leather jerkins, looked frozen to the core.

I gazed out towards the murky west. Darkness would come early and we had no wish to spend a second night on the road. We moved off again and I tried to look out of the window, but when I opened it Clarissa complained of the draught.

'Do you wish to kill me?'

I didn't think I had better tell her the truth so I said nothing.

It was already dusk and I must have lapsed into a doze because all at once I felt everyone around me begin to rouse themselves.

'Are we nearly there?'

'Down that way, in the valley.'

Ignoring Clarissa I opened the window again and leaned out. There was nothing to see, only trees and a narrow ribbon of a track. I felt immersed in excitement, then without warning, the woods gave way to a wide tumbling valley and there, nestling in the natural fold of the land was the outline of an imposing house.

'Look!'

'That,' said my mother, clutching her cloak about her, 'is Kilcreggan.'

★　★　★

The house was way beyond my imagining. I had expected something compact yet formal, but from a distance it represented a sprawling, ancient mass. Later I learned that it had over a hundred rooms but for the moment, trying to take in every detail, I could not believe that this solid, castellated fortress belonged to our family. The long narrow windows seemed to watch our approach in much the same way as I stared back.

The evening was windless and the air hung heavy with moisture that seemed to hover over the landscape. Everywhere there was the feeling of abandonment, of neglect. Bushes twisted in a tormented attempt to reach the light, weeds trailed wantonly across what was once a driveway. The ghost of once formal gardens still left an insubstantial impression on the rain-soaked ground.

As we drew closer, I could see that lights burned in some of the rooms. By contrast the rest of the house looked black and unfathomable. Sir Julius trotted ahead, giving Lisburn an undeserved thwack with his crop. The horse snorted and tucked in his rump but did not retaliate.

The servants must have heard us coming, or perhaps a lookout had espied us long before but as we pulled up in front of the porchway, the door opened and a gaggle of people came out to greet us. From round about others emerged from paths through the undergrowth to take the horses and begin the business of unloading our goods.

'Sir Julius. It's good to see you, sir, so it is.'

I guessed the man who welcomed us was the bailiff. Sir Julius had many tenants and his day-to-day business was conducted locally on his behalf. The man removed his cap and stood bare-headed in the semi-darkness. I couldn't make him out clearly but he looked sturdy, weather worn and from his speech he was Irish, perhaps a convert to our faith for Sir Julius would never trust a Catholic to act on his behalf. He had dark hair and the blue of his eyes was reflected even in the half light.

My stepfather did not respond, merely threw Lisburn's reins in the man's direction

29

and strode towards the house. A straggle of maids bobbed uncertain curtseys as he reached the front door.

Abel dismounted and handed Shamrock over to a groom with the warning, 'I shall be coming to see in a minute.' I knew that he would ensure that the animals were well cared for.

Meanwhile he was the one to hand Mama from the carriage and take her arm to guide her to the house. After the depredations of the journey her limbs were stiff and she clung to him like an elderly woman.

A young girl, probably about my own age, waited for Clarissa and me to descend. She bobbed a hesitant greeting.

'Well, take my hand!' Clarissa barked at her and made a business of getting down the step and arranging her skirts. A gust of wind from nowhere tugged at her bonnet and she gripped it tightly, pushing the maid out of the way. I followed behind, declining the young girl's help but giving her a smile of thanks.

As we walked into Kilcreggan House, I had the feeling of entering a cavern, bordered as we were on all sides by ancient, roughly hewn stone. A huge fireplace occupied the centre of one wall and a mixture of wood and imported coal threw out a welcoming combination of heat and light to meet us.

Ahead was a fine heavy staircase, blackened with years of smoke from the hall, and leading up to the family rooms. From ground level the kitchen and service rooms and servants' quarters spread out in three directions.

Mama had reached the top of the stairs and Clarissa and I followed behind.

'I'm Sorcha, your personal maid, ma'am.' A pretty young woman with that delicate combination of pale skin, even paler-blue eyes, and fine black hair greeted her. Her cheeks flushed as she bowed graciously in front of Mama. I saw Papa watching them, his eyes on the girl. I did not like what I saw. His gaze made me uneasy. My heart went out to Sorcha in the way that I felt pity for the deer Sir Julius liked to chase about his estate at Meath, driving them on to exhaustion only to take pleasure in their destruction. Beware, Sorcha, beware!

As we made our way along a corridor, an army of paintings partially hid the panelled wooden walls. I caught a glimpse of portraits, men and women in costumes from the time of Queen Elizabeth to our own King George. There were hunting scenes and several views of the house. In the distance I could hear the chink of crockery, the echoing buzz of activity from below stairs.

One by one we were escorted to our chambers. Mine, I was delighted to find, was mine alone. There was to be no sharing with Clarissa. I could hear the echo of her voice in my head: *Karenza, blow out that candle, I cannot sleep with its glare. Karenza, I must have a night light. I must have the windows open, closed, the fire alight, the blaze extinguished.* A dozen other complaints rang through my thoughts. Thank goodness I would be spared all that.

Like the hallway, my room was panelled. Ancient fur rugs of wolf and fox and rabbit covered the floor. Other skins had been sewn together and lined with wool to provide an old-fashioned bed cover beneath which sheets in local linen appeared to have been laundered and aired and pressed, for which I was grateful. A peat fire burned in a tiny grate but the damp was still discernible in the air.

Having prodded the mattress and held my hands out to the blaze I explored the rest of the room. A panelled cupboard stretched the length of one wall and cautiously I opened the door to see what was inside. It was empty.

Any further explorations were interrupted by a knock at the door and, in answer to my call, the girl who had handed us from the carriage poked a timid head into the room.

'Himself says you're to come at once to have supper.'

'Thank you.' I followed her back into the corridor looking about me as I went. Opening a door for me, she gave another curtsey and scurried away.

As I stepped inside I felt as if I had gone back in time. Whoever had built this castle, perhaps 200 years ago, had had aspirations to embrace the knightly path. As with the hall, the room was positively cavernous, the high walls draped with banners and tapestries. Ancient helmets and spears criss-crossed between the wall hangings. Way up above, the ceiling arched like a cathedral, supported by oak beams that had started life in the mists of time. It was magnificent.

Fires burned in both fireplace and braziers and along the centre of the room a long oak table was set out with delicate china that bore the Rowborowe crest. Along with the elaborate silver candlesticks, the tableware looked incongruous in this setting. Papa had imported fine English chairs with legs as spindly as those of a thoroughbred. They seemed positively ephemeral in contrast to the heavy settles and benches and the table itself.

'You are late. Take your seat.'

I did so, aware that Clarissa was glancing at

me with her superior smirk. To Papa's right, Mama was seated, looking tense and tired.

We ate in near silence, the meal served by two male attendants. I could sense that Papa was in a bad mood and I kept my eyes lowered, giving him no excuse to find fault.

'Karenza, do not slurp your food.'

'I beg your pardon, Papa.'

Once he had eaten he seemed to thaw a little. One of the servants poured him a third or fourth goblet of wine and he sat back and spread his legs, looking us over to get our attention.

'Right. Tomorrow I shall be riding into Cork. I have business there. You will all make it your business to check up on the household. I want a complete list of everything in the house that is not acceptable. The place is slovenly, a disgrace. I shall be hiring a man to design a new house then this monstrosity can be pulled down.'

I felt a jolt of shock. Surely he could not mean it? He continued, 'Any laziness on the part of the staff and the offender is to be dismissed. On the spot. Before I leave I shall call them together and spell out what I expect.'

I thought of the poor souls who depended on this house, this estate for their very existence but I said nothing.

Rising from the table, Papa said, 'Make sure that you are thorough. If you are not then I shall find out. I want a firm hand here in all things.' I saw Clarissa square her shoulders savouring the prospect and my dislike for her deepened.

In spite of these feelings, the journey had made me tired and that night I slept well. Next morning, as soon as I was certain that Sir Julius had left, I dressed and prepared to explore. For the moment it was not raining so I decided to take Shamrock and ride around the grounds, nothing too strenuous for he would be tired after his long journey, but a little light walking would do him no harm. First though, I must call and see Mama.

I was sorry to find that she was still abed. As I walked into her chamber she was sitting up under the great canopy of the half tester, surrounded by bolsters, her face taking on the yellowish sheen of the linen.

'Karenza, are you well?' Even her voice sounded tired.

'Very well, Mama; yourself?'

She gave a tiny shrug as if anything more energetic was beyond her. 'Such a tiring journey but I shall be well enough if I rest today. Papa has agreed that I shall stay in bed. While he is away, you and Clarissa can begin to set things in order.'

'This old place . . . ' I wanted to convey to her the dignity of the house, to express my respect for it and ask Mama to intercede with her husband to protect it, but before I could find the words, she said, 'Sir Julius is really displeased with the way things are here. It is so old and unfashionable.' From her tone I knew that it would be useless to say more.

Again I wondered if this was where she had lived with my father and if so, how she could bear to let this interloper destroy it. I looked across to the bed. She had closed her eyes and was dwarfed amidst the bolsters.

Had Sir Julius come to her last night? When he was at home his visits to her were nightly. Quickly I pushed the thought aside. I was about to confess to my plans for the morning then I thought better of it. What she didn't know couldn't worry her. As quietly as I could I crept towards the door so as not to disturb her. I gathered my cloak, hat and gloves from my room and escaped.

I had no trouble in finding the stables. Abel was in the yard talking to one of the grooms. As soon as he saw me the conversation stopped and he turned towards me.

'Good morning, Miss Karenza. I trust you are rested.'

'Thank you, I am.'

'*Dia dhuit.*' The other groom greeted me in

Gaelic and, although I understood, I replied in English. Papa does not approve of us encouraging the Gaelic language, a great pity for I find it mysterious and exciting and have taken the trouble to learn some of its mysteries. However, best to start off as I would need to continue.

To Abel, I said, 'I thought I would take Shamrock for a walk, just around the grounds.'

He looked unhappy. 'I don't think you should ride alone. We are strangers here. There has been trouble in the district, local men stirring up ill feeling over land rights. Perhaps I should come with you.'

I was about to object then I stopped myself. Perhaps, just perhaps, I would find a way of asking him what he knew about my father.

As soon as the horses were tacked up we rode across the yard, away from the house, through a gate in the wall and down towards a coppice of trees. The watery haze of last night had cleared but the ground beneath our horses' hooves was soft and uneven. Here and there small, brown, thick-coated cows, the property of various tenants, clustered in twos and threes amid stunted oaks, watching our approach. Ahead, the valley swept on down, drawing us into it as if by magic. We had gone perhaps half a mile when above us on the rocky incline I saw a young child guarding about half a dozen sheep. He or she — I could not tell which from the tangled hair and grimy rags that bundled a too thin body — stared at us with the same shuttered look of the cows. Already in the child's eyes I could see the beginnings of the familiar rage.

'How much land does Sir Julius have here?' I asked.

'Nigh on a thousand acres I believe. Some of it is demesne land, cultivated on his behalf by the tenants, much is rented out to the tenant farmers themselves.' He paused a moment to guide his horse around a boulder which blocked the path before continuing. 'Some have big enough holdings to make a go of it but many have just an acre or two, poor land only good enough to grow potatoes.'

At the thought of the poorer tenants, I felt the familiar unease, not wanting to be faced with their wretchedness. It seemed so unfair that Sir Julius should own all this, and yet he came here hardly at all whereas the people who depended on it for their very lives, had nothing that they could call their own.

'Are there many tenants?' I asked.

'Around a hundred or so I believe.'

'Who owned the land before Sir Julius?'

I thought I detected a hesitation before

38

Abel said, 'I couldn't rightly say. Perhaps you should ask your Mama.'

I think he knew that he had made a mistake even as he spoke. I did not let it pass. 'Why my mama?' I asked. Before he could think of an answer, I said, 'She owned it, didn't she, after her husband died?'

'She's told you, then.'

'I . . . found out.'

Abel shrugged. I swallowed hard and forced the next words out. 'I know, too, about my father's mistress.'

He didn't reply. Like Pandora I had opened a box and let out all kind of ills. What would happen now?

Abel drew to a halt. He did not look round and his voice was low and serious. 'A warning, missy. Don't ever, ever, repeat such things. Not in front of your mother. Never in front of your father.' The force of his words filled me with fear.

Shakily I said, 'He's not my father.'

'Be that as it may, he has all the power of a father.'

'But none of the love.' I felt afraid and tearful but I had to carry on. We had ridden for about another half a mile and I had noticed very little. Now we reached another gate in the continuous stone wall. Across the other side the land seemed to dip away ever

39

more steeply, rocky and tumbling.

'Is this the boundary of the estate?' I asked, to calm myself.

'It is.'

'And over there?'

'The village of Killimagree. That belongs to Sir Julius too, most of it.' He stopped as if to turn back but there was something in his manner that made me suspect he did not want me to go on.

'What sort of people live in the village?'

'No one that you would want to meet.'

'Not my father's mistress?'

'Miss Richborowe!'

'Ashburn. My name is Ashburn.'

He seemed at a loss for words. Turning his horse so that it was across my path, he said, 'People around here have long memories. They do not forgive easily. There is no one, no one, around here whom you should meet. Now, let us ride back.'

I was about to demand that he move out of my way. He had no authority to stop me, but he said, 'Have you no thought for your pony? He is tired. He should go no further today.'

To this I had no answer. Retaining all the dignity I could manage, I turned Shamrock and began the journey back the way we had come. I knew that at the first opportunity I must visit Killimagree. Alone.

3

My chance to leave the estate again did not come for over a week but, in the meantime, I discovered several interesting things.

It seemed that the reason for our move to Kilcreggan was twofold. First and foremost, Sir Julius had become involved in a scheme to develop a linen works. This he planned to do in conjunction with several other local landowners.

Although much of the land was poor, there were large swathes which would be suitable for the cultivation of flax. True, at the moment these were rented out to local men who struggled to make a livelihood with their crops and cattle but this it seemed, was only a minor inconvenience.

As Sir Julius explained to us at supper on his return from Cork, 'As soon as the flax is in production there will be plenty of work for all. Men women and children will have as much work as they can manage, what with the cultivation, the preparation, and spinning. Every cottage within miles can be fully occupied if they are willing to work hard.'

'Will they want to give up the land?' I

asked. If Sir Julius took control of it then the local people would have no right of tenure at all.

Sir Julius's eyebrows shot up. 'Want?'

I felt my face grow hot under his scrutiny. Leaning towards me, his voice low and chilling, he said, 'You seem to forget: this is my land. I shall decide to what use it will be put.'

In spite of his tone, I stood my ground. 'But what will the tenants eat in the time before the flax is grown but after their crops have all gone? Where will they graze their cattle?'

He glared at me. 'That is not your concern, madam.'

I expected some kind of punishment for daring to question him but for once the cloud of his disapproval disappeared quickly. Things were going well. He was in a good humour and did not order me to my room.

As the pudding was served, I thought of the child I had seen in the valley guarding the sheep, of the owners of the cows I had passed on my ride with Abel, and of the families who laboriously tilled the poor soil. What small independence they clung to was about to be swept aside. I remembered Abel's conversation with the new stable boy in Dublin. Sir Julius already slept with a pistol under his pillow. This latest scheme could only lead to further trouble.

While we all listened, Sir Julius expanded on a plan he had to bring in skilled weavers from the Continent, then to construct a canal that would take the linen cloth down to the River Lee and right into Cork. From there it would be shipped onward to the lucrative markets in England. There was also a growing market across the Atlantic in Pennsylvania but before he could take advantage of that, something would have to be done about the law which prevented direct trading between Ireland and the colonies. Sir Julius who had a seat in the Irish Parliament had been vociferous in his criticism.

In order to protect his interests, twice a year he went to England. By dint of much expenditure of time, of fulsome flattery and by lending the king money which would never be repaid, he usually succeeded in extracting some concession over matters that concerned him. I guessed that the question of direct trade with the colonies would be one of his missions on his next visit.

The second reason for our move to Kilcreggan it seemed, was to make the closer acquaintance of the Monroe family. Sir Fulton Monroe was a Scottish peer. Like my own father, his land had been given by the king, not to him personally but to one of his forbears who had served King Charles I well at the time of the Civil War. Charles II, aware of the value in having devout Protestants in all places of authority, had ordered the reward. The king had been generous and in spite of a hiccough when King James came to the throne, Sir Fulton had built upon that opportunity with great success.

Sir Fulton was father to an only son, twenty-five and unmarried. Apart from having extensive Scottish holdings, the Monroe lands in County Cork bordered the Kilcreggan estate on two sides. Sir Fulton was a potential partner in the linen project and a joining of the two families would be of great benefit to both. Clarissa, my shrewish, unprepossessing stepsister was to be the means of this association and it was apparently agreed that she should meet the boy before their betrothal was announced.

'How do you feel?' I tried to imagine what it must be like, about to be united with someone you had never seen. A few days before, a miniature had been delivered for Clarissa's approval. It showed a long-faced, rather sallow young man, laced and bewigged, powdered and silk clad. To my mind he looked weak and weedy. His mouth had a petulant thrust that even the skills of the artist had failed to make attractive.

Clarissa shrugged in that dismissive way of hers. 'He is rich,' she said, as if that answered everything.

Cavendish Monroe had been away in England at the University of Oxford and then touring in France and Italy. Once the wedding was arranged, there were plans to send him and Clarissa back to Europe for an extended visit before they set about raising a new dynasty of Richborowe — Monroes.

I knew that Sir Julius was rich but Sir Fulton, it seemed, was positively opulent. My stepfather was investing a huge amount in this marriage in the hope of further gain later on. Solicitors had already been to the house to discuss the details of Clarissa's dowry. Mama had made timid suggestions about a suitable wardrobe for her stepdaughter's journey. There were even plans to buy the young couple their own house in Dublin.

Until now the thought of marriage had not really interested me. Looking at my stepsister, two years my senior, for the first time I wondered if some similar fate might not be planned for me, nothing on this scale of course, but doubtless I would have some value in the marriage market. I was assailed by a sudden rush of resentment knowing that I would have little say in the planning of my future. How could that be right? Meanwhile, Cavendish Monroe and his parents, Sir Fulton and Lady Elizabeth, were to dine with us the following evening.

The Monroes arrived in a very dashing carriage drawn by two striking sorrel horses. It must have taken a great deal of time and money to find two such beautiful animals, not only in terms of size and colouring but in the details of matching blazes, white socks and black points. Eamon Shaughnessy, the bailiff, was there to open the carriage door and lower the step so that Sir Fulton and Lady Elizabeth could descend. Special matting had been put out in the courtyard to protect their shoes as they took the few steps from the coach to the front door.

I watched the arrival from the alcove above the entrance way. The family appeared to be dressed as if for some court occasion, a masque perhaps, the coats of the men and Lady Elizabeth's gown in matching plum-coloured velvet.

Sir Fulton was huge in height and with a girth the size of a well-fed bull. By contrast his legs were spindly, their gangly length emphasized by the tightness of his white breeches, the elegance of his narrow, jewel-encrusted slippers. Lady Elizabeth looked like a miniature version of her husband, as if they were some particular breed that could be identified by its conformation.

A moment later the prospective bridegroom came into view and I realized immediately that the portrait painter had used all his skill in presenting an acceptable likeness of this broomstick of a man. Certainly if he was part of a litter then he would have been drowned at birth as a runt. Could these two round parents have produced such a twig?

At that moment, Mama came along the corridor. 'Karenza, what are you thinking of? Come down immediately, our guests are here.'

I followed her down to find that Sir Julius and Clarissa were ready to receive the visitors. As we hurried in, Sir Julius turned and gave us a thunderous glare, hissing, 'You're late!' His head swung back to greet the arrivals and his expression changed in one smooth grimace.

'Sir Fulton, dear Lady Elizabeth, welcome to our most humble residence!' Sir Julius was fulsome in his apologies for the shortcomings of the house. I longed to come to its defence but thought better of it. If ever I were to voice my feelings it would give my stepfather even greater pleasure in destroying something I already held dear.

We were all introduced, Sir Fulton pressing flaccid lips against our hands as he peered with interest down at our bosoms. Lady Elizabeth appeared to feel that she was doing us a great honour in acknowledging our existence.

'And Lord Cavendish, this is my daughter, Clarissa.' My stepfather smiled smugly as he swept my stepsister forward like a magician producing a rabbit from a hat.

'Most awfully pleathed to make your aquaintanth.' It was a few moments before I realized that Cavendish had deliberately adopted the disconcerting fashion of speaking with a lisp, that and pronouncing his rs like ws, so that when Sir Julius remarked on the weather, Cavendish observed, 'You're quite wight, it's waining.'

I glanced at Clarissa to gauge her reaction but she seemed unmoved. Back like a ramrod she gently inclined her head as her shortly-to-be-fiancé rambled on about his travels, extolling the 'Wonders of Wome' and his visits to 'Fwance' with the 'Fine bwidges over the Wiver Theine.' I wondered how I would maintain a serious expression through-out the evening.

Venison, partridge, pork and beef were on the menu. Again Papa could not apologize enough for the simple fare, explaining that

48

the staff at Kilcreggan were really no more than *'ignorant peasants'* and that the Monroes must certainly come to Dublin where he would lay on a *'banquet fit for a king — or for Lady Elizabeth!'*

I had been to the kitchens earlier in the day and seen how hard everyone had worked, how hard they had tried to make this meal a success. Secretly I hoped that Sir Julius would overeat and die of an apoplexy!

At last we ladies were able to withdraw to leave the men to more serious matters. I breathed a sigh of relief but I had forgotten that we would be burdened with Lady Elizabeth.

'Do you find your time at Richmond Park pleasing?' Mama was trying hard. Richmond Park was the name the Monroes had bequeathed to their neighbouring estate.

'One finds a singular lack of society.' Lady Elizabeth's Scottish origins were evident in her voice. She looked around the room as if thinking of buying it and deciding against it.

Bravely, Mama replied, 'It would please me greatly should you wish to visit at any time. Perhaps we could discuss Clarissa's trousseau.'

'I hardly think there is much point in discussing it here. It must surely all be ordered in England — that is assuming that

49

you ever go to England?'

Mama looked flustered. I said, 'Papa goes twice a year but he always leaves us behind.'

Mama gave me a horrified look as if she feared that Lady Elizabeth might repeat my calumny. Quickly, she added, 'I am in a certain condition and Sir Julius is naturally anxious about my health.'

Lady Elizabeth looked bored. Turning to Clarissa, she asked, 'Do you play piquet?'

'I do, ma'am.' Clarissa gave a rare, rather alarming, smile which appeared to enchant Lady Elizabeth and the older woman drew her aside and began a low-voiced conversation which left Mama and I to our own devices.

When the men joined us they seemed to be in a good humour. Papa was positively jovial. 'I am pleased to announce that everything is arranged. Sir Fulton and his family are leaving the district in a few days but I think my beautiful daughter has made a sufficiently favourable impression upon young Cavendish.'

'Heah heah!' Cavendish gave Clarissa an exaggerated bow and Lady Elizabeth crowed with delight.

My stepfather puffed his chest out like a turkey cock. 'Then we should drink a toast to the young couple.' While we voiced our congratulations he rang the bell and the maid, Sorcha came in answer to his summons.

'Champagne!'

She nodded without meeting his eyes and hurried from the room.

My stepfather's cheeks were bright red and his eyes had a slightly unfocused look. For the moment he was genial but I had seen him like this before. Once the excitement was over, once the guests had gone, his mood was quite likely to swing from jolly to vicious with alarming rapidity. I glanced across at Mama and noticed how tense she looked, how hard she was trying to maintain a calm, welcoming façade.

Lady Elizabeth called Cavendish to her. Taking his arm and Clarissa's, she drew them both closer as if to confirm their proposed union. Papa and Sir Fulton wandered across to the window, continuing some conversation that had occupied them over the port. Mama stood close to the fireplace, unconcerned that the heat might redden her skin, holding the mantelshelf as if to give herself support. I knew that she longed to sit down but dared not do so unless her husband gave the signal. I turned my head in the direction of Sir Julius, hoping that I might catch his eye so that I could point out to him Mama's distress

51

but he ignored me. Only his conversation with Sir Fulton drifted across to me.

'You'd be best advised to seek a legal means,' Sir Fulton was counselling. 'There must be something. After all, they're Catholics, aren't they? Apart from the other business, there must be a way to get them out lawfully.'

'I hope so. That land is ideal for flax. Besides, the homestead stands bang in the way between your land and mine. I want it gone.' He stood fulminating for a moment then added, 'In any case, their very presence here is an affront to my wife.'

'Does she know who they are?'

'I've never mentioned it to her. People round here know better than to discuss it.'

Sir Fulton sighed expansively. 'Patience, dear fellow. You will get your wish sooner or later. There are always means and ways.'

At that moment the girl returned with the champagne and I was left to reflect upon what Sir Julius was up to, who he was planning to destroy. The mention of my mother in this connection had me thinking the impossible. Surely he did not mean the Kilbrydes?

'Splendid!' Papa took Lady Elizabeth's arm and insisted that she come to sit next to him. 'Soon we will be related, and I am indeed the

52

fortunate one.' He flirted with her and she bridled like a young filly. Mama had flopped gratefully into a chair and I went to stand close to her.

The cork popped, the liquid was poured and Sorcha came round with a tray, serving the ladies first as she had been instructed. She came to my stepfather last.

Until that moment he had been paying little attention but now, as he reached to take the glass, he stiffened. 'What's this?' His colour darkened and his already unsteady hands began to shake.

'Sir?' Sorcha looked at him with frightened eyes.

'This? These are not champagne glasses. Where are the proper glasses?'

'I — ' She looked at a loss.

Mama said, 'Julius, I'm sure our guests will understand . . . '

'Understand? What do we employ these people for if they can't do a damned thing right — begging your pardon, dear lady.' He took Lady Elizabeth's hand and kissed it, still breathing heavily with outrage.

Sorcha was frozen to the spot, not knowing what to do. Surprisingly, Sir Fulton came to the rescue. 'Don't fret yourself, my dear man. We have the same trouble. These Irish are pig ignorant. Pig ignorant. It is the burden we have to bear. Many's the time I have resorted to the cane to try and beat some civilization into them but all to no avail.'

Sorcha gave a little choking sob. I wanted to comfort her but to do so would only make matters worse. 'Nice champagne,' I said instead. No one took any notice.

For a moment we were all like actors in a tableau, holding our breath and waiting, then Papa let out a long-suffering sigh. 'You're right. You can't expect intelligence from this scum.' Reaching out he grabbed Sorcha's arm and pulled her roughly towards him. He lowered his voice and spoke close to her ear, his body touching hers. Pushing her away, he added, 'Get out.' She let out a little whimper and bowed her head as she scuttled away. Sir Julius puffed out his chest and grinned at Sir Fulton. 'I'll deal with her later.'

★   ★   ★

As the door closed behind the departing guests, Sir Julius turned with the self-satisfied smirk of a man who feels he has done well for himself. Without a word he returned to the drawing-room and poured himself a brandy. Mama, Clarissa and I trailed after him.

'Well done, my pet.' He called Clarissa to him and put his arm around her shoulders.

54

Her lips twitched into a grimace resembling his and I was reminded of the drawings a child does with half circles representing smiling mouths. Their expressions had as much depth.

Papa looked restless. Moving from Clarissa he drained the glass and poured a second measure. He announced, 'Change of plan. Clarissa must go to England to prepare for the wedding.'

'When will it be?' Mama asked the question.

'In the spring. In the meantime, we will return to Dublin. I want to consult my lawyer there and you can start making the wedding preparations.'

'Where will the wedding be?' I asked.

'In London. I think that is fitting. We'll take a house somewhere suitable. Clarissa needs time to become acquainted with the right people. There is much planning to be done. It might even be appropriate to invite His Majesty to the ceremony.'

I could see him positively expanding with the prospects. At the same time I sensed Mama's fears. She wasn't well. By then her pregnancy would be well advanced. The journey would be too much for her. In my view the scale of this wedding was already getting out of hand. I controlled the urge to say anything by imagining that with luck the Monroe carriage would meet with an accident on the way home, perhaps go off the road and the hapless occupants sink into the bogs, never to be seen again.

Papa was looking at Mama and I saw his expression alter, become more hawk-like. He said, 'You'll have to do something with yourself. You looked quite dowdy this evening compared with Lady Elizabeth. I won't have you letting me down.'

'Julius . . . '

I don't know what Mama intended to say but he forestalled her with a sudden jerk of his head. 'Don't start giving me excuses. If it was your daughter, your brat about to make a suitable match you'd be rushing to spend my money.'

'I don't want to get married.' I glared at him, immediately regretting that I had not held my tongue, but it had the desired effect of turning him away from Mama.

He came towards me. 'Oh, don't you? What makes you think anyone would have you anyway? You don't have a penny to your name, only what I, out of the goodness of my heart, choose to give you. So don't. Take. That. Tone. With. Me.' Each word was punctuated with a poke in the shoulder. I resisted the urge to tell him that my mother's parents would see to my needs and tried not to meet his eyes. He began to pace the room, restless, looking for some outlet for his rising aggression.

'You're jealous. Both of you. You're jealous of my daughter.'

'Julius, of course we aren't. We are really pleased that Clarissa has made such a good match.' Mama's voice was appeasing, vibrating with barely concealed fear. When he did not respond, she asked, 'When would you like us to leave?'

'In a few days.' He was barely mollified.

Mama said, 'Would you excuse me if I retired? I am feeling rather exhausted.'

'You'll go when I tell you to.'

She and I stood still while Clarissa sank on to the sofa and smoothed the folds of her gown. 'Whom shall I have for attendants?' she asked.

'Whom would you like, my poppet?'

She began to name friends. I was not among them. The fire was burning low and Papa rang the bell. After a moment Sorcha came in, her eyes downcast. She seemed to be trying to make herself invisible.

'The fire.' Papa flung himself down beside his daughter. I watched him following Sorcha with his eyes. Sitting upright he said, 'When you have done that you can escort your mistress to her room and after you have finished you will bring me up a night-cap.' Sorcha seemed to shrink even smaller as if she truly wished to disappear.

At his cue, Mama gathered up her things and bent to kiss his cheek. 'Goodnight, dear.'

He jerked his head away impatiently, saying, 'Don't keep the girl too long. I am about to retire myself.' With a great show of leniency, he announced, 'If she behaves herself, shows herself willing to learn how to behave properly in a gentleman's house then I may be prepared to overlook that foolish embarrassment of this evening.'

His eyes were already undressing the girl and there was no mistaking his meaning.

We all retired to our separate rooms. Clarissa and I had chambers in the west wing of the house while Mama and Papa were located in the east. Having said our goodnights, I went into my room only I did not undress. As soon as I was sure that Papa had retired to his chamber I left mine and crept back down to the drawing-room.

I sat on the sofa to wait but this made me nervous so I went to the window and pressed my face close in a vain attempt to see outside. Inside, the glass was damp with condensation and outside runnels of rain trickled patterns

58

across the pane. Beyond it was a black morass.

The drawing-room door opened and Sorcha came in, a picture of anxiety. She jumped when she saw me. I said, 'You finish up in here and I will take Sir Julius his night-cap.'

I saw the fear fall away from her. Her entire body seemed to throw off invisible bonds. 'Thank you, Miss Karenza.'

Since the first day I had set eyes upon her she had reminded me of someone and at that moment I realized who it was. 'Are you related to Eamon Shaughnessy, the bailiff?'

'He's my father, ma'am.'

I had an idea. I said, 'Your father didn't look too well earlier. Perhaps you should check on him before you retire.'

'Thank you, I will.' She gave a jerky little bob and fetched me a tray with a glass and a bottle of brandy.

'Would this be the right glass?'

'It is.' I smiled at her. 'Goodnight.'

Leaving the room I made my way to Papa's chamber. I was more than a little nervous. In thwarting his plans I might be making things worse, but I didn't know what else to do. Anything seemed better than leaving Sorcha to his mercy without at least trying to help.

Summoning all my courage I knocked on

his bedroom door.

'Come!'

I opened the door and stepped inside. He was already in bed, a stripy night-cap on his shaven head, his wig upon the stand nearby.

'Right, come over here.' For the first time he looked up and seeing me his eyes grew first wide and then narrowed with spite. 'What are you doing here?'

'Good evening, Papa.' I tried to be at my most cheerful, a dutiful daughter concerned for his comfort. The glass on the tray was trembling so I quickly put it down on the bedside table. Before he could ask, I said, 'I'm afraid Sorcha's father isn't well, so I sent her to attend to him and offered to bring this up for you.'

There was nothing that he could say. I could see the impotent rage in his eyes. For a moment I wondered if he would give way to his anger. No one would intervene if he chose to punish me. No one would even ask what I had done to incur his wrath. Standing beside his bed was the most lonely place on earth. Like facing a viper, any movement, any change of expression might cause him to strike.

'Get out!' The words came out sharp and clipped. Eternally thankful, I curtseyed to him and backed towards the door. Only as I turned the knob behind me did I release my own fear, breaking into a run to get away from it and not stopping until I was in my chamber and under the covers, safe from the ogres of the night.

4

For the next few days Sir Julius spent much of his time on business in Cork for now that our stay was being cut short he had to conclude his affairs quickly. At the same time the weather turned colder, the wind coming from the east and accompanied by prolonged and vicious spells of rain. In the circumstances I could think of no convincing reason to leave the house. Meanwhile the time was ticking by. Soon we would be returning to Dublin and I had learned nothing of the village nor found a way to establish if Orla Kilbryde and her mysterious child really did live close by. I decided that I must make some tentative enquiries and the only place I could think of to start, was the kitchen. Therefore, after breakfast on the third morning following the Monroe visit, I made my way there.

'As Lady Richborowe is indisposed, perhaps I should visit Killimagree and take any supplies that might be needed to the poor,' I suggested to Maraid Doneally, the cook. Maraid was a scrawny woman of uncertain years. Widowed, as far as I knew landless, she still had that determined grip on life that ill fortune alone cannot loose. Visiting the poor was what we had done in Waterford and Meath, suitably chaperoned, of course, by several of Papa's workers. I pointed this out to her, adding, 'Surely the tenants will expect it?'

Maraid's answer was blunt. 'Don't you be thinking of going there, missy. T'would be a mad thing for you to be doing.'

Was she saying that the people were dangerous? I asked: 'Does your family live in the village?'

'Indeed they do, but it's no place for a — ' She hesitated, lamely adding, 'For a young lady of quality.'

'Why? What do you think would happen if I went there?'

At that moment Eamon Shaughnessy came in, blowing on his fingers to instil some warmth into them. She threw him a warning glance. 'The young mistress here is concerned about the villagers, but I've been telling her it's no place to be visiting.'

'And right you are too.' He added force to the cook's pronouncement, helping himself to a bowl of tea and a lump of still warm bread before moving to the fireplace for comfort. I watched him ease the stiffness of his back and thought that indeed he did look unwell.

'Sit you down,' I suggested. He hesitated as

if sitting in my presence was not the thing to do but when I insisted, he perched himself on a stool close to the blaze. I returned to my subject. 'Surely the people wouldn't harm me? They must know that if anything bad befell me then Lord Richborowe would punish them severely. Besides, if I know what they need, I may be able to help them.'

Eamon shrugged. 'The villagers expect nothing of Sir Julius. In any case, there are always those who might act without thought as to the consequences. Desperate people will do desperate things, you know.' He looked embarrassed.

'What are they desperate about?'

'Just things.'

'Like what?'

He glanced at Maraid and she stepped in. 'Well, as an example, Padraic O'Connell died just last month. He was a good man, Padraic, hard working, had his own land, about twenty acres, which is a rare thing for one of the old faith these days. He had five sons. The four youngest have long since moved away to make their own future, there being little enough round here. Only Ciaron, the eldest boy, stayed behind to help his father. By rights, now Padraic is dead, the land should go to him. Padraic even made a will leaving Ciaron the land but they are both Catholics.

If Ciaron wants to claim it then he will have to deny his religion, otherwise the land will be split into five parts and shared between all the sons. That's the law. Not one part of the land is rich enough to support a family.'

She sniffed, wiping the back of a floury hand across her nose and then thumping her dough with concentration. Her voice low, she added, 'Meanwhile certain persons are making a claim to it. As Protestants they can take any land they choose by what they're calling 'Discovery'. In my book, that means theft.' She glanced quickly at me and I knew that she meant my stepfather but before I could comment she said, 'Anyway, Ciaron is so angry he makes threats.' She paused in her pastry-making, giving a long sigh. 'I'm begging your pardon, missy if this upsets you. I shouldn't be talking like this but — but there are others, too, who have their grievances.'

I had no answer. In the end I could only repeat, 'But surely they would not hurt me?'

I wandered around, making a trail of floury footsteps across the stone slabs, trying to see into the big iron pot that hung over the trivet, comforted by the heat thrown out into the room, and waiting for Eamon to go so that I could return to the subject. When at last he heaved himself reluctantly up from the fireside and went back outside, I decided that I had nothing to lose. I asked Maraid outright, 'Is there a family nearby called Kilbryde?'

She shot me a glance then looked quickly back at her pastry. 'Aye. There are Kilbrydes around here to be sure.'

I didn't know what to say. I didn't know how much the villagers were aware of. For all I knew they might know a lot only they were unlikely to admit to anything that embarrassed their landlord. Lamely, I offered, 'I know a family called Kilbryde in Dublin. I believe they have relatives in this area.'

'I doubt if it would be Riari.'

'Riari?'

'Riari Kilbryde. He and his mother have Otters Lough, a place down the valley.'

'They own it?'

She shrugged. 'As far as I know it belongs to some Protestant Irishman, but he seems to have given it to the Kilbrydes. I don't know the details.' From her expression I guessed that she knew all the details.

I fought to appear calm. Riari Kilbryde. Could this be my brother?

I asked, 'How old is this Riari?'

'About your age I should guess.'

Just as I was fishing around for something to say, anything to cover my confusion,

Maraid said, 'They'll not be anything to your friends though, missy. They — they're wild people. That Riari's a law unto himself. There's nothing he's not capable of.'

Wild. Like my father? I could hardly contain myself. I asked, 'What's the mother called?'

'Orla Kilbryde. Never been wed. A fallen woman and no mistake.' Maraid sniffed her disapproval. 'They'll not be the people you're looking for.'

I didn't ask any more. Somehow I found an excuse to leave the kitchen and raced up to my chamber, bumping into Clarissa on the way. I tried to move past her but she blocked my path. She said, 'How much have you done towards drawing up the list that Papa wants?'

I bit back the urge to say 'Nothing,' telling her instead, 'I've just been down to the kitchens.'

'Where are you going now?'

'Out. I'll check the outside.'

'In this weather? I'll tell Papa!' Her words were lost as I slammed my chamber door and struggled into my riding habit. Going out like this in the full knowledge of the household was madness but I didn't care.

Outside there was a steady, stinging rain. Within minutes I would be soaked. I made a dash for the stables, praying that Abel would not be there. To my relief, he wasn't, only Seamus, the Irish groom I had met earlier.

'*Dia dhuit.*' I spoke to him in Gaelic and he looked pleasantly surprised. I asked, 'Please will you saddle up my pony. I have a short errand to run.'

He merely bowed his head. He did not know me and had no reason, no authority or indeed even interest in questioning the wisdom of my riding out alone. I fretted with impatience as he brushed Shamrock down and fetched his tack with the slow, measured pace of a countryman. At last he led the pony into the yard and helped me to mount.

'It's monstrous wet,' he observed.

'I'll not be long.'

I pushed Shamrock straight into a canter. He seemed to pick up my mood because immediately he was fighting for his head, glad to escape the confines of the stable. As soon as we were out of view of the house I slowed him down. The ground was uneven and slippery and I had no wish to fall. In spite of the keen wind I felt warm, partly from the energetic ride, mostly from the exciting thoughts that raced in my blood. Today at last, I might meet the brother I had never known and the mysterious woman who had stolen my father's heart.

That it should be a brother seemed

somehow less painful. Although my father had not known either of us I could hardly bear the thought that another girl like myself, should have had a right to his name — except that she would be a bastard. With shame I felt glad, although in my heart I knew that it did not really diminish her in any way. Such prejudice was foolish, illogical but I could not help but draw comfort from it. Whatever the circumstances, I alone had a right to my father's name.

Shamrock tossed and jogged. We were riding into the wind and I had to push him hard to stop him from turning around. He did not know the countryside, he did not like the stinging rain. Every leaf, every shadow made him snort and threaten to gallop off.

I avoided the track that led down to Killimagree village heading instead straight on up the valley where Sir Julius had implied to Sir Fulton that the house of his unwelcome neighbours stood and where Maraid had also indicated that Otters Lough was to be found. The village lay down to my left and on the other side of the hill to my right was Monroe land. I had to concentrate on the ride, picking my way around boulders, splashing through peat-tinged streams, negotiating tussocks of dying wiry grass and padded mounds of sphagnum moss. When at last I paused to look about me I saw ahead a low, white house above which a plume of smoke wavered in the damp air. 'Come on,' I said to Shamrock. 'We're nearly there.'

We had only gone a few more yards and I was totally preoccupied with what I was going to do, whatever I was going to say, when I heard a shout. 'Hey, you! What the divil are ye doing down there?'

I stopped dead and looked about me. Higher up the valley a single figure was riding towards me. I hesitated, unsure whether to go in his direction or to turn back but before I could do either, the shaggy pony on which he was mounted began to slither down towards us. 'Don't!' he shouted. 'Don't in the name of Heaven go any further!'

My heart beginning to thump, I steeled myself for his approach. He was so heavily wrapped in furs that I could hardly make him out, except that he was certainly a local man, a native Irishman. I began to feel uneasy.

When he was a few yards away he slipped from his mount and began to scramble his way towards us on foot. 'Don't be moving, now.'

'I — ' Carefully he reached out and grabbed Shamrock's bridle, pushing him back a few paces and turning him away from where we had been going.

'How dare you! What do you think you're doing?'

'Saving your life. Are ye completely mad, riding out here when you don't know what you're about?'

Before I could answer, he said, 'Another few steps and you'd have been in the bog. In places there's no bottom to it. You and himself here would have been over your ears in minutes.'

The cold hit me then, not only through the dripping riding habit that was now limp and heavy on my body, sucking in the cold wind, but at the sudden shocking knowledge that we might have died out here, alone and undiscovered. As if picking up my thoughts, he said, 'They would never have found you, never have known your going.'

For the first time I really looked at him, what I could see of him, swathed as he was in a fur cap, a thick fur jerkin and the familiar woollen Irish shawl across his shoulders. He was young, thin-faced, and there was something about his expression that suggested he was used to taking knocks from the world but would die rather than show that he minded. His slim, well-shaped mouth turned down at the corners as if he found the world and everything in it a cause for cynical amusement. Strands of thick black hair were

71

plastered to his forehead and across his hollow cheeks. His eyes, light blue and black fringed, searched my face as he in turn studied me.

With the knowledge of who he might be, my world seemed to jolt, tilting crazily as if everything I had known before was somehow suddenly askew. 'Is that your land over there?' I asked.

'Sure and why wouldn't it be?'

I held my breath, faced with a revelation.

He caught his pony and leaped effortlessly onto his back. He did not have a saddle but a thick woollen cloth was fastened over the animal by means of a plaited girth.

'And who might you be?' He began to clamber back up the valley side, driving his pony forward with his heels and leading Shamrock as if I was some child rider.

Should I say: I am your half sister, I didn't know that you existed until a few weeks ago. I am pleased to make your acquaintance?

In reality I knew that I was in no state to cope with his response. Some sixth sense stepped in. Aloud, I said, 'I am Miss Richborowe. We own Kilcreggan.'

Technically that was now my name, for upon his marriage to my mother Sir Julius had legally made me his daughter although usually I am at pains to let people know that he is not my father. In this isolated place with this unknown stranger, this alien Irishman who might possibly be my brother, I felt it wise to hide behind my stepfather's power and standing.

'Are you now?' He looked round at me with interest. 'So you're the daughter.' He pulled a quizzical face and the sight of his half-amused, half-cynical grin set my heart beating faster.

'You're Riari Kilbryde,' I said.

'I am.' He looked surprised. 'Have they been talking to you about me? Have they warned you what a divil I am?' He suddenly grinned, transforming his expression to one of boyish good humour. 'Are you lost or something? Whatever else brings you up here on such a morning? I can't believe you came especially to see me.'

I wondered what he would say if he knew that was exactly the reason. I didn't know how to respond. We were back on the path and Riari hesitated, glancing down at the house a few hundred yards further along the valley. 'Did you want to warm yourself and get dry, or had I best escort you home?'

I didn't know what to say. I couldn't go back without seeing Orla Kilbryde, but being alone with this man, in these extreme circumstances, felt dangerous. My mother would surely die if she knew the truth.

'Is your mother there?' I asked.

'She is.' He raised an eyebrow. 'Are you afraid of being alone with me?'

'No, I — ' I couldn't tell him how much I wanted to see her, that I wanted to find out what it was about her that had lured my father away from my mother and into her arms.

He shrugged and made his own decision. 'Come on. We'll ride back to the house and get you something warm to put round you, then I'll be taking you home.'

Now that the decision was made I tried to claw back some of my dignity. 'There's no need for you to lead me. I can ride perfectly well.'

He shrugged. I'm sure you can, but keep to the path or I'll not be responsible for you.' He let Shamrock go and began to trot ahead, seemingly oblivious to the ruts and hollows that abounded along the track. I knew that it was a challenge and I would not let him win. I squeezed Shamrock on, keeping pace with him.

As we came up to the farmhouse I was surprised by its size, by the good condition of the thatch and the recently whitewashed walls. That the stone was thick I could see by the depth of the window recesses and the breadth of the doorway. Now that we were close I could also see that the cottage had been added on to an existing building and behind Otters Lough were the partly ruined remains of a fortification, nothing large and rambling like Kilcreggan, but a solid, much older place that still provided outhouses and barns and stabling for the farm. For a moment, fascination with the house distracted me from the momentous meeting to come.

Riari held out his hand to help me dismount. He raised a challenging eyebrow as I hesitated. Pretending indifference I grasped his fingers and slid to the ground then he took both ponies and led them through a stone archway around to the back. There, he shut them both in separate stalls. I followed behind, the pressure of his grip leaving an impression in my palm.

'Come on then, come and get yourself warmed now.'

My head was swimming and I felt utterly out of control. Here I was in a different world, one that had occupied my waking moments ever since the overheard conversation between Abel and the new stable boy. Now my imaginings were about to be made flesh. Riari opened the cottage door and went ahead, nodding to someone inside.

'You're back soon . . . ' A woman surfaced from the gloom on the far side of the fire. When she saw me she stopped, waiting for an explanation. Without taking her eyes from me she asked her son, 'And who might this be?'

I could only stare at her. Somewhere in my thoughts were angry words, the truth I should tell her about what she had done, how she had betrayed my mother, how she was no better than a whore. But I said nothing.

I don't know what I had expected — someone old, for was she not from a time before I was born? True, my mother was not old but she had lost her youth, perhaps lost hope. I thought of Mama as staid, ageless, hardly in terms of a woman at all. In contrast Orla Kilbryde, pulling her shawl closer about her shoulders, was slim and tall and never would you forget what she was. Her hair was loose and clean and tumbled in burnished black-brown waves about her shoulders. Unlike her son's, her eyes were gypsy dark, her features strong. Her bosom was thrust firmly against the wool of her shawl, which she held in place with slim though work-worn hands. Her tight grip emphasized the neatness of her waist, the gentle curve of her hips, her straight, proud back. She was beautiful.

I deduced rather than heard Riari introduce me. My rank, the name of my supposed
father did not appear to impress her, neither
did it seem to rouse in her any sort of
hostility. Instead she said, 'Come along in,
girlie. Ye'll catch your death. Over to the fire
now and quickly.' I must have looked shocked
or ill for she guided me towards the
welcoming peat, pushing me down onto a
wooden stool. I was so close that the wool of
my riding habit began to steam. To Riari she
said, 'Give me that cloth there,' and when he
did so, she proceeded to towel my hair and
hands dry.

'Something to warm her?' Riari asked. His
mother gave him a look that questioned the
wisdom of his suggestion but gave a barely
discernible nod and moments later he
brought me a wooden bowl which contained
a colourless liquid. She said, 'Drink this down
now, it will put blood back into your veins.'

I took a gulp, choking as the harsh liquid
scalded my throat. 'Steady girl, sip it.'

For a moment I wondered if they were
trying to poison me, but already I could feel
the drink heating its way down into my belly
and along my limbs. It was life-giving.

Orla asked, 'You're from Kilcreggan House
are you not? What ever are you doing so far
from home? And alone too.' She tutted, a

77

maternal noise, and for a moment I was enchanted by the sound of her voice, her very presence.

As I sat close to the fire, Riari spoke to her in Gaelic. He did not glance in my direction, but I knew that he was talking about me and I picked up the gist of what he was saying although it did not make sense.

'You remember what I said, about the daughter, about what we should do? Well, should we not take advantage of the chance? Now? There'll never be a better time.'

Orla shook her head, glancing at me to see if I understood. I feigned ignorance. She said, 'You cannot. You are unprepared. Besides, I want no part of it. That way surely leads to disaster.'

I held my hands out to the fire, pretending to be indifferent to their conversation, hoping that it might begin to make sense. Unease stirred in my mind. Surely they could not be planning to kill me? Riari made an impatient gesture and Orla said, 'She is not what I expected. One would have thought the old man's spawn would be as offensive as he is.' I realized then that they thought I was Clarissa.

At that moment a dog began to bark, a fierce warning sound that tells of the approach of strangers. Riari went to the window and peered out. He gave a snort of displeasure and hurried to the door, stepping outside. Orla Kilbryde in turn moved across to the window and I followed her. What I saw made my heart jump. Riding into the yard were three men, Abel Carter, Seamus the groom — and Sir Julius.

As I watched, my stepfather dismounted and went to push Riari out of his way but he stood his ground. Their voices were loud enough to be heard. 'Get off my land. You are not invited here. What is it that you want?'

'Where is she? What have you done with her you Irish . . . ' With surprising agility, Sir Julius wrong-footed Riari, stepped swiftly aside and strode towards the cottage, flinging the door wide. With a dramatic outstretching of his hand, he called to me, 'Where are you, girl? What has he done to you?'

Any explanation froze inside of me. Wordlessly I handed Orla back the empty bowl. Sir Julius looked at it. 'What filth have you been filling her with — you and your disgusting spells!'

'Papa, I got lost,' I started.

'Lost? What do you mean by leaving the house unaccompanied?' I saw the naked anger in his eyes, then as if remembering where he was, he said, 'Thank God that you are safe.' He nodded towards Seamus, adding, 'If this man here had not had the sense to tell me we might never have found you.'

'I'm sorry.' Among the myriad feelings that bombarded me was the fear that I had brought trouble to the Kilbrydes, that and the humiliation of being chastized in front of them.

'There's no harm done.' Orla spoke up calmly and Sir Julius threw her a vicious look.

'No harm? This girl is compromised. If ever it became known that she had been alone with . . . ' He could think of nothing bad enough to describe them and I saw Riari begin to bristle.

Fearing disaster, I said quickly, 'I think we should thank Mr Kilbryde for saving my life. I nearly rode into the bog.'

Sir Julius silently fumed. All the time he was looking around the cottage. There was something avaricious in his expression as if he was assessing its worth to him.

Abel and Seamus stood uncomfortably in the doorway. From their manner I guessed that while they would do whatever their master asked of them, their loyalties were being torn between the man who gave them a living, and their own kind, simple labouring men who lived and worked this land.

Riari said, 'I'll fetch your daughter's pony.'

'You do that.'

As soon as he was out of the room, Sir Julius turned viciously towards Orla. 'You heathen whore! Did you think to gain some advantage over me? Well, let me tell you, the time will come sooner than you think when you and your bastard will be off this land!'

'Papa!' I could not stand by and listen. I said, 'It is all my fault. I lost my way. Mistress Kilbryde has been kind to me.'

Sir Julius swung round, the force of his anger now directed at me. 'Mistress Kilbryde? I think it's time you learned the truth about Mistress Kilbryde. Just you wait till I get you home. You'll be sorry you ever left the house. You'll be sorry you ever came here.'

'Leave her!'

Abel had gone outside to take charge of the horses and Riari walked back into the house. In his hand he held a heavy club, the head gnarled and polished into a hard, vicious-looking weapon. As he stood there he thumped it meaningfully into the palm of his hand. Walking around Sir Julius, he said, 'She may be your daughter but that gives you no right to ill use her.'

I gave him a warning look, begging him to desist, knowing that it would only make matters worse. Riari said, 'If you want to vent your rage on someone then come on outside.' Pointedly he threw the shillelagh aside and stepped back, spreading his arm to invite Papa to precede him through the door.

I saw my stepfather hesitate. He was out of condition. This young man, my half-brother, was fit, hard, used to harshness. Sir Julius was soft, in the habit of letting others fight his battles.

I took my chance. 'Papa, I am truly sorry for causing you this worry, but the weather is getting worse. Should we not be getting back?'

He glanced at me, assessing the wisdom of what I said. To Riari, he barked, 'Keep away from my family or it will be the worse for you.'

'Nothing will give me greater pleasure.'

I quickly made for the door, throwing Orla a grateful look. I did not even glance at Riari, not wanting to give Papa any reason to renew his attack. Inside I felt thoroughly humiliated. Outside it was raining heavily. Silently Abel helped me to mount and then held Lisburn still while Sir Julius struggled into the saddle. With a vicious thwack of his crop he hit the horse hard across the rump and set off back up the valley, taking the path that Riari had shown me. In silence the rest of us rode behind, waiting for the storm to come.

★ ★ ★

As we rode back my thoughts see-sawed from the dizzy knowledge that I had found my brother to the bleak prospect of facing Sir Julius's wrath. Apart from my own ordeal I was worried about Mama. Papa would waste no time in pointing out what a wicked young woman I was and how my mother had failed to raise me to obedience and chastity and all the other supposedly female virtues. Poor Mama was unwell. She needed peace. Perhaps if I could be truly penitent instead of challenging him Sir Julius might mellow, although in my heart I already knew that the prospect of punishing me and, indirectly my mother, would be too great a pleasure to deny himself.

Ahead the house lay low and sprawling at the southern end of the valley, almost black in the wintry light. I longed for its shelter yet dreaded the confrontation to come. At last we clattered into the courtyard and Sir Julius and I dismounted leaving Abel and Seamus to see to the horses. Neither man looked directly at me but I could feel their sympathy stretching out in invisible waves. It was poor comfort.

In silence, Sir Julius and I walked to the entrance and, as we reached the door, it opened and Eamon Shaughnessy and his daughter were waiting for us. I knew immediately that something was wrong.

'Sir Julius, sir. Tis your poor wife. Taken ill she was soon after you left — the baby . . . '

My heart lurched and without waiting I raced up the stairs towards Mama's chamber. I could hear my stepfather puffing his way behind me. As I pushed open the door, the first thing I saw was Mama stretched flat on her back in the great bed, pale as the linen. The woman attending her stood back as we came in, her face grave.

Mama opened weary eyes and I could not read her expression for it seemed to combine relief that we were there along with extreme agitation. 'I'm so sorry,' she gasped. 'The baby . . . '

I took her hand and sank onto the side of the bed. 'Are you . . . ?'

'I think I shall lose it.'

She looked over her shoulder at her husband. 'Julius, please forgive me. The journey, I think it was too much.'

Papa said nothing, merely turned away and walked from the room. Mama gave a tiny moan and I squeezed her hands. 'Don't. Don't distress yourself. It is in God's hands.' My heart filled with pity for her, for her anguish, for her longing to bear a child that might rescue this marriage from its sterile, lonely state. Mama closed her eyes and I became aware of how wet I was. My riding habit clung to me like a cold, cloying burden. I signalled to the maid and whispered, 'I will just go and change and then I will come and sit with her.'

Before I could reach my room I encountered Clarissa coming from the drawing-room. She gave me a disparaging look. 'Trust you to spoil everything.'

'I don't know what you mean.' I tried to walk on but she stood in my way, sniffing indignantly.

'Now I suppose we shall have to stay here instead of going back to Dublin.'

'You needn't stay on my account — or my mother's.' I thought how lovely it would be if she and her father went and left Mama and I behind.

She looked almost pitying. 'Do you think Papa would allow you to remain here alone after what you did this afternoon?'

'I didn't do anything. I went for a ride and became lost. Some local people saved me from wandering into a bog.' From her look I knew that she regretted their intervention. I said, 'I am going to change my clothes and then sit with Mama.'

'No, you won't. Papa wants to see you in the drawing-room at once.' It was there again, that barely concealed pleasure at the prospect of trouble, whether for me or the servants or the peasants made no difference. Clarissa thrived on other people's misfortunes. I realized how much I hated her. As I went to walk away, she added, 'I'm glad that your mother might miscarry. The last thing I want is another brat like you to spoil my life.'

'Or to take your father's affection!' I shouted at her, my anger brimming over. 'You're afraid she might have a son and you won't inherit, aren't you? You don't care about anyone except yourself.'

'Sssh!' Clarissa looked back towards the drawing-room, afraid that we should be overheard and I knew that I had spoken the truth. Turning my back on her I strode away to my room whether shaking from the cold or with anger I no longer knew.

As I undressed I realized how cold I was, my skin as chilled as marble. In an effort to instil some warmth into myself I rubbed my body with a cloth but the numbness had penetrated deep into the heart of me. I thought of the fiery liquid that Orla Kilbryde had given me. That had worked, heating me from the inside. I shouldn't think about them. It was disloyal to Mama and yet at the memory of Orla and her son I knew how much I wanted to see them again.

When I was dressed I made my way to the drawing-room. With each step fear trickled in my stomach. To protect Mama I would try to face this ordeal with as little fuss as possible, not raise my voice if Sir Julius made unfair accusations, not cry out if he resorted to whipping me, but as my hand reached for the door handle it trembled so much that I didn't know if I had the resources to go through with it.

I forced myself to enter the room and as I did so I was surprised to see my stepfather slumped in a chair drawn up close to the fire. A bottle of geneva was open on the table beside him and in his hand he clutched a glass, his face turned towards the flames. He looked round as he heard me and I was amazed to see that his cheeks were wet. He was crying! Hastily he wiped his face with the back of his hands and sat up.

'Papa?' At the sight of his distress I forgot my own anxieties.

'I want a son,' he blurted out. 'I must have a son. You do see that?'

In the short time while I had been changing, he had very quickly got drunk but never before had I seen it affect him in this way. I had walked in expecting to face his anger and instead here was a stranger, blubbering like a small child. I didn't know what to do or say. Almost as if I wasn't there, he said, 'I know it isn't me. Other women . . . ' I had heard the rumours, that he kept other mistresses and that they had borne live children. I waited.

'Don't you see?' he said again. 'Everything that I have worked for. Everything that I have. What use is it if I don't have a legitimate son?'

'You've got Clarissa.'

He didn't seem to hear. He raised a trembling glass to his lips and drained it. 'You do understand, don't you? A man without an heir is a laughing stock.' I was out of my depth so I said nothing. Turning to face me, appeasing, frighteningly reasonable, he said, 'Tell me you understand. I must get back to Dublin to set my affairs in order. I — I'll see that your mother is well provided for.'

'You're not ill?' I asked, wondering if he might be dying.

'Ill? No, of course I'm not. Don't you understand, girl? If your mother loses this baby then I must do what they did in Biblical times. I must put her aside and take another wife.'

It was too much for me to cope with. I couldn't begin to see what it might mean for Mama and me. Where would we go? How would she react? In spite of everything, in spite of Sir Julius's cruelty and harshness I feared that Mama would still view it as some terrible failure, a shame upon her. And what of the land? What of that part of the estate which was hers by right? Where did that fit into Sir Julius's plans for his linen crop?

He was staring at me and I managed to say, 'When will you be leaving?'

'Tomorrow. I must get back. I must settle things for Clarissa's wedding too. I wouldn't want the Monroes changing their minds.'

Perhaps it was something in my expression at the mention of his daughter for his old self began to emerge once more. He said, 'I'm leaving the groom, Carter, behind and Shaughnessy will look after things in my absence. You, madam, will not leave the house. If I learn that you have disobeyed me than I shall punish you as you deserve. Once your mother has recovered — one way or the other — Carter will bring you both back to Dublin. In the meantime heed what I say or it will be the worse for you.'

'Yes, Papa.' I curtseyed, grateful to have avoided a beating and made a hasty retreat, my mind in a whirl. Outside in the corridor I stopped to catch my breath. It was all too much, my stepfather leaving, my mother perhaps being divorced — and me being left behind to find out all that I could about the Kilbrydes.

5

Sir Julius and Clarissa departed for Dublin the following morning. I spent the night on a couch in Mama's room and to my knowledge her husband did not even come to say goodbye. Meanwhile she slept peacefully and by daylight the threatened miscarriage had not happened.

'Is Papa very angry?' Mama sounded anxious and I bit back any retort that would add to her fears. She drank a little beef tea, lying back after a few sips as if the effort of swallowing was too much for her.

'I think he is just disappointed.' I chose my words carefully. 'But why are you worrying? You haven't lost the baby yet. If you rest and stay calm perhaps all will still be well.'

She did not reply, but I knew that her mind was abuzz with unspoken doubts. For ages I sat there trying to formulate the right words, then I blurted out, 'If you don't have another baby then wouldn't it be better if you weren't married to Sir Julius?'

She raised herself from the pillow. 'Karenza, you must not even think such a thing! I *am* married to him. He's my husband, that's all there is to it.'

I could not help but persist. 'Just suppose though, that there was only you and me. Would we not be happier, even if we were poor?'

'Please don't.' She fell back again, clearly worn out by the thought. I knew that my remarks distressed her but somehow I wanted to prepare the way so that if he did divorce her then she might see that it was not the end of the world.

She said, 'How could I leave him? Where would we go? Anyway he would never tolerate it. Such a thing is out of the question.' We were both silent then she said, 'If I should lose this baby then next time perhaps I should stay in one place. If I rest from the very beginning perhaps everything will be well.'

At the thought that she should go through this again I had difficulty in controlling my words. I merely repeated, 'Perhaps you will not lose it.'

I wondered how I would feel if she did indeed give birth to another child. A boy would certainly put Clarissa's nose out of joint and that in itself would be some comfort. Supposing it was another girl though? True she would be my half-sister but she would also carry the Richborowe blood and with it all their greed and spite. It was a futile thought. I reminded myself of my own maxim: that there is no point in worrying about something that might not happen.

Mama fell asleep and immediately I thought of the Kilbrydes. How could I find both reason and opportunity to go there again? It would be easier if I could win either Abel or Seamus over to my side, but fear of my stepfather would outweigh any pressure I might be able to bring to bear on them.

After a while I hit upon a rather unlikely excuse — that on my journey of yesterday I had mislaid a brooch which I felt sure I had lost at Otters Lough. Immediately I realized that there was a snag to that. When the brooch could not be found would not suspicion fall upon Orla? She might even be accused of taking it. In that case I would just have to play the fool and confess that I had been mistaken and that it was at home after all.

Full of misgivings I paced the room. Surely Riari would see through such a transparent subterfuge? Already he was suspicious of my visit of yesterday. In view of Sir Julius's arrival they would hardly welcome me back a second time.

Then there was the household. What reason could I give to have an interest in the

Kilbrydes — other than the one that certainly Abel knew about and possibly everyone else. Given the circumstances they all wished me to keep away from Otters Lough. My going there could only bring trouble. I tried to be sensible. I would have to be patient. Best to take each day one at a time and take advantage of any opportunity that may arise.

While Mama slept I wandered around the house, in spite of myself enjoying the sense of freedom now that Sir Julius and Clarissa were away. From the parlour I looked out across the valley, the long, narrow defile where streams intermingled with boulders the size of houses, where cows picked their way unerringly from hump to hump and where the Kilbryde land came face to face with ours. The wind had picked up, driving the clouds west and a very low sun forced its way through the greyness. It was several hours before it would grow dark. I knew that it was foolish but I could not stop myself from going out to the stable, just to visit Shamrock.

There was no one there when I arrived. The temptation to ride was too great. I would not risk leaving the boundary of the estate, but at least I could establish a pattern and begin to ride out daily. Taking my saddle and bridle from the rack I tacked Shamrock up and led him outside. Already he was jogging, ready for anything and I was hard put to mount him before we were trotting across the cobbles and in the direction of the valley.

When we reached the gate that led down to the village I stopped. I was tempted to go there but quickly dismissed the idea. Why do anything that might later prevent me from riding to Otters Lough? I turned a reluctant Shamrock back and comforted us both by jumping the hummocks that skirted the path.

Abel was in the yard when I rode in. I had been gone less than half an hour so before he could say anything, I dismounted with the words, 'I've just been as far as the gate. He needs toning up.' He didn't comment, merely took Shamrock's reins. I knew that he wasn't fooled.

At the house Mama agreed to try a little cold poultry with some fresh bread and a glass of red wine to help restore her blood. I thought she looked better, more colour in her cheeks and as she nibbled daintily at the meat I decided to try a new approach.

'Mama, did you live in this house before, with my father?'

She shook her head. 'Our home was about two miles from here, nearer to Papa's regimental headquarters, on the other side of the valley.' She faltered as if memories were trying to intrude. With a visible effort she pushed them aside and began to speak to me as if I were a visitor to whom she was imparting social chit chat. 'Kilcreggan House was, of course, part of the Ashburn estate and Richard, my husband, would have been happy to live here but I found it too rambling and dreary.'

Clearly my father had paid more attention to her wishes than her second husband. I thought of the house, alone and abandoned. 'This place was empty then?' I asked.

Mama looked uncomfortable. 'Not exactly. Local people, tinkermen and the like set up a sort of camp here. Richard didn't seem to mind but when Papa — Sir Julius, that is — received the estate, he turned them all out and moved in here himself.'

'So where you lived with my father, was that your share of the property?'

She nodded, wiping her lips with a cloth.

'What was it called?'

'Conlan's Bluff.'

'Who was Conlan?' I was distracted by the thought of the house's history. Mama shrugged her shoulders. The past had little interest for her. I asked, 'Who lives there now?'

'Nobody. It stands empty.' She sniffed in sudden irritation. 'Why must you ask questions all the time?'

I wondered if the displaced tinkers from Kilcreggan had perhaps moved there. I hoped that they had. I asked, 'Where did they go, the people who had been living here when Sir Julius moved in?'

Mama looked uncomfortable. I had seen the expression many times before when she was hard put to justify something concerning my stepfather. She said, 'I'm afraid some of them put up a fight. They tried to set fire to the house. Two men were shot. But Papa did have the law on his side.'

Her words shocked me. 'You don't believe that!' I could see it all, poor people with little to call their own, pushed out with no thought as to their future. What else could they do but strike back? I asked, 'What about the women and children? Did no one take them in?'

Mama had no answer. I could see that she was growing increasingly upset. As kindly as I could, I said, 'You don't have to defend him, you know.' Her bleak expression said everything. If she did not believe him to be right then she would have to admit to herself that their marriage was a terrible disaster.

I wanted to stop but for the first time she seemed truly exposed to my questioning. If I left it until another time she would find a way to avoid answering. There might never be another opportunity like this so I said, 'Do you know anything about the family who live at the head of the valley — the Kilbrydes?'

I saw the spark of anger in her cheeks. 'I don't know what you've heard, but it is all malicious lies.'

'What lies?'

I guessed she wasn't sure what I knew and was afraid that she might actually tell me the things she did not want me to hear. I waited.

Jutting out her chin, she said, 'The Kilbryde woman is a sinner. She had a child out of wedlock.'

'Whose child?'

She began to fiddle with the ribbons of her nightdress and I was reminded of that day in the drawing-room in Dublin when I had asked her about my father. As if reciting some well-rehearsed lines, she said, 'A man called James Delany. He is an Irishman but a Protestant. He and your papa were friends. The child is his. When — after your papa died, Mr Delany set the woman up at Otters Lough.'

'He owns Otters Lough?'

'Of course he does. Who else, do you think? That's his boy up there.' She looked away from me and I felt certain that she was lying. Pausing for breath, she added, 'Afterwards, Mr Delany married the sister of a captain in

Papa's regiment. A year later she died in childbed.' Her face clouded and there was something mystified about her expression as if she was not sure that she had got the story right. She said, 'He has remained a widower ever since.'

'Did you like him?'

To my surprise her cheeks grew hot. 'There is nothing wrong with that. He might be an Irishman but he is also a gentleman. Besides, he was Papa's friend and his lawyer.' Again she hesitated, adding, 'Of course I could not employ him professionally in view of his relationship with that woman.'

I didn't ask why. Surely his personal life would not affect his business dealings with my mother, not unless . . . ? Could it be that Mama was jealous of his love affair with Orla Kilbryde — assuming that such a thing had ever taken place? Perhaps she had nursed some secret feelings towards him? Either that or she could not forgive him for setting Orla up at Otters Lough because he was acting not on his own behalf but for my father? It was all too confusing.

In the meantime Mama continued, 'The Delanys have two hundred acres further on down towards the coast. Papa — Sir Julius, doesn't have any time for them. He doesn't approve of upstart Irishmen who become

Protestant just to further their careers.'

'Is that what he did?' She did not reply.

I thought again about Mama's house, Conlan's Bluff, where she and my father had lived. What was it like? Now it stood alone and empty unless, like Kilcreggan, poor, landless people had indeed colonized it. I doubted it though. On his wife's behalf Sir Julius, would make sure that no one benefited from it. If Mama had not married Sir Julius then one day it would have been mine. My stomach churned with acid resentment. I tried to push the anger away resolving to go there when the chance arose. So many things that I wanted to do and know.

Aloud, I said, 'So Mr Delany married someone else, even though he had a son?'

She avoided the question. 'He's done well for himself. Everyone respects him.' She hesitated. 'He still looks after Mistress Kilbryde and her son although, of course, he never acknowledged the boy as his own.'

Could that be because the boy was not his child at all? I waited for her to elaborate but she did not. On the surface, what she had told me made as much sense as what Abel had said. Perhaps after all Riari Kilbryde was not my brother but the son of my father's friend, a friend that my own mother had

99

nursed some secret affection for? However was I to discover the truth?

I had a strange feeling that I had escaped from a cage and now that I was in the open I didn't know what to do or where to go. Pursuing the Kilbrydes had been my sole objective but if what Mama said was true, then there was no point.

I thought of Orla Kilbryde's kitchen, the dark, smoky warmth, the feel of her work worn hands rubbing me dry. Had they ever touched my father? And what of Riari? Did I want him to be my brother or not? Perversely, at that moment I wanted to see them more than ever, to try and untangle the web for myself and to decide once and for all if Abel's or Mama's tale were true.

Mama said, 'I am feeling drowsy. I think I will sleep for a while.' She was dismissing me and the doubts were there again. Was she afraid that I might probe further and find the holes in her story?

'Sleep well, Mama.' I kissed her dutifully on the cheek and wandered away to absorb all that I had heard.

By next morning I had no doubts about what I was going to do. While Mama remained abed, I went straight down to the stables and finding only Seamus there, ordered Shamrock to be tacked up. 'I know

100

where I am going,' I said to him. 'There is no need to say anything to anyone. I will be back by tea-time.'

He glanced at the sullen clouds but said nothing, helping me into the saddle, then nodding a silent farewell.

This time I kept to the upper path, all the while scanning the horizon in case Riari should suddenly appear. I felt different now, more in control. For the moment, unless I learned otherwise, I could assume that I was not his sister but merely a neighbour. The knowledge gave me a strange sense of freedom yet there was something else. Disappointment perhaps — or relief? When I got there I would use the excuse of the brooch to explain my arrival.

Riari was in the yard as I rode in and at the sight of me he pushed back his cap and scratched his curly black thatch of hair. A smudge of mud dissected his right cheek like a duelling scar and I thought of my father killing a man. Already my confidence was beginning to ebb and Riari's questioning stare further unnerved me.

'I think I left something behind yesterday,' I said, slipping clumsily from the saddle.

'Did you now? And what would that be?'

His eyes, shrewd, knowing, seemed to see through my pretence and I could feel my cheeks growing red with the deception. 'A brooch.'

'I haven't seen it.'

'Well, now that I have come this far perhaps I should just check. Besides, I should like to see your mother.'

'And why would that be?'

'Because I like her.'

'She'll be pleased to know that.' I ignored the jibe and walked behind him towards the farmhouse. He said, 'I suppose you know that you are trespassing when you ride along the ridge?'

'How, trespassing?'

'Up as far as those trees yonder, that's my land. I don't welcome outsiders using it for their own purposes.'

'How else can anyone get here?'

'They can't. But I like to be the one to choose who visits.'

I felt mortified, as if I had broken some unspoken etiquette in coming here uninvited. The words stung too, an unwarranted criticism of me personally. To cover my embarrassment, I said, 'I thought it was your mother's land. Anyway, if you don't want me here . . . ' I was about to flounce off but he gave an indifferent shrug.

'I didn't say that. I'm just a little confused as to why Sir Julius Richborowe's daughter

102

should honour us with her company again.'

I didn't have time to answer because we had reached the farmhouse and Riari pushed open the door, ushering me inside. Yesterday I had been too concerned with seeing the occupant to pay much attention to the cottage. Today, I took in the details.

The door gave directly into the kitchen-cum-living room. It was long and low and Orla was sitting at the table, carding wool. She was near to the small, square window, taking advantage of the light. At some point the farmhouse had been enlarged, for further along, a second window was set into the wall and in front of it, its legs dug into the earth floor, was a loom. Its presence took me by surprise. With all Sir Julius's talk of a new linen venture I had assumed that nothing of the sort existed in the neighbourhood.

'My goodness.' Orla stood up and I knew that she too was surprised to see me. I felt even more uncomfortable, not knowing what to say.

Riari had no such trouble. 'Look, Mother, Mistress Richborowe has decided to honour us with another visit so soon.'

I looked to her for help and she said, 'You are more than welcome. What about your father, though? Will he not be angry with you for coming here?'

'He has gone back to Dublin. I — I had to exercise my pony so I took the only path I knew.' I relayed the story of the brooch but Orla informed me that it had not been found.

'Are you sure you had it when you arrived?'

'No, that is — perhaps I forgot to pin it to my habit.' I could feel my cheeks burning.

Orla dismissed the subject. 'Anyway, it's welcome you are. Come and get warm. Would you like some tea?' She pronounced it in the Irish way, as *tay* and I nodded my thanks. While she hung the kettle over the fire, Riari backed towards the door.

'I'll be going then. Tis you, Miss Richborowe has come to see.' I looked at him to see if he was making fun of me but he looked serious. Orla busied herself taking rough pottery mugs from the blackened dresser that stood along one wall and fetching a ewer of milk from a pantry leading off the main room. 'I have no sugar,' she confessed, 'but if you'd like a little honey?'

I reminded myself that these people were probably poor and declined the offer.

When the *tay* was brewed I held the mug between my hands, savouring the warmth, liking the rich taste liberally dashed as it was with creamy milk.

I still felt embarrassed, not knowing what to say. Should I own up, explain who my father was and see what she said? Should I let her know what I had heard about her?

I looked around the room again, my eyes returning to the loom. Orla followed my gaze. 'We grow our own flax,' she confirmed. 'Riari grows it, I spin it and he weaves what cloth he can in the winter months. We even bleach some of it for our own use. The rest brings us some small income.'

Again I wondered what Sir Julius would think. I had the impression that he thought linen production was something over which he would have a monopoly. Clearly it was not.

To break the silence Orla said, 'Do you intend to stay long, Miss Richborowe — at Kilcreggan, I mean?'

'Until my mother — until my stepfather's wife is well again — she threatens to miscarry.'

'I'm sorry to hear it. A child is a wonderful thing.'

She looked wistful and I found myself asking, 'Have you no other children?'

Her expression strangely tender, she said, 'I was unlucky. My husband died before Riari was born. I have never met another man I would want to share my life with.'

'Your husband?'

She looked as if she was debating what to

tell me, then she said, 'Kilbryde is my maiden name. My husband was English. Our marriage was kept very quiet. There were reasons.'

Things were beginning to slide out of control. What was she saying?

She gave me a philosophical smile. 'Nothing is what it seems, Miss Richborowe. My husband was raised a Protestant, but before he died, he embraced the true religion. He and I were wed by a priest, in extreme circumstances.' She faltered. 'I do not think I should be telling you all this.'

Clearly she was not talking about Delany. I asked, 'What is your married name?'

''Tis no matter.'

I couldn't push her, but all the time I knew that she was meaning my father. How could he have married her if he was married already?

My voice threatening to betray me, I asked, 'Was the man not already wed?'

Her eyes registered mild surprise at the question, but she said, 'In the eyes of the English law he was, but . . . we . . . we were truly in love — a marriage made in Heaven you might say. Once he embraced the true faith whatever had gone before had no meaning.'

I jumped to my feet, my concern for my

mother blinding me to everything else. I began to shout, 'What about his wife? Don't you think she had any meaning? Don't you think she deserved his time and company, his last hours?'

Her expression was confused. 'I don't know what you have heard, but he did nothing to hurt his first wife. Everything that he had went to her. She was spared the knowledge of our union. I — I should never have said anything about it.'

I was at the door, fighting with my tears, my sense of outrage. As I opened it I shouted, 'It is my mother you are talking about. *My* mother, *my* father! You were only his whore. He would never have married you. He couldn't.'

'You are his girl?' She seemed oblivious to my anger. Coming close, she turned me towards the light. 'Let me look at you. Yes, I can see you have his eyes. And his sense of justice.'

I was struggling to hold back the tears. I blurted out, 'I heard all about you. I wanted to see you, and to see what my — what your son was like.' There, I had said it, given the rumour, the fantasy a reality. There was no going back.

'Your brother.' She nodded, a thoughtful smile touching her lips. She said, 'Look at him and you will see the ghost of your father. I'm so sorry, my dear, I had no wish to hurt you. I didn't know who you were.' She expelled her breath, considering what I had told her. After an age, she said, 'Of course, I knew Alice Ashburn had a child but then your mother married the new owner of Kilcreggan and moved away. I had heard nothing of her since. This is such a surprise. It is all such a long time ago.' She sighed then added, 'But one way or the other your mother got her land back which is more than we did.'

'What do you mean?'

'Well, as we are Catholics, Richard could leave us nothing so he did the next best thing and left Otters Lough to his friend James Delany. James holds it in trust for Riari. It isn't the same though. It isn't truly ours, not in the way that Sir Julius Richborowe holds Kilcreggan. It will never be the same, and we were born here, have lived here for generations.'

I didn't want to admit to the truth of what she was saying although it confirmed everything that I already knew. Sir Julius and others like him had no moral right to the land other than that dictated by power. The familiar guilt began to gnaw at me, but I reminded myself that like the Kilbrydes, I was no better off. I had nothing that I could call my own. My mother, once mistress of her own share of this land had lost it as soon as she tied herself to my stepfather. Like Orla and Riari, Mama and I were victims. The only question was, what could I do about it?

Orla ushered me towards the door. 'The light is fading. You should be going. I'll ask Riari to escort you home.'

'No!' I didn't want to see his reaction when he found out who I was. I had no way of telling what he would think. While he believed me to be Clarissa, the daughter of his unwelcome neighbour, I could cope with his sarcasm, his resentment, but supposing he thought of me, Karenza, his sister, in the same way? Supposing it was not who I was but what I was that he disliked? I thought of his sharp, shrewd face, and did not pursue my thoughts except to acknowledge that somehow, in some undefined way, it was important that he should like me.

At the door, I said, 'May I come and see you again?'

'Of course.' Her expression changed, a frown playing about her brow. 'But be careful. Your stepfather feels he has good reason to hate us.'

'Why?'

'Let's just say he won't feel happy until he owns the entire valley and as things are, we don't intend to let him have his way.'

I knew that she wasn't telling me the whole truth but I left it. Coming outside with me, she led the way round to the stables. Of Riari there was no sign so she brought Shamrock out herself and assisted me to mount.

'You are sure you know the path back?'

'I do. Thank you.'

'Well then, go straight home and — Karenza?'

I reined in and turned to face her. She reached out and squeezed my wrist. 'Don't think badly of me. Never would I have chosen to love another woman's husband, but sometimes nature is stronger than our wills.'

I nodded, half in love with the idea of such grand passion, half condemning her weakness in giving way to it.

As I rode off, she called, 'Slan agat. Goodbye, my dear. One day you will understand. You cannot be your father's daughter without falling in love.'

As I cantered Shamrock towards Kilcreg-gan, I thought: when it happens, please don't let it be with the husband of another woman.

6

I left Otters Lough buffeted by a whirl of emotion. Whether wittingly or no, my mother had lied to me. Unless Orla herself was lying (and why should she?), Riari Kilbryde was definitely not the son of James Delany but of my own father, Richard Ashburn. He was my half-brother, and next to my mother the nearest blood relation that I had. Did Mama know this or did she genuinely believe that Orla had not been her husband's mistress? The knowledge enveloped me. As I rode, I teased out every feeling, excitement, fear, a kind of wild elation. All the time I wondered which version did I want to be true? I was too confused to work out all the implications.

In spite of the earlier warning I paid little attention to where I was going, relying on Shamrock to pick a safe route home. I reasoned that in one afternoon I had become a different person. Living with Sir Julius we were part of the cream of Irish society but now I knew the truth I was living a lie. It was surely no coincidence that I felt instinctively more at home in the modest farmhouse where Riari lived and where my father had longed in his heart to be. After all, I was my father's daughter. I did not take after Mama either in looks or temperament so I must surely take after him.

As I rode I wondered about that other home, Conlan's Bluff, where my parents had lived together and where presumably, I had been born. If I wanted to find out who I truly was then perhaps the answer would be there. Or perhaps I needed to meet Mr James Delany, my father's friend.

I was taken by surprise when Shamrock slowed at the gate leading back through the boundary wall. I had been so preoccupied throughout the ride home that I had noticed nothing.

Seamus was in the stable-yard but I did not enlighten him as to where I had been. Let them all think that I had been merely riding around the estate. As I crossed the courtyard to the house, I thought: tomorrow or the day after I will make a visit to Mr James Delany's house. He must know the truth. Perhaps he will make my father come alive for me in a way that nobody else can or will.

I couldn't ask Orla. It would be too much like prying and as for Mama, she closed up like an oyster whenever my father's name was mentioned. Thinking once more of the Kilbrydes I did not know when I would see

112

them again. To do so was to think about making changes, to publicly acknowledge the truth. I was not sure that I was ready for the repercussions.

To my surprise, Mama was sitting in a chair when I reached her room. I was about to explain that I had been riding in the grounds but her expression warned me that she at least was aware of the real reason for my outing.

'Where have you been — and don't lie to me!' Seeing my guilty face, she continued, 'You've been to see them haven't you, the Kilbrydes?'

Her mouth was set in a firm line and her eyes glared hard as flint. I had never seen her like this before. In the face of her anger I said nothing, not looking at her. I could hear her tense breathing and out of the corner of my eye caught her agitated little movements.

At last she burst out, 'Whatever possessed you? How could you even think of seeing them? They're bad people, little better than outlaws. What could you want with the likes of them?'

I bit back the urge to say: *I wanted to know if Riari Kilbryde was my brother*, for to do so would surely bring the heavens down on our heads.

Mama continued to wring her hands, her

113

teeth clamped over her upper lip as if to hold back her anguish. Suddenly asserting herself, she said, 'You must not, you must never ever think of going there again, do you hear me? If Papa was even to get a hint of what you have been doing he would be appalled.'

'Why?' At the mention of his name I regained something of my spirit.

'Why? Because they are bad people, that's why. Because he expressly told you not to leave the house and you disobeyed him.'

'Who is going to tell him, you?'

Her eyes grew large as wagon wheels. 'How dare you speak to me like that! Is that what you want, that I should tell him? I should, you know. If he finds out from someone else he will be furious.'

I didn't think that anyone in the household was likely to say anything. After all, Sir Julius inspired only dislike, not loyalty, so why should anyone do so? By now, however, Mama had resorted to blackmail. Dabbing her eyes with a crumpled silk kerchief she whimpered, 'I really cannot stand the worry. I cannot tolerate the anxiety. Please, Karenza, please promise me that you will not go there again.'

'I — ' I wanted to argue, but before I could say anything, she added, 'I want you to swear on the life of your unborn brother or sister

114

that you will not go to that place again. If you have any feeling for me you will do so. Promise me now.'

'That's unfair!'

'How is it unfair? You break my heart when you are disobedient. Now I am telling you not to go there. Give me your word that you won't disobey me.'

I thought: supposing the baby dies? She'll think that it is because I have broken my word. It was an impossible situation. She drove her point home. 'If you do not promise then I am afraid that the worry will make me ill again.'

Against her words I had no defence. 'Well?' She looked at me with large moist eyes.

Suddenly a torrent of anger engulfed me. I shouted, 'Did you know that my father became a Catholic before he died?'

She seemed to grow physically larger as an answering indignation swept over her. 'What a wicked thing to say. How dare you. How DARE you!'

'It's true.'

In the face of her anger I regretted my words. She continued to issue forth a stream of outrage. 'I would never have thought that my own daughter would spread such wicked lies. What have I done to be treated like this by my own flesh and blood? Where did you get such a notion from? Don't tell me, those wicked people have been filling your head with slanders against your papa. Don't you see that they are using you to hurt me?'

'Why should they want to do that?'

'Because they are wicked.'

I shrugged. I couldn't think of anything else to say except the obvious — that my father had changed his religion so that he could marry the woman he loved. Angry as I was with Mama I could not do this to her.

'All right, I promise I won't go there again.' I mumbled it so low, so unwillingly that she made me repeat it.

With a sigh she sat back in the chair as if a great weight had been lifted from her shoulders. 'Remember now, this is a binding oath. You will not regret it.'

I could not agree with her.

She was silent for a while then gave me a bright smile as if ending our dispute once and for all. 'I am beginning to feel a little better. Perhaps we should be thinking of going back to Dublin.'

Something about her expression revealed her true thoughts: that she did not want to give me the opportunity to break my promise. With a moment of insight I guessed too that she did not want to leave Sir Julius to his own devices for too long. If I had heard the rumours about his other women then probably she had too. Did she know that he was contemplating putting her aside? Was she afraid that he would do so?

I said, 'I don't think you should even consider travelling, not if you want to safeguard the baby.' I resisted the temptation to add that if she decided to move back to Dublin then I would not be held to my promise as I did not want the baby's death on my conscience.

By and large she sounded relieved by the suggestion that she should remain at Kilcreggan. 'Perhaps you are right, dear. Perhaps I should wait a little longer. Tonight I will write to Sir Julius and tell him that for the time being I will stay here. I am sure he will understand if I explain about the baby.'

I nodded. 'I'm sure that's for the best. After all, he is keen for you to have the baby, isn't he?'

'Of course he is. A son would make such a difference to him.' She began to ramble but I stopped listening. Everything was so confusing. My stepfather had forbidden me to leave the estate. I had already defied him but no one was likely to tell him. I had now promised Mama not to go to Otters Lough but what if I happened to bump into Riari in some other place? Or Orla? Neither had I promised Mama to stay within the boundary walls. As she settled down to take a nap I thought that soon I would ride out and see what, if anything, I could learn from the mysterious James Delany.

The chance came the next morning when Mama handed her letter to Abel telling him to go to Dublin and to return as soon as he could with any news. 'Shamrock needs to be exercised,' I announced. 'I will ride with Abel a mile or two and then return directly.'

Mama looked agitated but decided against making a fuss, merely saying, 'Be sure to come directly home.'

It was a crisp morning, the ground hard beneath the horses' feet. We set out early so that Abel could make good time before darkness set in. We rode in silence, but I knew that he was aware of the arguments that had taken place the day before and, of course, I had already confessed to him that I knew about the Kilbrydes. I decided to challenge him outright.

'Abel, do you think it could be true that Riari Kilbryde is my half brother?'

'I couldn't say, miss.'

'But you don't think it's impossible?'

'Nothing is impossible.'

I waited and when he didn't respond, I added, 'I have heard that he might be the son

118

of Mr James Delany.'

'Have you?'

I sniffed with frustration. 'Don't play the fool. It is important that I know what you think.'

'Sometimes knowing things can only bring trouble.'

He kicked his gelding into a canter and I stopped talking as Shamrock fought to get in the lead. When we slowed down, I persisted with my questions. 'Do you think it could be true that my father became a Catholic?'

'Only he would know that, miss.'

'And the priest?'

'I don't know of any priests around here.'

I knew that that at least wasn't true. They might not advertise themselves, not admit to teaching the children in the hedge schools, or to taking mass in the houses and hovels in return for a good meal, but they were certainly there.

I asked, 'If a man changed his religion, would it free him from the obligation to his wife, that is if he was already married?'

'I know nothing about such things.'

It was clear that I wasn't going to get anywhere with this line of questioning so I decided to take another tack. I said, 'Do you know where Mr James Delany lives?'

'Aye. In a house called Falconridge on the

other side of Killimagree.' He nodded in the direction.

'Do you know him?'

'I know of him. He is a neighbour of Sir Julius.'

'And he was a friend of my papa.'

'Is that so?'

You know it is, I thought. Aloud, I asked, 'Do you know what sort of a man he is?'

'I've heard that he is rich, successful. He was born locally, a poor boy, but the people who owned Sir Fulton Monroe's land before he bought it took a liking to young Mr Delany and sent him to Dublin to be educated. I believe he studied the law and then he came back here and bought Falconridge House.'

'Where is that?'

'At the top of yon valley.' He nodded again in the direction of the sunset where Killimagree nestled at the foot of the hills.

I asked, 'What about Otters Lough? How did he come to own that?'

'I couldn't say.'

'Is he very friendly with the Kilbrydes?'

Abel ignored the question although I knew that he had heard me. I tried again. 'How did he and my father meet?'

He gave a sigh of exasperation. 'How do you expect me to know such things? Do you

120

never give up?' By way of response he pushed his horse forward again, leaving me too far behind to continue the conversation.

Our route was taking us nearer to Killimagree. When he slowed down again, I said, 'Perhaps I'll leave you here and ride back.'

'You are going directly home?'

'Of course.' I gave him a provocative look. 'No doubt you've heard that I've promised not to go to Otters Lough again.'

'Should I have done?'

I had no answer. Instead I turned Shamrock back in the direction of Kilcreggan. 'Have a safe journey.'

'I will. And — if I were you I'd forget all about the Kilbrydes and pay heed to what your own folk tell you. They only have your welfare at heart.'

'Good day, Abel.'

'Good day, miss.'

As soon as he was out of sight I changed direction, skirting the settlement of Killimagree and heading on towards the head of the valley where Abel had hinted that Falconridge stood.

By one of those quirks of nature, the folds of earth that had produced our valley running from north to south had also pleated the land creating a second valley off to the right that

121

lay from east to west.

As I rode I noticed two birds of prey circling the crest to my right. They seemed suspended on invisible currents. Falcons. The place was well named. The mournful cry of a solitary gull broke the silence, reminding me that the coast was only a few miles to the south. At that moment I got my first glimpse of the house.

It was built on the side of the slope, facing towards the south. To my surprise it was quite modern in construction, square, three storeys high, with a porticoed doorway and many large, paned windows at the front. Around it the ground had been levelled to accommodate lawns and terraces of flower beds, and the panorama of the valley provided a perfect vista. I remembered what Abel had said, that Mr Delany was a lawyer, not a farmer. Falconridge had none of the workaday barns and outbuildings that marked Otters Lough and even Kilcreggan as working farms.

I reined Shamrock in and stood wondering what to do. In the distance dogs barked. Would they attack me if I rode nearer? If I did so, what should I say? Half of me wanted to turn back, but having come this far I knew that I would regret it later if I did not make some attempt to meet the man who had been my father's friend.

The main entrance to the house was now clearly visible and, as I rode a few more paces, the door opened and a man came out, two Irish wolf hounds bounding at his feet. I stiffened and Shamrock, sensing my mood gave a sudden and unexpected leap turning back the way we had come. Because I had not been paying attention he caught me off balance and as he flicked his back legs up, frightened by the feel of my skirts across his rump, he succeeded in unseating me. I fell with a jolt onto the uneven ground, a boulder jabbing me hard in the shoulder. Shamrock immediately cantered off several yards then stopped to graze.

The commotion alerted the man at the house and already he was racing towards us. For a moment I could only think of the pain in my shoulder. Holding my arm I tried to move it but it was too agonizing.

'Are you all right?' He bent down and seeing the way I held my arm, gently removed my hand and explored the injured place. He did so with such professional ease that I made no objection. He looked no more than five and twenty. I had expected someone older.

'Nothing broken there.' He began to manipulate my shoulder and under his fingers it moved, stiffly at first but gradually with greater ease. 'Do you hurt anywhere else?' He sat back on his haunches and studied my face. He was not very tall and there was a softness about him that hinted at a man who liked home comforts rather than the challenge of the great outdoors. His eyes, which were quite round in shape and blue, had a peculiar, sparkling quality that made him look as if he was permanently amused. I thought that I had seen him before but could not imagine where.

My rear felt bruised but I did not say so. 'I am unhurt, thank you.' Somehow I struggled to my feet, aware that my hands and knees were stinging.

'My horse spooked,' I said by way of explanation, hoping that he wouldn't ask how I came to be in the valley in the first place.

'Well, come along up to the house with you. I am sure you could do with a little something to restore you. You live near to here?'

'I was accompanying our groom on part of his journey. I had just turned back. He is returning to Dublin.'

If he realized that I had not answered his question, he did not show it. Instead, he helped me along, although in truth I could have walked well enough. As we neared the door, the dogs came to investigate. 'Down, my lovely boys!' He almost seemed to bark at them and they drew back, their noses raised, twitching to pick up my scent. I must have passed muster because they both wagged their tails before settling down under the shade of a great ash tree that grew near to the entrance.

'Are you Mr Delany?' I asked.

'Doctor Delany. I am a physician.'

Then I remembered where I had seen him. Here was the man who had come to my assistance at Ormonde Quay when the apprentices had hung the students up by their belts.

'Oh, I was under the impression . . . ' I spoke without thinking and he looked down at me with questioning eyebrows.

'I heard that Mr Delany was a lawyer,' I said with embarrassment.

'That is my brother James. This is his house. I am merely visiting.'

A man came across the yard at that moment, one of the servants, and the doctor said, 'There's a horse loose just down on the pathway. Go and catch him and take him to the stables. Check him to see that he is uninjured.'

I thanked him and we went inside. He showed no signs of recognizing me for which I was relieved. As we walked into the hallway I was immediately struck by the light airy feeling, the elegance of the drawing-room where Dr Delany escorted me and bad me sit and rest.

As I eased myself gently on to a couch he went to a sideboard, taking out glasses and a decanter and pouring two measures of Madeira which he brought across, holding one out to me. 'Your good health, Miss . . . ?'

'Ashburn.' I used my father's name because I could no longer bear to be thought the child of my stepfather.

My host's eyebrows shot up and his sparkling eyes asked questions. 'You are not Richard Ashburn's daughter, from Kilcreggan?'

'I am.'

'Well, well.' He nodded as if digesting the information. 'My brother was a good friend of your father,' he volunteered.

'So I believe.' My heart thumped uncomfortably. I wanted to appear calm and sophisticated but this tenuous link with my past threatened to overwhelm me.

'I did not know my father,' I managed to say. 'I was born after he —— '

'I was about eight. I remember the excitement around here.' He stopped. 'I apologize. This must be painful for you.'

'No! No really, no one will tell me about what happened. I want to know.'

'Not until I know your full name.'

'Karenza Ashburn. My stepfather is Sir Julius Richborowe. We are visiting Kilcreggan while Sir Julius makes plans for the estate.'

He bowed his head and I saw his eyes narrow slightly as if suspicious of what my stepfather's plans might be. He said, 'Liam Delany at your service.' His lips twitched with amusement as he added, 'My father was a peat cutter. When he died we were thrown upon the charity of the two Miss Englefields who used to own the land they now call Richmond Park. They took a shine to my brother James. I was just a baby.'

Something about his tone warned me that there might be unspoken family tensions here. 'I believe your brother has done well for himself,' I ventured.

Liam sipped his drink speculatively. 'You could say that. He hasn't wasted an opportunity to get on in life.'

'And you? Surely you too have done well to become a doctor?'

He gave me a 'who knows' look. 'Let's just say that medicine is the only profession open to a man of the old religion. Although we are nominally of the new faith, I still cling to certain traditions.' He shrugged his thoughts aside, adding, 'Not that I would have wanted to do anything else in any case. Helping the sick has its own rewards and I am not a man of great ambition.'

Talk of religion and ambition left me feeling uncomfortable. I had often heard Sir Julius bemoan the changing climate and how the British Parliament threatened to give in to the Irish Catholics because it did not want them to go the way of the French or the American colonists who were near to revolt. I thought of the peasants, of their poverty and sensed that in some way it was all tied in with what Liam Delany was hinting at. To get on to safer ground, I said, 'Did you ever meet my father?'

'Oh yes. He used to come to our house when I was young. We didn't live here then. Ours was a modest cottage on the old ladies' estate. Your father and my brother were very close. When . . . when the trial took place my brother was newly qualified. He defended your father's rights — not with the military, of course, because it was outside his jurisdiction, but he saw to it that your father's property and belongings were distributed as he wished.'

'Including Otters Lough?'

Liam raised his eyebrows again. 'What do you know about Otters Lough?'

'That my father gave it into the care of Mr

128

Delany in order that the Kilbrydes might live there.'

'You know a lot for a young girl.'

'I am not a young girl!' My cheeks grew hot.

'Well now, you are neither an old woman nor a young boy.' He grinned at me. There was nothing patronizing about his expression and I felt my tension ease.

'To be honest, I don't know very much,' I confessed. 'No one will talk about my father, or about what happened. My feeling is that my mother was cheated and that I have been done out of my father's estate — I think that Riari Kilbryde feels the same.'

'You know Riari Kilbryde?'

'He is my half-brother.'

His lack of denial confirmed Orla's story. At last it was formally acknowledged, not just by Orla who might have her own reasons for claiming it to be so but by someone not directly involved. I felt heady. Riari and I were kin, of the same blood. Perhaps I could do something to help him claim his birthright, ensure that he had outright control of the land our father had wished to leave to him. I brushed over how I might achieve this, imagining instead his gratitude which bathed me in a seductive warmth. I very much wanted his approval.

Liam was looking at me pensively. He said, 'My brother James is ambitious but he is also loyal to his friends. If the law changes, which surely it will before too long, then he will pass the land over to Riari as your father wished. In the meantime he holds it in trust.'

'Supposing he died?'

Liam looked surprised. 'Then I don't know.' Clearly he had not considered the implications although I hoped that James Delany himself would have done so and made provision for my brother. My brother! The words lifted me onto a crest. I desperately wanted to be known by everyone as somebody close to Riari Kilbryde.

Liam interrupted my reverie. 'If it is any comfort, I am my brother's next of kin. If, God forbid, I should inherit Otters Lough then I, too, would carry out your father's wishes.'

'Thank you.' Talk of my father in this way, as if it was real and something to be acknowledged, filled me with emotion.

Liam eased the tension by adding, 'If you came here hoping to see James I'm afraid you will be disappointed. He is away in Dublin.'

'It is no matter.' I comforted myself with the thought that when we returned to the city, I would find a way to make his acquaintance.

Meanwhile the day was slipping by. I suppose all in all I had ridden an hour with Abel. Now I had to ride back. Mama would be growing anxious. I tried to think of anything else that I wanted to know but nothing would come. I drew comfort from meeting Liam Delany again and in extending my connection with my father one tiny step closer.

I stood up. 'I really think I should be going.'

'Of course. I'll ride a way with you.'

'There's no need.' He ignored my protest and, ringing a bell, sent for the horses to be brought round.

Rather stiffly I struggled on to Shamrock's back, my behind feeling bruised against the hardness of the saddle. I watched Liam mount, hauling himself onto his mount, remembering the agile way in which Riari leapt on to his pony. Given a good horse I had no doubt that my brother would ride with consummate skill. As it was, any horse worth more than five pounds was denied to a member of the Catholic faith. In contrast, Liam, riding a handsome mare that must have cost at least thirty guineas, looked ill at ease, a sack of potatoes dumped askew in the saddle.

'Is that your horse?' I asked, remembering

131

that he too was a professed Catholic.

'My brother's. Riding is not my favourite occupation.' We began to walk down the valley and Liam talked companionably. 'I'm what they call a book worm. James rides better than I do, but your father was the truly athletic one. He could shoot a single leaf off a tree at a hundred paces and when he rode he was really foolhardy. I've seen him jump a solid wall higher than a man with no idea of what might be on the other side. His exploits were legendary.'

I was captivated. This was what I wanted to hear, tales of my father's derring-do. A surge of excitement welled in me and I wished that I was not Mama's but Orla's child, wild and rebellious like my brother. My brother. The thought was there again. Somehow, somewhere soon I would have to see him again.

As Kilcreggan came into sight, Liam said, 'Well, perhaps I should leave you here.'

His tone reminded me that Sir Julius was liked by nobody. Clearly Liam had no desire to meet him. 'He's away,' I said. 'My stepfather is away.'

'I doubt your mother would be pleased to see you riding with a single man and unchaperoned.'

He was right of course. I turned Shamrock to face him.

'Thank you for everything, for helping me and for . . . for the information you have shared with me. I appreciate it.'

He shrugged, looking embarrassed. 'I'll be returning to Dublin next week. I have more work waiting for me than any man could ask for.'

'Where do you live?'

'Great Britain Street.' He named the ancient highway. It was not so far away from our home. Liam said, 'I have my share of rich patients nearby but I also take my healing where it's needed, among the poor.'

I looked at him with new respect. Life was confusing. When I thought of my father, of my brother Riari, I was stirred by their sense of adventure, by an urge to be like them, a free spirit who would think nothing of flouting convention. But I also had a conscience that urged me find comfort in doing good, Christian things. Looking at Liam I thought that he symbolized the one way of life and Riari the other. Which sort of person was I? Perhaps I needed to try both ways before I would find out who I really was.

'Goodbye, Miss Ashburn.'

Liam raised his hat and turned the horse clumsily back the way he had come. It resisted and he spoke to it with sudden authority. I remembered the way he had spoken to the dogs. He might not ride well but he seemed to have a way with animals for the horse was already walking sedately back the way he had come.

'Farewell, Miss Ashburn. I wish you well.'

'Goodbye, Dr Delaney, perhaps we shall meet again.'

I waited until he was out of sight before riding on to the house. Once I was inside, I made for my room, avoiding going to see Mama. I still felt angry with her after yesterday's confrontation and I wanted to be alone to absorb the things that Liam Delany had told me. As I changed out of my riding habit I took time to examine my bumps and bruises. My entire body began to feel stiff and I rang the bell for Sorcha, ordering plenty of hot water to be brought up to fill a tub. I would have a long soak and enjoy the reverie. Tomorrow, tomorrow I would ride out again, not to Otters Lough, at least not directly. If God was good then He would point me in the direction of my brother and I would be able to speak with him, make myself known, seek his friendship and together we could begin to right the wrongs perpetrated on us both by Sir Julius Richborowe.

7

Next morning I awoke to a fog. It took me a while to realize that it was not outside but in my brain. As I went to get up, every part of my body ached and my head was as heavy as lead. This was clearly not only the effects of yesterday's fall: I was suffering from a fever. There was nothing for it but to stay in bed.

Mama came to visit me. She looked surprisingly well and through a stuffy haze I urged her not to come too close. She placed a cool hand on my throbbing head and sent for Sorcha, telling her to burn feathers in the room to assist my breathing and to bring me long drinks laced with a few drops of laudanum to ease the chill.

The cold grew worse and for several days I was confined to bed. For much of the time I slept. I had vivid dreams where my father came to meet me, wearing armour and riding the finest horse I had ever seen. He looked like a god. He did not speak to me and although I tried to attract his attention I seemed to be invisible.

Orla was there with Riari at her side. The sun shone and her glorious hair was loose,

135

tumbling down to her waist. She held out a scarf to my father and he rode over to take it from her, tucking it into his helmet so that it fluttered in the breeze. He said: *I will always be your champion*. I was captivated by Orla's beauty but it made me sad that it was she and not I who commanded my father's attention. Suddenly Orla seemed to see me. She called out: *See Karenza, Papa and Riari are the same person*, and both men turned to look at me. In that same moment, I awoke.

For a while I tried to hold on to the sense of wonder at being in my father's presence but I could not recapture the dream and when I finally opened my eyes, Mama was again at the bedside.

'Did I awaken you?' She looked flushed, demanding my attention and I struggled to sit up. She said, 'Abel arrived back this morning. He brings a letter from Papa.' I could see that she was burning to tell me about it.

'What does it say?'

'I am to stay here but Papa wants you to return to Dublin. Sir Fulton and Lady Monroe are planning to visit. Papa needs you to chaperon Clarissa.'

She gave a a shaky sigh. 'It will be very exciting. There will be outings and visits to the theatre. You will meet new people.' From her tone I guessed that she would like to have

136

been part of this. As if picking up my thoughts, she said, 'Of course, Papa is only thinking of me. He insists that I stay here to safeguard the baby.'

I wondered if he had already found someone as a possible replacement for Mama should she miscarry and wanted to keep her out of the way. It was not like him to be so concerned for her welfare.

'When do I have to go?' I asked.

'As soon as you are well enough.' I detected an edge of anxiety in her voice. Probably Papa had demanded that I should leave straight away.

I closed my eyes and lay back on the bolster. I did not look forward to the journey to Dublin but in my mind's eye I could visualize the city, our beautiful wide street and the thread of the river, the hustle and bustle of the citizens, and the prospect of concerts and plays that until now I had not been allowed to attend. Perhaps somewhere I would meet Mr James Delany.

Close on its heels came another thought: perhaps I shall see Liam, then almost immediately both possibilities were overshadowed by the knowledge that I would be leaving Riari. Orla would, of course, by now have told him who I was, but I needed to see him for myself, to know what he thought. In my ideal world I longed for him to admit how much alike we were, to tell me that all his life he had known there was something missing and that now he had found me his life was complete.

I asked, 'When will I be coming back?'

Mama hesitated. 'I don't know.'

Of course she didn't know. She would have to wait to find out whether Sir Julius intended her to remain permanently at Kilcreggan or to return later to Dublin. If she remained, then once the Monroes departed I might be allowed to return. If, on the other hand, her husband summoned her back to the city then perhaps I should never return to Kilcreggan with its all-important neighbours.

Once more we were both pawns in Papa's personal game. I turned away from her and closed my eyes, making a vow: If I was not allowed to return within a month, then I would run away and find my own way back, back to Mama and back to my brother.

Faced with my silence, Mama said, 'You had better rest now, child. Tomorrow you must get up and begin to regain your strength. Weather permitting perhaps you will feel up to travelling by Thursday.'

I knew that she was anxious that I should go. If I did not do so her husband would grow impatient. He was used to being obeyed without delay. In spite of his absence his influence still extended the miles between Dublin and County Cork. Closing my eyes, I wondered is there anywhere in the world that we can get away from him?

★   ★   ★

I managed to put off the parting until Friday although there was no opportunity to leave the house and visit Riari before we left. Fortunately a mild spell started on the Thursday which in some ways made travelling easier, although the paths were deep with mud and the going harder for the horses.

One of the maids, Niamh and another groom, Tomas, a cousin of Eamon Shaughnessey, were travelling with us. From the doorway, Mama waved us goodbye.

'You will take care?' I could read the anxiety in her face. It aged her, took away her personality.

I said, 'Of course Mama. I shall be quite safe and before long I will be back.'

She nodded but I don't think she believed me. Her lips quivered and I knew that there were things she wanted to say. I waited but with a deep intake of breath she forced a smile and waved me away.

'I hope you find Papa well.'

'I'm sure I shall.'

'And Clarissa.'

We went through the motions and I bit back the urge to tell her that I intended to come back no matter what. Anything I said would only add to her fears.

'Goodbye, Mama. Take good care of yourself.'

I pushed Shamrock on, glancing back once or twice to see her poor, solitary figure diminishing as we gained the roadway.

On the journey I often rode ahead with Abel while the other servants followed behind. He told me about the rainfall that had inundated large areas of Dublin on his last visit and how the gentry had amused themselves by sailing along the thoroughfares and right into the town. Many poorer people had been drowned, unable to escape from the flash floods that raced along the course of the river and across the mud flats. Fortunately our house is far enough away from the waterside to be unaffected but I felt sorry for those who had no means of escape.

Thinking of the poor of Dublin reminded me of Liam Delany. I asked Abel, 'You don't happen to know where the Delanys of Falconridge live in Dublin?'

I saw the subtle stiffening of his back as he

turned his deaf act on me. Undaunted, I continued, 'I happened to bump into Dr Delany the day I rode with you. He practises in the city.'

Abel visibly thawed. 'Ah. Mr Liam. He's a grand fellow. He works from the new hospital. It isn't completed yet and he gives much of his time for free when he isn't fund raising as well. He goes regularly to the Lazar Hospital too. A good man is Mr Liam Delany. He cares about people, not just the rich and powerful but the poor and weak. A grand man.'

I remembered Liam's gentle, smiling face. The thought of him was somehow comforting. Hopefully our paths would cross when once I reached the city.

We arrived in the late afternoon. It struck me how many different kinds of places there were in Ireland. Not long before we had been out in the countryside, surrounded by nothing but silence and green. Now the world had changed to grey and the very air was filled with the rumble and bustle of the city, the clattering of sleds, the clopping of horses' hooves, the murmuring of human voices. To my surprise I realized that I liked them both. Back there on the road was space and emptiness and a timeless quality that drew me to it, while here was variety and surprise

141

and stimulation. I wasn't looking forward to seeing Papa but in other ways Dublin drew me back.

As we turned into Sackville Street I was surprised to see a crowd gathered about halfway down, near to where we lived. Abel drew back for a moment and we all hesitated, waiting for him to confirm that all was well. Slowly we rode closer and as we did so I could see that indeed the gathering was right outside the entrance to our house.

'Whatever is happening?'

As I looked I realized that most of the crowd consisted of poor people. There was an air of excitement about them, the same anticipation that might precede a horse race, or a hanging.

'What is it?' Ignoring Abel I pushed ahead, riding as close as I could without trampling on the assembled gathering.

'What is happening?'

A grubby-looking man with ginger hair and blackened stubs for teeth turned towards me. 'Tis a fasting. Yon feller's fasting upon the owner, demanding retribution.'

I didn't understand what he meant. Craning my head over the top of the crowd I could see that there was a smaller huddle right by the railings. 'What is happening?' I repeated for the third time.

Abel took control, dismounting and clearing a passage so that we could approach the steps. As I pushed my way through I came face to face with a young man, draped in an Irish shawl. He was chained by the wrists to our railings. His face was grey, the hollows of his cheeks shadowed by the twilight, his garments frosted in the seeping damp. It was my brother Riari.

My heart gave such a jolt that I could only stare at him. In return he raised his dark eyebrows provocatively at me. 'Well, Miss Richborowe, I didn't expect to see you here.'

I continued to stare at him, making no sense of what I saw.

Behind me, Abel was urging me forward. 'Come away, miss.'

At last I managed to ask, 'Whatever are you doing?'

Riari's lips curved down in a sneer. 'It seems that someone has informed your stepfather that my father became a Catholic before he died. Sir Julius now claims that if such was the case, then my father had no authority to pass on any of his land so he is demanding it for himself. He spat symbolically over his shoulder. 'I would die rather than hand him Otters Lough. I intend to stay here until he retracts the claim.'

I felt positively shaken. Guiltily I remembered what I had said to Mama. Had she written to Sir Julius and told him? Surely not. And yet she was so in awe of him, so afraid, that perhaps she was unable to keep anything to herself for fear that he would find out and accuse her of disloyalty.

'How long have you been here?' I asked.

'Three days. There's a long way to go yet. I'll stay until I starve if I have to.'

'You aren't eating?'

'Of course not.' He sneered at my ignorance. 'This is the traditional way. There is no other.'

Niamh and Tomas hurried up the steps and into the house, unwilling to be drawn into any sort of dispute. With difficulty Abel held onto all four horses. His prods were becoming more persistent.

Riari nodded towards the man standing next to him. 'This is my friend and lawyer, James Delany. He is representing my rights.'

'Ma'am.' The short, sturdy, man at his side bowed his head. I was immediately struck by the resemblance to Liam although his face was older, more irregular in shape and it had a leaner, more reserved quality. My throat grew dry. Of all the people in the world, he was the one who might be able to answer all my questions. I stared at him, too tongue-tied

144

to be able even to acknowledge the introduction.

The memory of Mama's face, her flushed cheeks, made me stare at him. Was she, could she have been attracted to him? He was certainly not handsome. Neither had the years dealt kindly with him for his face was lined and his belly bulged beneath his waistcoat. But he looked kind, a quality which had been singularly lacking in my mother's life. I had not expected to meet him in these circumstances.

He said, 'So you are the daughter of Mr Richard Ashburn?'

I nodded, looking to Riari for some acknowledgement but he had closed his eyes. The weather was damp. It was growing cold. He looked ill and exhausted. He could surely not remain where he was?

Seeing my concern, James Delany was about to speak but he was forestalled by Abel. 'Miss Karenza!' He positively shoved me up the step. 'Go along now! This is no business of yours.'

'Oh, but it is!'

As he guided me away, Riari called out, 'You had best stay away from this. It is not your concern. My quarrel is with your stepfather.'

With that, I was pushed forward and the

door closed behind me. I stumbled into the hall and before I could gather my wits I was greeted by a bellow from Sir Julius. 'Get her out of here!' His face was puce with anger.

I looked around for anyone familiar but there were a gaggle of strangers, new servants brought in to prepare the house for the visit of Sir Fulton Monroe.

'Papa?'

'That scum out there is about to get everything he deserves.' Sir Julius positively fumed, his fists balls of anger. I wondered if he might hit out at me just to relieve his tension. I remained silent. He said: 'What is the world coming to when bastards and peasants think they can dictate to their betters?'

I kept very still, not wishing to provoke him with any gesture however slight that he might be able to interpret as disobedience. For the first time I noticed that there was someone with him, not a servant but a middle-aged man in a good quality coat and breeches, sporting a luxuriant golden wig.

The man said, 'Sir Julius, I must urge caution. The crowd is growing larger by the minute. Any attempt to disperse it might result in a riot with unknown consequences for your property, or even for yourself.'

Sir Julius harrumphed away, snorting like

an over-excited bull. The man in the wig added, 'Besides, the young man has his lawyer with him. It is the lawyer who holds the land, not the lad. He is a Protestant, a man of means. I cannot think it would be wise to challenge him. There is a goodly chance that you would lose.'

My stepfather blustered some more and after a respectful silence his companion, whom I assumed to be Mr Toby Burlington, one of the foremost lawyers in Ireland and Sir Julius's adviser in legal matters, added, 'I know, too, that you have an interest in growing flax, but the government are encouraging everyone to do so. I cannot see how you can hope to have a monopoly. If you try to take the production away from this young man he will still have the law on his side. After all, he may be a bastard and a Catholic, but in effect he is only a tenant, and he can justly claim to be doing what his landlord approves of.'

As Sir Julius seemed about to burst with rage, he added, 'Besides, you have your visitors to think of. It would not look good to have this sort of dispute when so much is at stake.'

'Paaah!' Sir Julius finally exploded, but like a balloon I could see him positively deflating. He said, 'Get rid of him then. Tell him

147

whatever you like.'

'I er — I don't think he will go unless he gets an assurance from your own lips.'

Papa positively trembled with impotent anger. Gently the visitor said, 'Perhaps if you can bring yourself to say that you will not pursue a claim to the land or interfere in his linen production then . . . After all, you can always change your mind at a later date.'

Taking a deep breath, my stepfather strode to the door and flung it open. Cautiously I followed behind.

'Kilbryde!' In the face of his presence the crowd subsided into silence. From the vantage point of the step, Sir Julius towered over my brother. His sword was at his side and for a terrible moment I wondered whether in the heat of the moment he might not draw it and run him through.

Riari met my stepfather's eyes. For a long, dramatic time both men stared at each other with mutual hatred, then Riari said, 'I want a verbal statement from you, in front of this assembly, and then the same thing in writing.'

Sir Julius who had clearly been about to make his own demands stood with his lips working like a breathless goldfish. I kept very still and the man in the golden wig gave a tiny nod of his head, urging his reluctant client forward.

'Very well. I have no need for your few paltry acres. Why you are making this fuss I cannot imagine.'

'Are you saying that you make no claim to Otters Lough?'

'Of course I don't make a claim to it. Why should I? There seems to be some silly misunderstanding here.'

'Then you swear to it before this gathering? And you will put it in writing?'

'Good God, man, if that's what you want.' Sir Julius pretended amazement, amusement even. He could be a good actor when he chose.

The crowd let out a collective sigh. It was tinged with regret for the fun was suddenly over. One by one they started to drift away.

Mr Delany bent his head and said something to Riari. I remembered how much I had hoped to be able to meet my father's friend and talk to him. Now there seemed little likelihood that I would ever be allowed into his presence. Indeed, the chances of seeing Riari again were slipping away.

Mr Delany released the chains and I watched Riari stretch his aching arms, massage his bruised wrists, his numb hands. I wanted to rush to his side and sooth his aching limbs but my stepfather still stood between us.

Before I could say anything, Sir Julius turned and pushed me inside. 'Get away from here or you'll be sorry.' I looked at Riari, hoping for some recognition but he was preoccupied with his own affairs. Reluctantly I went back indoors. The atmosphere was still taut with explosive tension. The best course of action seemed to be to retire to my room. I certainly had plenty to think about.

* * *

I did not see Sir Julius or Clarissa until the following morning by which time my stepfather had regained some of his equilibrium. As I came into the parlour for breakfast, Clarissa studiously ignored my arrival, but I greeted her with sisterly affection, determined to make the best of the time to come. If I was co-operative then at the end of the ordeal perhaps I might win permission to return to Kilcreggan.

As I listened to the conversation between Sir Julius and Clarissa I gathered that the Monroes had taken a house in the new development south of the river at Merrion Square. Clarissa unthawed sufficiently to confide that when she married she would be quite content to own a house in that neighbourhood. In the meantime, she and I

150

would be riding out in the park with Cavendish that afternoon. I was about to suggest that Shamrock would need a rest when Clarissa added, 'Sir Fulton has the most exquisite new carriage.' Clearly we were not to ride but be driven. Being ensconced with Clarissa and her betrothed in an enclosed carriage was not appealing.

Now that she had an audience, Clarissa became quite voluble, reeling off a list of engagements. That evening the Monroes were to dine with us and the following evening we were invited to a soirée with friends of Papa's at Palace Row where it was mooted that the viceroy himself might be present. In between times there were planned shopping sprees, a shooting party, a ball and a plethora of social get-togethers organized for the visitors' entertainment. I braced myself and prepared to be bored.

On being reacquainted with the Monroes my worst memories were confirmed. Cavendish with his foolish affectations, Lady Elizabeth with her innate snobbery and Sir Fulton with his penchant for losing control of his hands whenever we were alone, were about the least pleasant companions I could imagine. I tried to shut the thought of them out, thinking instead of Riari, wondering what he would tell Orla about his time in

Dublin. As I relived the scene outside the house, I regretted that I had not been braver. What I should have done was to chain myself next to him, a declaration of our kinship and of my hatred for my stepfather. Surely as I had done nothing he must think me weak and spineless?

So preoccupied was I with my own thoughts that it was several days before I realized that Sir Julius had added a new companion to our outings, and one whom I heartily disliked. The man was called Percival Wilkes and he had apparently made a fortune in shipping beef to Europe. It seemed that he was looking to diversify and Sir Julius had invited him to consider participating in the linen venture.

Mr Wilkes was essentially grey; grey hair, grey eyes (although liberally bloodshot), with grizzled moustachios and grey, unhealthy-looking skin. His clothes were of a similar hue although expensively adorned with lace and pearl buttons. There was something inherently degenerate about his appearance, a skeletal quality as if he had been worn away with ill living. The pores at the end of his nose seemed unnaturally enlarged and I fancied that perhaps this was to allow the geneva, which he imbibed in great quantities, some means of escape. His skin seemed to exude the very smell of the drink. When he breathed his lungs rasped, putting up an uneven struggle against the acrid fumes of a pipe which was invariably clamped between the brown stain of his teeth.

I wondered how Papa had become acquainted with such an unpleasant man and when I asked Clarissa, she replied, 'Why, they patronize the same clubs.'

'Clubs?'

She gave me a pitying stare as if amazed at my ignorance. 'Any gentleman who has influence in the town conducts his business at his clubs. Surely you know that?'

I did not want to confirm my ignorance so I remained silent. For the moment I was satisfied with her explanation, but a few days later, rising early and being the only one at breakfast, I could not help overhearing the servants' gossip. Through the panelling that separated the dining-room from the passage-way, I learned that both Sir Julius and Mr Wilkes were regular visitors to something called the Hellfire Club. This was, it seemed, a place of the most ill-repute housed at the Eagle Tavern in Dame Street and those who visited launched themselves into every form of dissipation imaginable. Although I was unclear as to what sort of dissipation they might mean, it did not sound at all like the sort of place to do business.

I felt deeply uneasy. From what I heard, other women were involved. Poor Mama. I wondered if Mr Wilkes also possessed an unfortunate wife but when I mentioned it to Clarissa, she said, 'Oh no, Mr Wilkes is free, although I do believe he is in the market.' She gave me a peculiar look which I did not understand so I chose to ignore it. In the meantime the routine of outings and visits continued unabated.

For the Friday of our second and final week, Sir Julius purchased tickets to a concert at the Music Hall in Fishamble Street. This was a charitable event to raise money for a lying-in hospital for the poor. When I heard where we were going I was somewhat surprised for normally Sir Julius would not have associated himself with such an event. On this occasion, however, it seemed that some very eminent people were expected to be present, hence my stepfather's wish to be seen as a generous supporter of the city's under-privileged. Indeed, the sale of tickets was so successful that they came with a request that the gentlemen should leave their swords at home and that those ladies who clung to the older fashion should refrain from wearing hoops. In this way the maximum number of patrons could be accommodated.

I was dismayed to find that once again Mr Wilkes was to be a member of our party, as was a lady called Eugenia Martin. Lady Martin was in her prime, a dark-haired, dark-eyed lady of not more than thirty, with a look of the Spanish about her. I was surprised that Sir Julius should bother about her, given that he had little time for the Spanish but to Eugenia, he could not have been more attentive.

'Is Lady Martin married?' I asked Clarissa.

The smirk was there again. 'You could call it that. Her husband is Sir Godfrey Martin. He is at least ninety.'

'Where does he live?'

'He owns much of Kilkenny. He's there now. They say he's dying.' There was dismissal in Clarissa's voice.

I felt shocked by her blatant disregard. 'Should his wife not be with him?' I asked.

'Really, Karenza, you amaze me.' Something about Clarissa's tone implied that there was more to this than I fully understood so I decided not to ask any more questions.

On Friday evening, I travelled to the concert in a coach with Clarissa and Cavendish and Mr Wilkes, whilst a second carriage conveyed Lord and Lady Monroe, Sir Julius and Lady Martin. Mr Wilkes insisted on sitting unnecessarily close to me

155

and although I kept edging away, he persisted in moving ever nearer, his hand coming to rest on mine as they lay folded in my lap.

'You have a fine figure, my dear.' He looked meaningfully at my breasts and I turned away, trying to ignore him. Undeterred, he continued, 'You can be sure that your stepfather wants what is best for you.'

I had no idea what he was talking about but I nodded politely, looking to Clarissa and Cavendish to distract him but they seemed absorbed in each other.

The Music Hall was packed indeed. Our seats were placed so close together that whichever way I moved, my body was pressed against my neighbour and given the choice of touching either Mr Wilkes or Lord Monroe, I froze into myself and prayed that the evening would soon be over which was a pity for the ensemble played delightful music by Mr Handel and Mr Purcell.

Looking about me I was delighted to see Liam a few rows ahead. The very sight of him seemed to calm the unease that had been with me ever since we reached the city.

I was looking to find an opportunity to call out to him when I realized that he was in the company of a pretty woman who, throughout the performance, leaned against him in a most intimate way. Her presence shocked me.

To tell the truth I was somewhat put out. Without having really thought about it I had labelled him as quite plain and therefore unlikely to be attached. Looking at him smiling at his companion, I revised my opinion. He might not be rugged or athletic in the way that many men, including my own brother Riari, were, but there was a certain attractiveness in his appearance, not least in his wide, good-natured smile and laughing eyes. If I were to be honest with myself I was affronted because he was with a beautiful girl whereas I was squashed between these two elderly lechers.

I looked around to see if there was any sign of James Delany but I could not see him. Much of the time I heard nothing of the concert, wondering instead how I would ever find the chance to meet my father's friend and finally learn the things that I wanted to know.

As the concert drew to an end I hoped to have a chance to speak with Liam but he did not appear even to see me. As I watched, hoping to attract his attention, he was swept along by a group of friends, all laughing and joking. Their very sociability left me with a terrible sense of isolation. I did not want to be here with Sir Julius and his hateful companions. With a sudden surge of longing I yearned to return to Kilcreggan and to the valley that led to Otters Lough.

By the time we began our journey home it was dark and, once again, I was seated next to Mr Wilkes. To my horror, as we drove along he reached out and tried to slip his hand under my skirts.

'How dare you!' I pushed him away, indifferent to the fact that I might be embarrassing him in front of Cavendish and Clarissa but they said nothing and in the gloom I realized that they were locked in an embrace.

Seemingly undeterred, Mr Wilkes took my hand, resting it in his lap where to my disgust I could feel the bulge of his manhood. I tried to pull myself free but he held tight to me and my tugging seemed to excite him. I could not quite believe it when he said, 'Better get used to it, my dear, Sir Julius is quite agreed.'

'I don't know what you are talking about.'

'Come along now, you aren't a child.'

'You aren't suggesting that I should marry you?'

He chuckled, an unhealthy, rasping noise. 'Not marry, no. I've always been of the belief that blossoms are better by the bunch than singly.' As I struggled to free myself he pushed harder against my hand and then,

158

with an audible outpouring of breath, relaxed his hold.

'Stop the coach!' I leapt away from him disgusted by his very presence.

At this Cavendish and Clarissa were forced to tear themselves apart.

'Karenza, whatever are you doing?'

'This man molested me!'

There was silence. At last, Clarissa, lowering her voice, said, 'Don't be so foolish. You owe a lot to Papa. At least you could be nice to his friends.'

'Nice? This man assaulted me!'

Mr Wilkes gave a jovial little chuckle. 'Nonsense, dear child. You are imagining things. Don't fret now. We'll sort it all out with Sir Julius later.'

Throughout the rest of the journey I kept as far away from him as possible while Clarissa and Cavendish, faced with my undivided attention sat reluctantly apart. I felt a little sorry for them for within a day or two Cavendish would be leaving to accompany his parents back to Scotland. It would then be several months before Clarissa and possibly Mama and I joined them in England to meet the right people and purchase Clarissa's trousseau. They might want to make the most of their time together but for the moment I could think only of myself. I needed their attention to keep Mr Wilkes at bay.

The other coach had reached Sackville Street before us and, as we made our way inside, Lord and Lady Monroe, Sir Julius and Lady Martin were already in the drawing-room drinking wine. Sir Julius welcomed our party with a great show of bonhomie. I knew that it did not extend to me and before he could object I excused myself and went straight to my room. I was still shaking, wondering how to handle the delicate matter.

I must have been upstairs for perhaps half an hour when there was a peremptory knock at the door, which opened before I had a chance to answer. Sir Julius stood in the doorway, breathing heavily from the exertion of climbing the stairs. Quickly I stood up, alarmed at the sight of his angry expression.

'What have you been doing?' he asked.

'Doing? Nothing.'

'That's not what I heard. I hear you have been upsetting my friend Mr Wilkes.'

'Upsetting him? He behaved in a most unseemly manner.'

Sir Julius tossed my objections aside. 'That's enough, girl. Mr Wilkes is a very influential gentleman. He can do our family a great deal of good.' He came a little closer, his head tilted back, looking at me as if seeing me properly for the first time. 'You're quite a presentable piece. If Percy was in the marriage market then I'd make sure that you were his choice, but as it is he isn't inclined to matrimony so we'll just have to go along with the way things are. Given time I might be able to persuade him round, but either way it doesn't really matter. He's got more money than you can imagine. More even than the Monroes. By the time I've finished with him that money will be ours.'

'But . . . ' I was too stunned to reply.

As he talked, Sir Julius adopted that foolish, benign look that affects some men in their cups. It reminded me of the day he told me that he might have to divorce Mama. He reached out to touch my face but I jerked away. He shrugged. 'Anyway, there's nothing for you to worry about. It is all done with my permission. It's time some man taught you what it's all about. Might as well be one who can give us something worth having in return.'

'You aren't suggesting that I — '

'Not suggesting, telling you.'

I couldn't believe what he was thinking. Aloud, I said, 'I can't. I won't! You must be mad to suggest it. He's the most foul, depraved — '

Sir Julius hit me hard across the face. The

161

move was so fast, the change of mood so unexpected that it left me reeling. Grabbing my arm he pulled me to him. 'That's enough of that. There's no can't or won't about it. You will and that is all there is to it. Percival is coming over tomorrow. The Monroes will have gone by then. If he feels inclined to remain for a few days then so he shall. And you will do all that you can to make him welcome. Now. Get you to bed. I've made your excuses downstairs.' He threw back his head, looking at me with derision. 'You had better get as much sleep as you can tonight because tomorrow you'll probably get very little, not if I know old Percy.'

With that he left the room, leaving me in a state of disbelief. Nothing in my life had prepared me for this moment. Whatever his failings I had somehow believed that in the end Sir Julius would protect me. Now I knew otherwise. What would my mother do? What would she say if she knew? It would surely kill her. Meanwhile, I could not, would not, stay.

Without waiting a moment longer I changed from my evening gown into my riding habit, fumbling in my attempt to make haste. Once I was dressed I crept down the stairs, my heart in my mouth in case I should be discovered, but they were all still in the drawing-room.

162

Cautiously I crept out through the back door and hastened away in the direction of the stables. By this time tomorrow, with God's protection, I would be well on my way to Kilcreggan.

8

I don't think anything could have prepared me for the nightmare of that journey. By the time I crept from the house it was after midnight but there were still people in the streets, mostly drunkards and homeless men and women for whom night or day made little difference.

I felt like a mouse creeping out into the night, exposing itself to every threat imaginable — cats, dogs, birds of prey, flailing hooves — the violence of man. As I scurried towards the stable I prayed to God to protect me. By concentrating all my thoughts inside my head I managed not to look about me, hoping that in some way I would become invisible. Whether or not my prayers were answered I can't be sure but I reached the stables without mishap.

I arrived in total darkness. At first I could not even guess which box housed my own Shamrock. Sometimes the horses are moved around so that they were not always in the same stall. When I eventually located him I then had the problem of finding his saddle and bridle in the darkness and tacking him up. While his companions continued with their comforting business of crunching hay, Shamrock snorted his objection, holding his head so high that I was hard pushed to reach him. Swinging his hind quarters around I had great difficulty in lifting the saddle onto his back and then reaching the girth which dangled on the far side of his belly.

At last I had him ready and pulling hard on his bridle I managed to drag him reluctantly into the yard where I made a business of mounting. Only after what seemed an eternity did we leave the stable-yard and set out for Great Britain Street which leads out of the city and towards the west.

I comforted myself with the knowledge that we must surely pass within a few yards of the Delanys' house and I tried to guess which one it might be. Should I knock at a door and ask them to help me? Of course I could not. It was one o'clock in the morning and anyway, they might consider it their duty to return me to Sackville Street. If, on the other hand, I was to tell them the reason for my escape then who knew what might follow? It struck me that neither of them was the sort of man to let a wrong go unpunished, and to bring further trouble between them and my stepfather would be madness. Resolutely I kept riding.

Before long the row of houses gave way to poorer habitations, then occasional work-shops and stores and finally to open land. It was still almost completely black. We could only make slow progress for poor Shamrock, now thoroughly subdued, needed to feel his way along for the moon was no more than a sliver of silver light. As we drew further into the countryside I remembered the bog in the valley leading to Otters Lough. Supposing we encountered something similar out here, alone and miles from anywhere? We would surely be lost. As I rode, with only Shamrock to hear, I snivelled to myself like some abandoned orphan.

As the sky began to lighten I set my course by the sun's rising, hoping that I was not totally confused. I longed to dismount and find somewhere warm and dry to sleep, but we still had many miles to go and I had to arrive, if possible, by daylight.

As the morning wore on my thirst got the better of me and I stopped at a stream to drink. The water was brown, whether from the gentle erosion of the peat or from some contamination in the stream I neither knew or cared. At my side, Shamrock rested his muzzle delicately on the surface of the water and took his fill. He then proceeded to tear at the poor, sparse grass on the bank and much as I wanted to hurry on, I had not the heart to stop him. My own stomach felt little more than a shrivelled spot somewhere in the centre of me, made the colder by the water I had just imbibed.

I don't know what distance we had covered but as darkness threatened again I had no idea where we were. Poor Shamrock travelled with his head lower and lower, his legs barely propelling him forwards. For the last hour I too walked, my boots water-logged with mud, rubbing against my stockings until my heels were raw. There was no escape from the throbbing pain in my toes, my aching legs, the gnawing hunger in my stomach or the stinging hurt of rain against my cheeks.

No longer could I think straight. Inside my head were a series of visions, pictures of warm, happy occasions, of tables loaded with food and great log fires, of music and laughter. Forcing my eyes to focus through the icy drops of rain on my lashes, I located a hollow beneath a twisted oak tree and leaving Shamrock to wander, I curled up and shrunk into myself.

I knew nothing, until from a great distance a voice roused me, echoing into the reaches of my mind. '*Conas a ta tu?*' I managed to open my eyes and found myself staring at an old woman who was bending over me. I closed my eyes again then opened them, registering the soft feel of goose down beneath me, the heavy warmth of covers over me.

'*Cad is anim duit?*'

'Ashburn,' I replied sleepily. 'My name is Karenza Ashburn. And I am well. *Taim go maith.*'

I felt peculiarly at ease. True, my limbs felt stiff, my toes itched with the familiar torment of chilblains and my lips were cracked from exposure to the elements, but in all other respects I felt remarkably well.

'My horse?' I looked at the old lady.

'He is taken care of.'

I relaxed. I should be worrying about where I was and what I was going to do but I couldn't find the energy. Here, in this soft coccoon of a bed, it was too cosy.

The old lady took up a bowl of soup and insisted on spooning a few mouthfuls between my lips. Obediently I opened and closed my mouth, like a fledgling. I felt like a child again, cared for, safe in the comforting protection of an adult. When I had finished drinking, the old woman looked pleased.

'Well, my dear what a fright you gave us. Whatever were you doing, out there alone?'

'Where is this?'

She smiled. 'Lost, are you? You're at a place

168

called Falconridge.'

'Falconridge?' I sat up with disbelief. 'How did I get here?'

'One of our shepherds found you down at the mouth of the valley. And a good job he did, too, or dead you would be by now.'

I shook my head, overwhelmed by the course that events had taken. 'I have been here before,' I said. 'I met Dr Delany.'

'Did you indeed? Well he left this very morning.'

I sat up. 'Did he know that I was here?' Try as I might I could remember nothing other than the aching weariness of my journey, the cold and hunger and then waking up in this bed. Had I seen Liam? What might I have said to him? What must he think?

The old lady asked, 'Was it him you were trying to reach?'

'No.' Surely by now he would have sent word to Kilcreggan! My thoughts were interrupted as my companion held out a folded paper.

'Mr Liam was sorry that he had to leave but he asked me to give you this.'

He had seen me then. My hand shook as I took the letter. Breaking the seal, my eyes misty with weariness and fear, I read: *First the quay at Ormonde, then here at Falconridge, next at the Music Hall, now*

169

under a bush in the valley — where will you turn up next? No more dangerous wanderings now! Be sure to drink the potion I have left with Maire. Do not worry. I will not give you away. L.

I felt a sudden lifting of my spirits. He did remember me from the day we saw the apprentices. He had seen me at the concert although he had not acknowledged me. I hadn't thought of it at the time but in view of the company I was with, that was hardly surprising. Most of all though, he was not going to tell anyone where I was. I felt such a surge of gratitude towards him. He was probably the kindest, most intuitive man I had ever met.

As if picking up my thoughts, the old lady asked, 'Do you plan to stay here?'

Liam's note had not exacted any promise from me that I should do so. Aloud, I said, 'No. I — I was making for my brother's house at Otters Lough.'

The old lady gave me a quizzical look. 'Your brother?'

'Riari Kilbryde.'

I saw her surprise and wondered whether I should be saying it. I had no guarantee that I could rely upon her silence. What sort of trouble might I be bringing to my family by this public acknowledgement? And to Orla?

170

Instead, should I not be going home to Kilcreggan and to Mama? For a moment my resolve nearly weakened, but then I reminded myself that if I went home, the shock of my arrival and the reason for my running away would cause her as much grief as my disappearance.

Besides, it was Riari I wanted to see. Riari.

'Well,' the old lady said. 'Just you rest now. Once you are strong enough someone will escort you to Otters Lough. Do you wish us to send a message to say that you are safe?'

'No. No, thank you. They are not expecting me.'

She bowed her head and left me and in the warm glow of the room I closed my eyes and thanked God for my mysterious delivery.

In fact I was weaker than I thought and when I attempted to rise from the bed that evening, my legs refused to hold me. It was not for another two days that I was up and dressed and ready to leave.

'*Go raibh maith aguth*. Thank you very much.' I squeezed the old lady's hands. 'You have been more than kind to me.' I indicated my clean, sponged garments and dried and oiled boots.

'Nonsense, now. Do you have any message for Dr Delany?'

'No. Just convey my thanks to him for his kindness.'

She bowed her head and watched at the doorway while I mounted the horse awaiting me. It was not Shamrock for his poor legs were still swollen and had heat in them. Instead they lent me the thirty guinea mare that Liam had ridden so inexpertly on my last visit here. There was something comforting in taking his place in the saddle as if his spirit still remained to take care of me.

A groom came to accompany me and together we began the descent into the valley. I didn't quite know what to think. What was I going to say when I reached Otters Lough? What would they think, Orla and Riari? Would I be welcome, or would my presence be an embarrassment to them? Perhaps I should change my mind and go home to Kilcreggan. But even as the thought came to me I had visions of Sir Julius arriving in a great rage. Might he not carry me directly back to Dublin, back to the odious Percival Wilkes?

The groom did not talk so I was left to these thoughts. Soon I recognized the familiar landmarks that showed the way to Otters Lough. As we skirted Kilcreggan and entered the valley, I said, 'You can leave me now. I would rather make the rest of the journey

172

alone.' I did not want him witnessing my arrival, overhearing the explanations and perhaps seeing me turned away by unwilling hosts.

'If you are sure, miss.'

'Perfectly. And thank you for your time.'

'Tis welcome, you are.' He raised his hat, bowing in farewell and turned his horse back. The hunter tried to follow but I pushed her forward and after a moment's refusal she gave in, picking her way along the already familiar path that led to the farmhouse.

'Oi!' I heard the shout before I saw anyone and as I looked towards the direction of the sound I saw Riari standing at the gateway, watching my progress along the path. At the sight of him my entire being seemed to be overtaken by some tidal wave of tension. I was on a knife edge, waiting.

'What the . . . ' I realized that he had been looking at the horse rather than the rider and until that second he did not realize who it was. 'God Almighty. What are you doing now?'

I knew immediately that coming here was a mistake, but it was too late to turn back. 'Good day.' I spoke to him in Gaelic then reverted to English. His probing gaze flustered me and my next words were

173

foolish in the extreme. 'I — I've left my stepfather's house. For ever.'

'Have you now?' He walked across and caught the hunter's reins as we drew near. 'Well, you'd better come inside. My mother is milking the cow but she'll not be long.'

I'd had the foolish notion that when next we met he would hold out his hands and say: Welcome, Sister, I've waited all my life for this moment. I forced myself to say, 'You do know who I am?'

'Miss Richborowe.'

His indifference threatened to pull me under but I struggled on. 'I've never been that. My father was Richard Ashburn, the same as yours.'

'So they tell me.'

I waited for him to respond but he did not. He merely indicated that I should go on into the house then turned away to take care of my horse.

I felt increasingly humiliated. Coming here was a terrible mistake. I should leave at once and go home although that entailed facing Riari again and asking for my horse back. More explanations, more humiliation.

I thought again of my mother. Of course, I should have gone home. Once she learned that I had run away she would be out of her mind with worry. My promise came back to me. Was this not enough to make her miscarry the baby? And it would be all my fault. No! I checked myself. It was the fault of my stepfather, her husband who was willing to use me for his own ends. She would never want that. For a crazy moment I thought that perhaps she could come and live here too, until I remembered that she and Orla had both been rivals for my father.

'Karenza, my dear, whatever has happened?' Orla came into the kitchen, wiping her hands on her skirts. I noticed how red and work worn her fingers were, but as she held them out to me I was glad to clasp them and rest my cheek against hers.

'Now, tell me what has upset you. Riari said that you looked distressed.'

He did? My spirits lifted a little. Perhaps he was not totally indifferent to my feelings after all. I said, 'It is difficult to explain. To be honest I have run away. I have been with my stepfather in Dublin and he keeps bad company. I could not stay and become the harlot of one of his friends.' My words brought back the memory of Percival Wilkes and I shuddered.

Orla pushed me to sit on the settle near to the fire. 'Indeed you could not. What does your mother think to all this?'

'She does not know. I came directly here.'

'You rode from Dublin? Alone?'

'I became a little lost. I ended up at Falconridge where Mr Delany's servants took me in.'

'I see.' She did not look as if she saw at all but she said nothing, taking the kettle from the trivet and beginning to make tea.

'What do you plan to do then?'

I hesitated. How could I say outright: *I plan to stay here*, not unless she invited me. Instead, I said, 'I don't know.'

'Well, while you are thinking about it, you must stay with us. That is if you don't mind sharing a bed with me?'

'Of course not. You are very kind.'

I accepted the bowl of tea and sipped it as my fears subsided. I was too tired to think about the future. I said, 'I will happily work for my keep.'

'Will you now?' She smiled as if the idea was amusing.

'I am good with horses,' I said in my defence. 'And I can sew well although I hate it.'

'We won't ask you to sew then.'

I knew she was making fun of me so I chose my next words carefully. 'Will Riari mind if I stay here? I — I get the impression that he doesn't like me.'

Her expression softened and she reached

176

out to touch my arm. 'Why should he not like you, child?'

I remained silent, unable to tell her about the great void that claimed me whenever I thought of his lack of approval.

Carefully, Orla said, 'I think it is taking him a little time to get used to the idea that he has a sister, that's all.'

'It's taking me time as well.'

9

It is amazing how quickly we slipped into a routine. Every day I helped Orla with her chores, seeing to the cow and the sheep, making cheese and butter, fetching potatoes which were stored on slats in the barn, cooking mutton stews with the vegetables saved during the summer months, making colcannon, spinning the flax into yarn.

This was the hardest task. I had been taught how to spin at home, but Orla had that gift for producing fine yarn of a coveted, regular thickness. In every spare moment she would take up the distaff and her fingers caressed the flax fibres with a gentle pressure that twisted them smoothly into a continuous thread. I watched, bewitched by her movements, envying her the unconscious skill. By contrast, my own efforts were poor and I wondered if I should ever master this craft — or could the flax be angry with me because of who I was and be determined to spoil my best endeavours? In this place where my stepfather was so deeply hated, I could not entirely laugh the foolish notion away.

At first Orla tried to give me the easiest

jobs around the farm, but I was determined not to be viewed as someone too superior — or useless — to pull her weight. When the weather became too bad I volunteered to clear the yard when it became impassable with mud. Soon my hands were as rough as hers and my cheeks took on the rosy tint of a country girl. I did not care. I worked so hard by day that sleep, deep and dreamless, came easily at night. I refused to think beyond the morrow and the comforting routine that we followed.

Only Riari disturbed my peace. Much of the time he was outside, working past darkness and when he did come in to eat or pass the evening until bedtime, he said little.

On days when it was too harsh to work outside he sat with his back to us, hunched at the loom weaving the brown linen, gleaning what little light he could from the small square window which faced to the south. This waterlogged climate suited the yarn perfectly and the damp from the earth floor spread like invisible fungus through the loom, keeping the cloth moist and workable.

When it grew too dark to see he sometimes paced restlessly, poking the peat with angry stabs to encourage a little more light and heat, or gazing out into the black emptiness as if he might penetrate its gloom. I feared

179

that my presence was unwelcome and if only I would leave he would find some sort of peace and settle.

When I tentatively suggested it to Orla, she merely replied, 'Riari is a man of the outdoors. He can never rest easily if he is caged inside.' I took small comfort in the knowledge that I was not the sole cause of his discontent.

When he was away from the house, I allowed myself to examine the cloth he had woven, wondering at the regularity of the weave, the subtle variations in colour that gave it a fine, marbled appearance. The webs stood in a neat pile waiting for the spring when he would sell them at the fair to be bleached and perhaps exported as far as England. I found it hard to believe that anyone could produce such a fine finish from such unpreposessing material and I longed to have the words to tell him of my admiration. Instead we did not speak and the void that longed for my brother's approval grew gradually deeper.

On those rare occasions when he was more forthcoming he spoke in Gaelic, addressing his remarks to his mother. This, too, made me feel in the way, humiliated, not knowing how to break through the barrier of his indifference. The longing niggled at me day and night.

After a while I realized that I must return the hunter to Falconridge and collect my own Shamrock. At the thought of leaving the confines of Otters Lough my fragile sense of safety began to ebb away. I had no wish to step beyond the valley or even beyond the farm itself. For a wild moment I wondered if Riari would go on my behalf, but I did not know how to ask him.

One damp morning, Orla sent me across to the byre to see if I could find any eggs. Although it was winter, one or two hens were still laying and she wished to enhance our larder by making a rich pastry filled with berries she had collected and dried that autumn. They now sat soaking in a bowl on the table.

'Even one will do,' she called after me, as I wrapped her shawl about my shoulders and picked my way across the yard.

As I went inside the barn the first thing I saw was Riari bending over one of his sheep and examining her hooves for any signs of foot rot.

'I've come to see if there are any eggs,' I called out, not wanting him to think that I had come into his company without a reason.

He did not acknowledge my remark, merely cursed under his breath as the ewe

181

kicked out at him, narrowly missing his leg.

For what seemed like forever I poked in all the likely corners but I could find nothing. A mouse, disturbed by my explorations scurried up the wall and through a tiny hole. To break the tension, I said, 'Tomorrow I must ride out and return the hunter. I need to fetch my pony.'

Still he did not comment. The nightmare journey from Dublin had stolen my courage, but I did not have the nerve to ask him if he would come with me. Instead, I heard myself say, 'Would you be happier if I left here?'

He was so long in answering that I didn't think that he was going to do so and when he did, his words were muffled so that I did not catch them.

With sinking heart, I added, 'I feel that I have outstayed my welcome.'

'Why should you think that?' He turned in my direction and his eyes held mine, challenging me to explain myself.

'You don't seem to like me.' To my own ears my words sounded increasingly foolish but I found the silences unbearable. My tongue began to run away with me. 'It is not my fault that my mother married Sir Julius Richborowe. I know that you hate him but you are luckier than me. At least you have this farm. I have nothing.'

He swung round, wiping his hands on his breeches and his eyes were dark with suppressed anger. 'I don't have this farm; Delany has it. He lets me use it as an act of charity.'

In spite of myself I could not let it rest. I said, 'That's not true. Your father left the land for you — for your mother. One day the law will change and it will be legally yours.'

He sniffed derisively. 'Who told you that? Delany? You think that will happen if I just sit back and wait patiently?'

I didn't know how to answer. In the end, I said, 'You made your point when you came to Dublin. What else can you do?'

He did not answer my question, instead saying, 'Anyway, it isn't just this farm. Look as far as you like. Once everything you see belonged to my father.'

'Our father.' I could feel myself being left out.

'Our father.' He looked surprised at himself for agreeing with me. With a sigh he let the sheep go and stood up, his hands resting on his haunches to ease the stiffness caused by crouching. 'It's different for you; you've always had everything.'

I was offended by his assumption. My life with Sir Julius flashed before me with all its pain. 'That's what you think. What have I had? Oh, there have been nursemaids and governesses and fine clothes, and I learned to play and sing and sew, but I haven't had the right to be myself. Not like you. I would gladly trade it all for this,' I looked around the dark echoing barn, adding, 'At least you have been free to make your own decisions. When Sir Julius married my mother he even stole my identity.'

I saw Riari suddenly tense, straining his ears in the direction of the yard. 'Someone is coming.'

At that moment I, too, heard the sound of horses. Riari frowned. 'Stay here.'

As he spoke he stepped outside. I sidled up to the doorway and peered out. My heart nearly stopped, for there, riding into the yard, was Sir Julius accompanied by two grooms.

Riari strolled across in his direction.

Sir Julius remained mounted, looking down at my brother with ill-disguised contempt. 'Where is she?'

'Who?'

'You know who. Richard Ashburn's brat.'

Riari spread his hands. 'Only my family live here. I don't know who you mean.'

Sir Julius smacked his crop impatiently across the flap of his saddle. 'Don't play the fool with me, Kilbryde. You are on borrowed time.'

Riari was unmoved. He asked, 'Is there any reason why whoever you seek should be here?'

Sir Julius turned to his companions. 'Search the place.'

'Just one moment!' Riari stepped forward. His manner was such that both men who had been in the act of dismounting, struggled back into their saddles.

To Sir Julius he said, 'You have no authority to come here and certainly no right to go into my house. If you try to do so then I will stop you by whatever means I must, as a trespasser. I have the law on my side.' The gravity of his words was belied by the even tone but it had an effect.

Sir Julius looked to his men. 'Go to the stables. See if the girl's pony is there.'

Riari spread his hands in acquiescence. 'If that will satisfy you, then do so. What has happened to this girl? Has she become lost or something?'

Sir Julius fretted in the saddle. 'I'm the one who is asking the questions.' He glanced down at his hip where a pistol rested to hand.

The grooms came back into the yard shaking their heads. Riari said, 'If she should happen to turn up here then I will escort her home — that is if she wishes to come. Meanwhile . . . ' He spread out his arm, indicating the gate, waiting pointedly for Sir Julius to leave.

Impotent, unwilling to start a brawl in which he might be hurt, Sir Julius said, 'If ever I learn that she has been here and you have kept her against her will, I'll burn this place to the ground.'

He did not wait for Riari to respond. Swinging his mount around he started back across the courtyard.

Before he could go any further Riari called out to him, 'Richborowe, I hear that you intend to start your own linen venture here. I hear that you have already issued notices to your tenants increasing their rents, threatening to bring your own men in if they cannot pay. Be warned: if you try to evict one tenant from his holding you'll have all of us to deal with.'

Sir Julius turned back. Supported on each side by a groom he rode across to where Riari stood. Without saying a word he raised his crop and brought it down hard in my brother's direction. Only Riari's quick reaction prevented it from landing across his face. In a flash he grabbed Sir Julius by the arm, hurling him from the saddle and into the mud. The two mounted escorts looked from one to the other but did not move.

As my stepfather puffed and struggled on

the ground, Riari said, 'This is your last warning: leave the villagers alone. And keep off my land.'

Beetroot red with rage, Sir Julius staggered to his feet, brushing ineffectually at the mud. As he bent to pick up his crop, Riari placed his boot on it. 'Just go. And don't think of drawing that pistol of yours because I'll have it out of your hand in seconds and if I had possession of it there's no telling what I might do.'

Sir Julius was too outraged for words. Puffing and snorting like a stallion, he grabbed the reins of his horse, wrenching its head round and struggling into the saddle. From his superior height, he said, 'I won't forget this, Kilbryde. And sure as I own this valley, you will come to regret it.'

Without looking back he rode away, his companions following behind. I guessed that later they would regret not having come to his assistance.

As they disappeared from view, I realized that I had been holding my breath and with a great gasp I released my fear.

Thank God that no harm had come to anyone. And when it came to it, Riari had not given me away. He had said that only his family were present. Was that his way of acknowledging that from now on we were kin? My spirits soared.

As he came back into the barn, I said, 'Thank you.'

He gave me an appraising look. 'I guess you had no wish to return with him?'

'Never.' I hesitated. 'Is he really planning to evict the men from his land?'

'No doubt about it. He wants to bring in skilled men from other areas. Most of his tenants are already behind with their rent. In no way can they pay more. It is a madness. They have no security so they do nothing to improve the land and every year it grows more poor and arid.'

There was a moment of uncomfortable silence. I wondered how it would all end. Riari broke into my thoughts. 'What is it that you plan to do then?'

Was this his way of saying that I could not stay here forever? I thought back to our disrupted conversation. I said, 'I want to gain my freedom. Like you, I want my own land.'

For a moment he circled the barn, thinking. I was reminded of the restless way he paced the house. Perhaps his thoughts were always busy, driving him on. The hint of retreating hooves was now no more than a distant echo, swallowed up by the other sounds of the countryside. Riari stopped and drew in his breath as if to speak, checking himself before he did so. Finally he said, 'How far would you go to get back what was yours — ours?'

'I don't know.' I was still trembling from Sir Julius's visit. I had no idea where this conversation was leading.

He went to stand near the doorway, gazing out across the yard. I could hardly hear his words above the wind. He said, 'There is a way, if you have the nerve to take it.'

'What?'

He looked round at me. 'That stepsister of yours.'

'Clarissa? What about her?'

'She's the heiress, isn't she?'

'Yes.'

'There you are then.'

'I don't know what you mean.' I moved a few steps closer to him. His eyes were diamond sharp with his thoughts, but at the same time there was a calculating look about him. He smiled to himself as if the enormity of what he was thinking amused him. It scared me.

He said: 'When your sister marries whatever she has will pass to her husband, is that not right?'

I nodded uncertainly. Now I thought of it, this was what had happened in Mama's case. Sir Julius had married her for the land. That was what Abel had said. But Cavendish Monroe was heir to such a fortune that Kilcreggan was only a minor addition to his estates. This could not be the only reason that he was marrying Clarissa.

I said, 'My stepsister is betrothed. She is to be wed next year.'

'Then we need to act before then.'

'How?'

Again he looked directly at me, but this time his eyes were challenging, or perhaps taunting. He said, 'If she married me then I would be the one to get the land.'

'You?' I couldn't imagine it. Clarissa agreeing to marry Riari? I blurted out, 'She would never do that.' I was afraid I might have offended him and wanted to explain what she was like, how she looked down on anyone poorer than herself, how the only thing that mattered to her was wealth and position.

He seemed immune to my response, asking instead, 'Did she choose her proposed husband?'

'No, of course not.' I frowned, not knowing where the question was leading.

'Exactly. Her father chose for her. Her value to him lies in her good name, in who she is. Take that away and what have you got left?'

'I don't know what you mean.'

He met my eyes again and I felt my skin grow warm under his scrutiny. He leaned back and studied me. 'Take you now. Don't you realize that by running away you have thrown away your value in the marriage market? In *their* marriage market? You are soiled goods, Sister, compromised. You have no worth any more.'

'I — ' Tears started to prick in my eyes at his assessment of me.

Riari said, 'It makes you cry? Does it matter so much to you? Do you want to be a commodity to be sold in their world? You probably do, it's all you've known.'

'No. I don't!' I began to see what he meant although not where his thoughts were leading. I asked, 'What does this have to do with Clarissa?'

Suddenly he grinned, an expression of exhilaration that transformed his face. I felt heady at the sight of him. He beckoned me closer, a boy with a secret he longs to share. 'Are you brave, Karenza Ashburn?'

'I think so.'

His look questioned the truth of my answer but he carried on, 'Are you willing to gamble? If you do what I want then you'll be breaking the law in a very big way. The penalty could be the highest, although if we are careful then there is no reason why we should not succeed.' In that second, bathed by the intensity of his look I would have done anything to keep his approval.

'What do you want me to do?'

'I want you to bring your sister Clarissa here.'

'I can't! What for?'

His answering grin bewitched me. 'Because I intend to compromise her. Once there is any doubt about her virtue, her good name, your Cavendish what's-his-name will drop her like a hot potato.'

'What are you going to do?' I thought of Percival Wilkes and my heart beat far too fast. Whatever I felt about her, I could not, would not put Clarissa in danger. 'What are you going to do to her?' I repeated.

'Nothing. Only hold her for a few days while I parley with her father.' He looked affronted that I might think otherwise. Thawing, he said, 'It isn't what I do that matters, it's what they think I might have done.' The prospect clearly amused him. 'If I were to despoil her then I'd face certain execution as a rapist, but if I let there be doubts as to her condition then she'll plummet in the marriage market. Only someone interested in getting his hands on the land will be willing to take her then, and that will be the last kind of suitor your stepfather will want. Especially if it was me.'

I was confused. A thought occurred to me. 'If that's the case, why should Sir Julius agree to you marrying her?'

'Because I shall let it be known that she is carrying my child.'

'You can't!'

'I can't?' There was something magnetic about him and I was engulfed in an almost exquisite anguish at the thought of all those years I had been denied the knowledge of him. 'You can't,' I repeated. 'For one thing you're a Catholic.'

His face hardened again. 'Do you think I'd let that stop me? My father changed his faith to get what he wanted. I can do the same. I'll take the oath. I'll swear allegiance to that fat king of yours across the water if that's what it takes. What does it matter as long as I get my land back?'

There was something about the depth of his bitterness that chilled me. In that moment it seemed there was nothing he would not do to get his own back on the people who had cheated him.

Uncertainly, I asked, 'What about me? What will I get from all this?'

'What do you want?'

What did I want? I didn't know. At least, I

did know that I didn't want Riari Kilbryde to marry my sister. The reasons were too complicated.

I said, 'I can't do what you ask. For one thing, when they find out, you'll be hanged. Besides, Clarissa is in Dublin.' But even as I spoke I suspected that she was with Sir Julius at Kilcreggan, waiting to see if I had come back there.

Riari turned to me and grasped me by the shoulders. His touch shot through me like fork lightning and his eyes burned with his sense of mission. 'Is it because you are afraid?'

'No.' I shook my head ignoring the uncertainty inside.

'Come on then, what do you say? You claim that you're my kin; what are you prepared to do, little sister, to get back our birthright?'

'I — ' I had no words.

I saw his brow begin to darken, his eyes grow cold. 'I'm asking the impossible, aren't I? At heart you're still one of them.'

'No! I'm not.' I scrabbled round for some way to explain what I felt but nothing came. All I knew was that I did not want to lose his good opinion. I remembered the conversation he and Orla had had the first afternoon I came to Otters Lough. At the time I had not understood it but Orla had said: 'I want no

194

part of it'. This was what they had been talking about, kidnapping the daughter of Sir Julius Richborowe. She must know the gamble that he would be taking. He risked losing everything, even his life. I asked, 'What about your mother?'

He did not acknowledge the question and my fears deepened. Looking into the hypnotic depth of his eyes, feeling the intense pressure of his fingers against my arms, I knew that I had no choice. From somewhere deep inside my head I heard myself say, 'All right, I'll do it.'

10

That evening, I said to Orla, 'I think I should go home. My mother will be worried about me.'

She put her sewing aside and gave me her attention. 'Of course you must, if you so wish.' For a moment she studied me, then, as if reading my mind, she said, 'Have you thought about what you are going to say to her? It won't be easy to explain your reasons for running away — or where you have been all this time.'

She was right. I would have to give Mama some explanation. I could think of nothing to tell her except the truth. By now, however, Sir Julius would have given her his own version of events. Who would she believe? If she accepted my story then any pretence that her marriage was acceptable would, surely, be dashed. On the other hand, if she did not believe me — my stomach began to churn at the prospect.

In spite of everything I still wanted to spare her any pain. Try as I might, I could think of no satisfactory alternative so I pushed the subject aside. I said, 'Tomorrow I will ride across to Falconridge and collect Shamrock then I'll go home.'

'Would you like Riari to go with you?'

My brother was sitting near to the hearth mending a piece of leather harness. He had his back to us but all the time I was aware of his presence. I glanced round at his crouched figure. His face was half in profile, shadows playing across his cheekbones, giving him a predatory, almost hawkish look. I knew that he was waiting for me to say that I needed his company. Once we were alone he would surely use the opportunity to further press me about abducting Clarissa.

I said, 'No. No, thank you. I will be better on my own.' From his changed posture I sensed his amusement — or was it disdain? He knew that I was having second thoughts and I was assailed by conflicting emotions, on the one hand wanting only to keep his approval and yet needing to protect us both from what was surely an act of folly.

The knowledge of my parting hung over the evening. With misgivings I thought that I had been happy here and now that Riari had acknowledged me as his kin I could have been even more content. I did not want to leave.

Although he hadn't said so I knew that he did not wish Orla to know about our discussion. Of course, she would be afraid, afraid for him, afraid of the consequences. All the anxieties came rushing back and quickly I pushed the thought of that, too, aside. With luck, Clarissa would have remained in Dublin and then I should be able to do nothing about it.

A hundred times during the night I changed my mind. To avoid thinking about the kidnapping I tried instead to envisage my arrival at Kilcreggan. Would everyone run out to greet me like a prodigal son, rejoicing in my homecoming? But Sir Julius? What was I to say to him? What would he do?

I tried to imagine a scenario where Sir Julius was away but Clarissa was present. Should I try to persuade her to come with me to Otters Lough? What reason would I give? And if I succeeded, how could I let Riari know?

That line of reasoning led me no further so I sought about in my mind for something more certain. There was nothing. I wondered if Mama was still with child which led me naturally to ponder on Sir Julius's intentions with regard to Lady Martin. If what they said was true and her husband was at death's door then she must be an attractive prospect as a widow. If Mama lost the child I wondered how far Papa would go to regain his freedom.

Immediately a worse thought occurred to me: if Sir Julius had made up his mind to have Eugenia Martin then a pregnant wife would be a hindrance indeed. Could Mama actually be in danger? I had few doubts that my stepfather was ruthless enough to take any action — even murder, to get his own way! The image was so vivid that I sat upright in bed, stifling a scream of terror. Beside me, Orla stirred and I fought back my nightmares. Once she settled I lay back again but I could not stop from tossing this way and that, seeking for a means of escape.

I remembered what Riari had said, that I was now valueless in the marriage stakes. If Papa remained married to Mama and if Clarissa married Cavendish, what would my future be? I would either stay at home for ever, an ageing and much despised spinster, or I would be forced to earn my own living, perhaps as a governess. On the other hand, Papa might use me as bait to entice the likes of Percival Wilkes into some lucrative agreement. Nowhere were there comforting answers.

Next morning Orla and Riari prepared for my departure. My brother brought the hunter round to the door for me while Orla insisted that I take her shawl to protect me from the threatening rain.

'You know that you can come back here, don't you, if all else fails.'

'Thank you. I do. You have been very kind to me.'

'Nonsense.' She gave me a quick hug. 'You are like the daughter I never had.'

I felt a surge of regret because during my stay we had not talked of my father. It was almost as if while I had been here I did not need to think about him. Now that I was about to leave I felt compelled to claim him as my own once more.

In silence, Riari reached out and grasped me about the waist, lifting me into the saddle. '*Slan agat*,' he said. 'You will be in touch?'

I read the message in his eyes. He was relying on me to set his plans in motion. I nodded, too overwhelmed by his presence, by what he wanted me to do, to speak.

Taking a deep breath I turned the hunter away from the farmhouse and began to journey home. When I glanced back Orla and Riari were standing together watching me. I wondered if I would ever see them again.

★ ★ ★

At Falconridge nobody questioned me about where I had been or where I was going. The Delany brothers were absent and I didn't

200

know whether to be disappointed or relieved. On my arrival, I merely handed over the hunter and received my pony in return. I took courage from their lack of curiosity. I had assumed that my family would have scoured the countryside looking for me and that news of the circumstances of my disappearance would surely have reached Falconridge. Perhaps I was mistaken. Sir Julius aside, perhaps my running away was regarded as really of no great import, either that or the enquiries had not reached as far as the Delany house. I hoped that my reappearance would be greeted with equal calmness at Kilcreggan.

It was strange to ride Shamrock again after all this time. I think he was pleased to see me and I took comfort in the knowledge that he was a true friend. As I rode back along the valley I reached the point where I could either turn right towards Kilcreggan or left and back to Otters Lough. My instincts were to turn left but I knew that I had to go home. Surely they must be concerned about me? I prayed that they would be so pleased to see me that the enormity of my running away would be forgiven.

The sight of the house set my blood racing so that my head was filled with the whoosh of it. My legs trembled against Shamrock's flank

201

and I felt an answering quivering along his ribs. 'Good boy, we'll be all right,' I assured him.

'Holy Mother!' Seamus was the first to see me and came running across the yard to meet me. 'Mistress Karenza, sure can it really be you? What a sight you are for sore eyes!'

'Good day, Seamus. Is my mother here?'

'Your mother and your sister.'

'Sir Julius?'

'No, missy. He left only this morning for Dublin.'

I breathed a sigh of relief. 'Are they very angry with me?'

'Angry? No — at least, your poor mama has been in great distress.'

I slithered to the ground, feeling instantly guilty. 'And her health?'

'Well enough, all things considered.'

I could not actually bring myself to ask him about the baby but from his tone I concluded that she was still with child.

The news of my arrival seemed to flit ahead of me and, as I walked through the door, I came face to face with Clarissa. Her hostility was almost tangible. 'What brings you back here? Haven't you done enough damage?'

'I don't know what you mean.' For a moment I thought that she was not going to let me pass and I had to squeeze by her to get into the hall.

'Karenza, oh my dear, dear girl!' From the gloom Mama gave a wail of anguish as she came rushing towards me, throwing her arms about me and clasping me tightly to her. 'My dearest daughter, wherever have you been? Praise to God you are safe. Are you hurt?'

'Mama, I am well. I am so sorry to have distressed you but there were reasons.'

I glanced around at Clarissa and she shot daggers at me. I turned back to Mama. 'Perhaps we could speak alone.'

Mama hesitated and for a moment I thought that Clarissa was going to insist on accompanying us. I realized that now she was betrothed, my stepsister's opinion of herself had risen even higher. Mama, ever timid, was in danger of becoming subservient to her. Turning to Clarissa, I said, 'Please do as my mother wishes and leave us.'

Clarissa began to expostulate, then, with a toss of her head, she retreated towards the stairway. Over her shoulder she said, 'Just wait until my father hears of this. You'll be sorry you ever came back!'

In the drawing-room Mama and I moved across to the fire-place. 'Oh my dear, I've been so worried. Out of my mind.' Mama continued to express her anxieties and I wondered what on earth I was going to say. She seated herself near to the fire, her hands clasped in her lap and waited. I took in the gentle roundness of her belly.

Eventually the words tumbled out. 'Mama, please forgive me for causing you such worry but it was beyond my control.'

'Why? How? Karenza, I must know what happened. Where have you been?'

I latched on to the last question. 'Mama, I am sorry that I cannot give you the details, but I have been under the protection of certain persons I encountered before I left Kilcreggan.' I had no idea what I intended to say next. I blurted out, 'They are decent people who have my welfare at heart.'

'The Delanys! I should have known it. Abel said you had been asking after them the day you rode with him on the road to Dublin. He said that you had asked after the Kilbrydes, too, but after what I told you I was certain that you would never go there.'

I felt my cheeks grow warm at the deception but I did not enlighten her.

Mama nodded to herself. 'The Delanys. I should have realized. True, Mr James Delany was your papa's friend but why did you not send word to me? You must have realized how worried I would be?'

I was as at loss. I did not want to tell her the truth. Taking charge, I asked, 'What did Sir Julius tell you?'

At the mention of his name I saw the too familiar tension grip her. 'Papa is sorely aggrieved. I do so hope that we can smooth things over before he returns. You have put him to such trouble and I am so ashamed that you neglected your duties in not staying to chaperone the rest of Clarissa's visit. Clarissa is most put out.'

'So I see.' I bit back the urge to tell her the truth.

She said, 'Were you welcome at Falconridge?'

'Mama, there is nothing for you to worry about.'

'I should write a note at once and thank them for their kindness to you, although it was remiss of them not to let me know that you were safe. Were you unwell that you did not write yourself? Anyway, why did you not come straight home?' The barrage of questions continued and the only comfort was that she did not give me time to answer them.

I asked, 'Are you in good health? The baby?'

'All is well, I thank God, although . . . ' Her face clouded and she bit her lower lip. 'Papa seems to have lost some of his enthusiasm for the baby. He — he seems quite distant. I think perhaps the worry over you has added to his burdens.'

I reached out and grasped her hand. 'Mama, why don't you leave here? What about the house you lived in before with my father, could we not go there? Surely it is still yours?' As she began to shake her head, I said, 'Why do you not consult Mr Delany about your rights to the property? Sir Julius cannot force you to stay here and if he does not want you then . . . '

'Oh but he does want me! Of course he does; I am his wife. It is just that he is such a busy man with so many responsibilities.' She gripped my hands tight in return. 'Karenza, please ask for Papa's forgiveness. He made mention of looking for a husband for you. It is so good of him. You must prepare yourself to make a good marriage.'

Something inside of me burst. I could not let the moment pass. 'You don't know the sort of man he had in mind. Anyway, marriage was not his first thought.'

'I don't understand.'

I struggled to find the right words. 'Mama, Sir Julius had someone in mind but I don't think he was interested in marrying me. Let's just say that I could have advanced Papa's business enterprises but not in the marriage bed.'

'No! You must have been mistaken. My dear, you don't know anything about these things. Believe me, Papa assures me that he has been to much trouble to ensure that you make a good marriage.'

'If that is what you choose to believe.'

'I do believe it. It is the truth. If only you would try harder, be more obedient, then life would be easier for all of us.'

'Not for me!' Outrage swelled within me. Nothing had changed here. When it came to her husband, Mama was no better than a slave. Against his power I was helpless.

For the first time I began to see Riari's proposition as something worth considering. What if Clarissa were to marry him? Would he not become the heir to Kilcreggan on his wife's behalf? When Sir Julius died (in the not too distant future, please God!) the property would pass to Riari and then Mama and I would have our right to the land safeguarded, for I was confident that he would take care of us.

Riari. I saw his face as clearly as if he was in the room. Riari, my brother with his oh so blue, questioning eyes, his disparaging grin and a smile that would surely charm Clarissa herself. The thought jolted me back to the present. No! Surely he in turn could never want her, would never succumb to her haughty form of snobbery? I felt heavy inside, jealously wanting to guard him for myself. At the same time I could see no alternative but to do what he wanted. I could no longer avoid the truth. Whatever else might happen, I did not want Clarissa to win my brother's love.

I felt indescribably tired. My mind rebelled against one more thought. For tonight I must sleep. Tomorrow things might seem clearer. As I sank into the welcoming familiarity of my bed, I vowed that I would not try to influence events. By the very nature of things, one way or the other, fate would decide its own way forward. Who was I to try to change things? As sleep claimed me I pledged that I would let nature take its course.

* * *

The next morning Clarissa was already at breakfast when I descended at first light. I bit back my annoyance, remembering what I had vowed the night before. I said to her, 'I am sorry if my departure from Dublin upset you. It was foolish of me to run away as I did. When will you be seeing Cavendish again?'

She gave me a superior stare, but then the

208

desire to talk about her fiancé overcame her other reservations.

She said, 'Papa is really angry with you. He will probably not permit you to come to England with us.'

'I am sorry.' Inside I rejoiced. Escaping from the epic of Clarissa's wedding with its tedious preparations would be a relief indeed. To keep her sweet, I asked, 'Have you decided what you will wear and where you will live?'

This opened the floodgates, and Clarissa regaled me with the infinitessimal details of her plans.

'I shall be so sorry to miss all the excitement,' I sighed, pretending a regret I should never feel.

She looked at me askance and I guessed she was thinking that if I was not present then she would be denied the pleasure of lording it over me. She said, 'Perhaps if I were to intervene on your behalf . . . '

'Would you?'

'Let's just wait and see.' This was the sort of power game she enjoyed so much. Hating myself, I said, 'Perhaps we could ride out some time. I've discovered a wonderful old ruin at the head of the valley. I could show it to you.'

'Perhaps.' She was losing interest. I fished around for something else to make an outing attractive. 'They say that there are white deer in the valley. They are very rare. If we could see them then, when Papa returns, he might take us to hunt them.' I hated myself for what I was saying, but I knew that I had found something to whet her appetite. Like her father, the prospect of hunting wild animals excited her and the thought of destroying something rare that few other people had seen would be a magnet indeed.

'Perhaps.'

'Shall we see what the weather is like? Tomorrow?'

'Perhaps.'

Once again I had difficulty in sleeping, wondering what I would do if Clarissa actually decided to accompany me. Now that it was a possibility I didn't want her to. What would we do when we reached Otters Lough? The idea of her being kidnapped was preposterous. I tried to draw comfort from the thought that if she did agree to come then I would have to take her somewhere else and pretend disappointment when we did not find the white deer.

The next morning dawned cold and bright, the perfect conditions for a ride out. As I came down to breakfast, Clarissa was already there. She greeted me with the words: 'I think today we should go and find the white deer.'

'Of course.' Everything began to slide out of control.

She said, 'We will take food with us and one of the grooms can accompany us.'

'No!' The word was out before I could stop it. Scratching around for an explanation, I said, 'The deer are very timid. The more of us there are, the less likely we are to see them.' Seeing her hesitate, I added, 'It is quite safe. I have been there alone, several times.'

To my relief she acquiesced but this momentary victory set free all those other worries. It was too late to let Riari know. All I could do was to ride in his direction and hope that he was there. After that it was up to him.

As we went down to the stables I began to wonder what would happen after the kidnap? What was I to do? Or say? How would I explain what had happened without implicating my brother and bringing about his downfall?

'Come along, Karenza, for goodness sake!' Clarissa was already mounted and waiting for me.

As we rode along the valley I explained about the bog and how it was essential to stick to the upper path.

'Who told you all this?'

Clarissa insisted on riding ahead and for a moment I thought how convenient it would be if she actually rode into the bog. It would not, however, solve the problem of getting the land back so I called out: 'Further to the right here.'

As she began to climb the slope I saw him, mounted on the pony, watching our progress. I was so shaken that I actually gripped the pommel of the saddle to stop myself from falling.

'That's far enough.' Riari rode out into our path, blocking the way.

'Who are you?' Clarissa gave him a haughty stare, challenging him to impede her progress.

'You are trespassing.'

'Nonsense.' She sniffed her derision. 'All of this land belongs to my papa. Get out of our way or I'll have you whipped.'

'Clarissa!' I tried to warn her, but her sense of her own importance made her impervious.

Riari sat back on the pony and smirked at her. 'I'd hate to argue a point of law with such an important lady but the name on the deed of this land is that of my godfather, James Delany. However, as you wish to ride freely over it, let me escort you.' He bowed his head and indicated that she should pass him which she did, booting her horse and tossing her head dismissively.

I looked at him and he grinned. There was

a rare warmth in his expression, reassuring me. I had no choice but to follow on behind.

Halfway along the path that led to Otters Lough, Riari called out, 'Take the turning to the right ahead.' I had not noticed the narrow track before, winding on up the side of the valley and skirting the farm.

Clarissa hesitated as if she resented being told which way to go but she followed his instructions. Curious, I brought up the rear, wondering where we were going.

I did not have long to wait. The path climbed steeply towards a ridge and as we breasted it, I had my first glimpse of the landscape on the far side. There, nestling at the confluence where two meandering streams briefly touched, was a white, stone house. It looked solid but deserted. Without being told, I knew that this was Conlan's Bluff where my parents had lived their lives together, within reach of the town and the garrison — yet sufficiently close for my father to visit Orla whenever he chose?

In other circumstances I would have been fascinated by the house and its part in my history. It was certainly more modest than I had expected, a single-storeyed stone dwelling. But then my father had only been a younger son, one still to make his way in the world. For my mother this must have seemed

213

humble indeed. Hungrily, I tried to memorize the details. In most ways it was similar to Otters Lough except that at some point the windows had been enlarged to let in more light and shutters added to keep out the winter winds.

I was too tense to think any more about it. Dimly I heard Clarissa ask, 'Where is it that we are going then? Where are these deer?'

She stopped her horse and turned towards me but at that moment, Riari said, 'This is where we are going.' He nodded towards the house.

'We? I was not talking to you.'

'No, but I am talking to you, Miss Richborowe. Allow me to introduce myself, I am Riari Kilbryde. Once, long ago, my father owned every acre that you can see from here. Every hill, every rock and stream, every tree and hummock they were all his. But that was before my father was executed, and before your father married Alice Ashburn and took the valley from her. I fear the time has now come to redress the balance, so you, Miss Richborowe, are to be my guest.'

'Don't talk rubbish.' She went to move on but he was off the pony and had hold of her mount before she could respond.

He said, 'You have nothing to fear but for the moment you are going to stay here.'

For the first time she looked alarmed, swinging round to reach me. 'Karenza! What is happening?'

I looked helplessly at her. Riari said; 'You, Miss Ashburn will ride back the way you came and inform Sir Julius Richborowe that his daughter has formed a new attachment.'

'Karenza!'

'Clarissa, don't be afraid. Do as he says. He won't hurt you.'

She twisted her head from side to side in confusion and then with a vicious movement, kicked out her foot aiming at Riari's face. Swiftly he caught her ankle in a strong grip, absorbing the blow and pulling her neatly from the horse. She fell heavily on to the path in front of him.

'That's enough, mistress. If we are to be husband and wife I can see that I shall have to teach you a lesson.'

'Husband and wife?' Her eyes turned black with disbelief.

'Riari, please . . . ' I spoke without thinking and Clarissa struggled to her feet. Shaking my brother off, she glared at me.

'Riari? You know this man?'

'I — ' I was speechless. He intervened. 'Just hold your tongue, madam. I'm not going to hurt you, not if you behave yourself.' Looking her over, he added, 'Much as it pains me, I

215

want my land back and it seems that the only way to get it is by wedding myself to you.' Seeing her amazement he said, 'Take comfort, Miss Richborowe, the prospect does not appeal to me any more than it might to you but desperate situations call for desperate measures. Now, your sister can ride home and reassure your father that you are unharmed. In the meantime, we will get to know each other preparatory to our wedding.'

'Karenza!!' Clarissa gave a wail.

Riari grabbed her firmly by the arm and pushed her ahead. Briefly glancing over his shoulder, he said to me, 'Let them know what has happened. Oh, and in case they think to take her back by force, there isn't a man in the village who will not come to my support, so I suggest that your stepfather gives in with good grace.'

With that he hauled Clarissa off in the direction of the house, leaving me to return and face the consequences.

11

The news of what had happened to my sister spread through Kilcreggan like a forest fire. At first I tried to shield Riari from any blame, but the more I was forced to explain it all, the more I began to realize that I could not hide his part in it. Only then did it dawn on me that he wanted me to tell, for how else could he claim Clarissa as his bride? The only thing I omitted was my own involvement.

As soon as she heard, Mama flew into a panic, sending a message hot foot to Papa in Dublin.

'Oh Karenza, whatever is going to happen? What will Papa say when he learns? Who is this wicked man? Do you think he will kill Clarissa?'

I tried to calm her. 'No, Mama, I am sure that he won't. What he wants is the right to marry her. Only in that way will he get back the estate which he feels belongs to him.'

'But I don't understand.'

Too late I realized what I was saying. It was no good pretending any longer. She would have to face the truth. I said, 'Riari Kilbryde claims that he is the son of my father. He says that in marrying you, Sir Julius took the land which should by rights belong to him. Now he wants it back.'

'That's a wicked lie!' She twisted away from me, but as I watched her, she grew visibly smaller, shrinking into herself as she tried to hide from the admission.

I said, 'I have met his mother. I think that what they claim is true.'

Mama sank, defeated, on to a seat, plucking at her skirts with agitated fingers. After a too long silence, she said, 'You never knew him. You never knew your father. He was so . . . ' I waited and her voice cracked with distress. 'I wasn't brave enough for him. Against that woman I had no chance.'

'I'm sorry.' I tried to comfort her but she was seeking her own solace in telling me how wild her husband had been, how godless and immoral was Orla Kilbryde.

'They say that she had dozens of men. Half the garrison. Why, that son of hers could belong to anybody.'

I remembered Orla's words, the certainty that there had only ever been my father. Gently I said, 'Mama, you know that isn't true. She is a good woman. I think she loved my father — as you did.'

My mother began to cry, a mournful, hopeless sound and I let her purge her grief.

All the time I wondered what might be happening at Conlan's Bluff. The thought of Riari alone with Clarissa raised its own spectres and I was hard put not to race over there and bring her back. Only the thought of Riari's anger prevented me.

It was three days before Sir Julius arrived in a flurry of dust and outrage. 'You!' He glared at me with hatred. 'This is your doing. How dare you lead her into such peril?' He paced the room, a glowering, dangerous figure. Taking a deep breath, he asked, 'What has been done to rescue her?'

I shook my head. No one, least of all Mama or I, had even considered mounting a search party. Sir Julius spat. 'Pah! You are useless, every one of you.' He swung round and grabbed me by the hair, twisting me around until I cried out with pain. 'This is your doing. She would never have ridden out unchaperoned unless someone encouraged her. Why did you not protect her?'

I swallowed back the desire to say that Clarissa was two years older than me and quite capable of making her own mistakes. With a great huffing and puffing he let me go.

Like treading on glass, I tried to explain it all. Resisting the urge to rub my bruised head, I said, 'There was nothing that I could do. When we were taken I had no choice but do as I was bid, to come back and let you know what had happened. I was specifically told to bring the message to you.'

His fists beat impotently against his sides as he sought for a plan of action. 'Right. Get every man together. I am going to take her back by force. When we get there I — I'll lock that bastard in the house and set fire to it. That will solve the problem of Riari Kilbryde.' From his froth-flecked lips and the wild glint in his pale eyes I knew that he relished the prospect.

For the first time I realized the importance of my role. He was quite capable of rushing in with terrible consequences. 'Papa,' I said, trying to appear calm and reasonable, 'what about Clarissa? How will you get her out without endangering her? Besides, if she is now . . . compromised, then would it not be better for her to wed than to spend the rest of her life living with the disgrace?'

What was I saying? Surely Riari never really intended to marry her so why was I putting it forward as an option?

'You think I'd let her marry that filth?'

'But — '

He spat the next words at me. 'By God! He shan't have her. I don't care what happens but he'll never get his hands on my land. I — I'd rather give her to Percy.'

With shock I realized then the depth of his hatred. Even Clarissa's wellbeing was second to his loathing for my brother.

'Perhaps Cavendish will still . . . ' I started, but the ice of his stare stopped me in my tracks.

Briefly I wondered why he hated Riari so much, not just now but ever since I first learned of his existence. Surely it was not on my mother's behalf? I could not believe that he was concerned about the wrong my father had done in taking Orla as his mistress. No, Sir Julius did not care for the hurt Mama might have suffered. There was something else. I felt suddenly sick with fear.

He rang the bell and one of the maids came in answer. 'Brandy!' he barked, still pacing the room. Mama had had the presence of mind to retire to her chamber with a headache. I was faced with the full force of his anger.

Restlessly he continued to pace the room, muttering beneath his breath. I stood looking at the floor, unwilling to provoke any sort of outburst.

'Right.' He stopped and drew himself upright. 'First thing tomorrow I will ride out there with every man I can get. If necessary we'll take her back by force.'

'Might she not get hurt in the mêlée?' I said again.

'Hurt? She's hurt already. She's no good to me now.'

'But surely . . . '

Of all the certainties in my life, the belief in Sir Julius's feelings for his daughter had been one of the strongest, yet now I realized how right Riari had been. Her value lay only in her name and her virginity. Take that away and she was of little use. Her needs, her feelings had no meaning. For a man like Sir Julius Richborowe, all the tenderer emotions, love, compassion, kindness were as nothing. Surely by our actions we had ruined Clarissa's life? I began to tremble.

Needless to say I passed a sleepless night. Try as I might I could see only disaster at the end of this venture. Just supposing Sir Julius gave way and Riari married Clarissa? What was to stop him from changing his will in favour of someone else? What would Riari do then?

I thought again of Mama. Supposing, just supposing she did indeed have a male child, then all of this would have been for nothing — unless? No. I stopped myself, but not quickly enough to avoid facing the dreaded question — that perhaps Riari actually wanted to possess my sister for herself? Surely not. He hadn't even met her, or had he? A wave of undiluted anguish swept through me. I didn't want Riari to marry Clarissa. In fact I didn't want him to marry anyone — except the one person he could not marry — and that was me!

The revelation was so devastating that I was numbed by it. I was in love, wickedly, sinfully in love with my own brother. God would strike me dead. I must never, ever, think of him and even as I formed the thought, the memory of his face, his body, surged through me like a rapier.

I was up before the rest of the household and already I had made a plan. Moments later, Papa descended, his mood black as peat, helping himself to a goodly measure of geneva from the sideboard as soon as he came through the door.

I said, 'I think I should come with you today, lead you to the place where we were taken.'

'Out of the question.'

I waited a respectful silence before adding, 'Unfortunately I don't think I can describe it to you. Once I get there, however, I will be able to direct you.'

He stared at me with his cold, malicious eyes. 'Are you trying to make a fool of me?'

'No, Papa, of course not. I simply want to

help get Clarissa back.'

He gave me a look that would freeze a furnace. Sneeringly he said, 'In any case, I can guess where he has taken her.'

Hopefully, I said, 'Perhaps you could negotiate her release if I agree to be held in her place.'

'Don't be stupid, girl. What have you got to offer?'

He was right. In his world I was of little or no value. In mine, I had my heart and soul to offer to the man I couldn't have.

While he fretted and fumed I endured the painful realization that for me there could be no happiness. Ever.

Nothing more was said and before Sir Julius prepared to leave I hurried across to the stables and gave instructions that Shamrock should be tacked up with the other horses. To my surprise there were already several mounts saddled in the yard. Clearly we were to be a big party and this in itself was cause for alarm. I fretted about how to warn Riari, but just as I was planning to leave straight away, I saw Sir Julius and several of the household servants coming across to the stables. Quickly I slipped back into Shamrock's stall. Better not to advertise my presence but to tag along behind.

Abel, coming into the stable block gave me

a shamefaced look. It seemed that he and Seamus were both part of the raiding party. Naturally they would be. They worked for Sir Julius, but I felt a sudden despair at the knowledge that Riari's neighbours and his fellow Irishmen should be forced to ride against him, held in thrall as they were by the wealth of their English landlord.

Sir Julius set the pace, thrashing his horse into an immediate canter. Soon some of the ponies were struggling to keep up. As we rode I wondered if I could find a short cut but the ground was too treacherous. Approaching the opening to the valley wherein lay my parents' former house, the party slowed. For a moment I thought they were planning their ambush, but as I pushed Shamrock forward I saw that the path was blocked by two armed men. Clearly Riari, too, had his supporters.

There was some low-voiced discussion and I just managed to catch the suggestion that Sir Julius should ride alone as far as the house to see his daughter and her kidnapper.

'Tell the bastard to come here!' Sir Julius spat his contempt.

Quickly I intervened. 'Come, Papa, I will ride with you.' Before he could show surprise at my presence or raise an objection I set off towards the house. Neither of the guards tried to stop me and Sir Julius, with a grunt of displeasure, rode after me.

There were other men on guard outside the house but my attention was focused on the dwelling itself. We were approaching it from the rear. Still staring at the windows as if I might see the scene inside, I dismounted and one of the guards took Shamrock's reins. 'Miss Ashburn.'

My surprise at being known was soon overtaken by the enormity of the situation. Without looking round for Sir Julius I crossed the threshold and into the house.

Inside, although much larger, it was not dissimilar to the Kilbryde kitchen, the same solid walls although the enlarged windows let in more light. Any furniture of value had long since been removed, leaving it virtually empty. It took me a moment to adjust to the changing light and to the vision of my brother Riari standing near to an old wooden table beside which Clarissa was seated on a stool. A third man holding a firearm, stood facing the door.

My eyes were only for my brother. Like a thirsty man I drank him in, desperate to know what had been happening. A strange, throbbing in my throat made it difficult to breathe. As he saw me he lifted his eyebrows with a quizzical movement. 'Miss Rich-borowe.'

226

At that moment Sir Julius pushed me aside, making for Clarissa at the table. 'Are you hurt, girl? Are you ruined?'

To my surprise, Clarissa did not leap from the stool and fling herself into her father's arms. Greeted with her lack of response, Sir Julius turned towards Riari.

'You've done it now, young man. You'll pay for this all right.'

Riari gave him a disparaging look. 'I already have.'

Sir Julius said, 'This place is surrounded. There's no escape. You will come with me. I am going to see you publicly flogged, then hanged.'

'I don't think so.' Riari nodded towards the still open door through which we could see Sir Julius's men in a huddle, surrounded by a group of Irishmen with an assortment of weapons.

Sir Julius's face darkened. 'You think you are going to blackmail me into letting you marry my daughter? Well, think again. I don't care what you have done to her. If she's soiled goods then she can die unwed. If she's in whelp then we'll have the bastard farmed out somewhere far away. No matter what, you aren't going to have her.'

Riari grinned, his eyes bright with the pleasure of inflicting pain. I clung to his every word like a lifeline. He said, 'You're too late. We're already wed. I've signed the oath of allegiance, a Protestant priest was fetched and we were married yesterday.'

Sir Julius's wrath was a shadow compared to my own disbelief. The lifeline snapped and I plunged towards the abyss below. Sir Julius stood like a goldfish, mouthing the air, lost for once for anything to say. At last, looking at Clarissa, he said, 'You didn't agree to this? It was done under duress so it can be annulled.'

'I agreed.' Clarissa's look challenged her father, a determined line setting about her small, pouting mouth.

Agreed? What was she up to? This was not possible. In a moment I would wake up and none of this would be true.

Riari said, 'If you are thinking of disinheriting her, then go ahead. Marrying her has been worth it just to see the expression on your face.'

Sir Julius positively blustered. Riari, frighteningly calm, said, 'Perhaps you'd like to escort my wife home. She needs a change of clothing, although from now on I will be responsible for her upkeep.'

Clarissa rose from the stool and walked across to the door. She did not even glance at her husband. 'Are you coming, Papa?'

Until this moment I had not known what

the expression a broken man, truly meant, but in my stepfather's posture, the expression of bleak shock on his face, I saw indeed that for the moment his world had collapsed about him.

Nobody took any notice of me. Sir Julius and Clarissa went outside followed by the armed guard. Only Riari and I remained.

There is a certain place just under your ribs where pain starts. Perhaps that is why they talk of a broken heart. Somewhere inside my chest a lonely void began to ache, a hole so deep that it could never be filled. This had been the point of the whole exercise but I felt betrayed in the most painful way.

'You've married her?' I asked.

'I have. It didn't seem worth taking any chances.'

'But — you don't love her?'

His face softened, a gentle smile tranforming it, transforming me. I wanted to cry, to throw myself into his arms and say, 'But you can't. I'm the one who loves you.'

He said, 'Don't worry little sister. There's nothing they can do. I meant it when I said I didn't care about the land. Not enough, anyway. Punishing him in this way is its own reward.'

'But why? Why do you hate him so much?'

229

He gave me a brief, glorious hug. 'One day I'll tell you.'

As my heartbeat subsided, I had a momentary vision of Clarissa and Cavendish locked in an embrace in the carriage on the way from the theatre. What about her feelings? Were they married in name only or — I couldn't bear to pursue that line of thought.

'What about my sister?' I asked.

Riari shrugged, the familiar sardonic grin shaping his mouth. 'Well, I suppose Sir Julius has had the last laugh, although he'll never know it.'

'What do you mean?'

'Well, you see, my bride was in fact already soiled goods.'

'You mean?'

'Ay. No virgin your sister.'

'Then . . . ?'

He looked questioningly at me. 'Then what?'

I couldn't ask him. I couldn't even bear to think of him making love to Clarissa. I repeated, 'But you don't love her.'

He took my arm and led me to the stool so recently vacated by his wife. 'Karenza, marriage has little to do with love. One day you'll find that out for yourself.'

I tore my arm free from him. 'I won't! I'll

never marry. I won't live a lie. Ever.'

He gave me a gentle smile. 'Believe me, little sister, sometime, somewhen, you'll follow the same path as the rest of us. You'll marry for convenience and you'll love because you can't help yourself.'

Looking into the bottomless blue of his eyes I knew that the second part of his statement at least was true.

★ ★ ★

I remember nothing of the journey back to Kilcreggan. I tried to find some small comfort in the knowledge that I had done what Riari asked, helped him to fulfil whatever ambition he was pursuing, but the cost to myself was great. Oh I cried, a great deluge of misery released into the empty countryside. I had not once believed that he would actually marry Clarissa and never had I considered that she might become a willing partner in whatever it was he was up to. For the moment I cried myself out. What did it all mean?

As the house came into sight several things happened at once. From downstairs I heard the sound of shouting, Sir Julius's voice raw with rage, and from upstairs a window suddenly shattered, accompanied by a scream of undiluted fury. Some unidentified object bounced into the courtyard accompanied by a shower of glass.

My instinct was to turn back, but for all I knew Mama might be the focus of my stepfather's anger. I could not creep away and leave her to his mercy.

Seamus heard my approach and came across to take Shamrock from me. 'Mistress,' he nodded politely, ignoring the furore that was continuing inside the house.

For want of something to say, he announced, 'Dr Delany is here.'

'My mother is not . . . ?'

'No, ma'am, he comes on a social call, or so I believe.'

My pleasure at the thought of seeing him was tempered with alarm. Surely he was not the cause of the commotion? Certainly the cacophany did not sound very sociable.

With a nod of my head I left Seamus and braved the arena.

Inside, Mama was seated on the sofa, her legs raised and her head tilted back, holding her nose. Liam bent beside her, dabbing at her face with a cloth.

'Mama?' I rushed to her side mindful of Sir Julius gazing out into the courtyard, his left foot beating a frenzied tattoo on the wooden floorboards.

'Miss Ashburn.' Liam rose to his feet. 'No

cause for alarm. Your mama has had a nose bleed. Nothing to worry about.'

I glanced up at the ceiling in the direction of a muffled yowling and he said, 'Mistress Richborowe is upstairs.' From this I deduced that it was Clarissa who had hurled the missile through the window.

I had forgotten the details of Liam's appearance. His broad workman-like hands with their short, clean nails held both of Mama's in his. Gently he squeezed them, reassuring her. 'There, Mistress Richborowe, you are getting your colour back now. No need to think of bleeding you. Nature has done her own work.'

'You are very kind.' She gave him a weak smile and closed her eyes.

To Sir Julius, Liam said, 'Perhaps it would be best if your wife were to rest.'

In response my stepfather shrugged as if what his wife did was of little concern to him. He was breathing heavily and I guessed that whatever had happened before, he had now burned his anger out. Speaking to the window he said, 'I have reached a decision. I am a busy man with important business to conduct. By their actions all three women in this house have disgraced me. I have no further wish to expand my affairs here. I shall return to Dublin and pursue the family

233

interests there and in Meath and Kilkenny.'

As he gazed out at the nothingness, Liam said, 'You will all be leaving Kilcreggan then?'

'Wrong. I am leaving. The women will remain here.' He drew in his breath several times as if to speak, then changed his mind, launching into another monologue. 'For once I regret that there are no longer nunneries to instil virtue into wayward wives and daughters. As it is, I shall have to make my own arrangements.'

What did he mean? Neither Mama nor I were willing to ask.

Liam stood up and stretched himself like a well-fed tabby. 'Is it your wish that I attend your wife and daughters in your absence, as their physician?' he asked.

'It is not. I do not wish for any man to come calling. None of them is to be trusted in male company. When I return to Dublin I will engage some suitable female to have charge of them.'

'Julius!' Mama let out a wail which had the predictable effect of drawing her husband's wrath.

Coming closer, his voice now low with venom, he said, 'You, Madam, are a disgrace as a mother. I married you so that you could care for the moral and spiritual welfare of my daughter. Look what you have done. You have let her become a slut.'

'I — ' Mama tried to protest but Papa was in full spate.

'As for your own spawn, God alone knows the extent of her folly. Behind my back she has been consorting with a rebel, a law breaker, a gypsy, heathen bastard whose only aim in life is to injure me. It is because of her that my own girl has been ruined.'

I could not accept this. I interrupted him, 'That's not true. Riari — '

He swung away from Mama and came towards me, menacing as a wild boar. I found myself backing towards the door. 'Riari? I'll give you Riari! You know who he is, don't you? Your good-for-nothing father sired him on that bitch up at Otters Lough. You and he come from the same stock, madam.'

'I know.' I took some small comfort in hearing my kinship voiced and in seeing Sir Julius's disappointment at my lack of reaction.

Liam took the momentary break in the tirade to say, 'Sir Julius, upsetting yourself and your family in this way is not good for anyone's health. I really think that you should — '

Sir Julius rounded on him. 'Get out! Don't you come here with your advice! If it wasn't for your brother's connivance that heathen

235

rabble up there' — he nodded in the direction of Otters Lough — 'would have been ousted long ago. Heed my words, Delany: I do not want you coming here again.'

Liam nodded his head in acquiescence. 'That suits me very well. I only called because I learned that your daughter had run away from Dublin and turned up at our house in great distress.'

'My daughter? She's not my daughter. Neither of them are. As from this moment I disown them both and the woman who, unfortunately, I made the mistake of making my wife.'

He was off again, ranting to himself. Liam turned his usually friendly blue eyes to me and they were clouded with concern. He said, 'Don't worry, Miss Ashburn, if you need me at any time then send a message and, of course, I will come.' He raised his voice. 'Good day to you Sir Julius. I hope that soon you will sort out your family problems to your satisfaction.'

Sir Julius did not answer and I followed Liam to the door. 'Thank you for your kindness.' I did not want him to go. He represented a bulwark against my stepfather's violence. He was kind, he was safe.

He made a helpless gesture. 'I fear that there is little that I can do without making things worse. Am I to understand that your sister has actually married Riari Kilbryde?'

Hearing him say it made it real again. I couldn't speak so I nodded my head. Liam bent closer. 'You look distressed. Are you concerned for her?'

'No.'

'For him then?'

I looked at the ground, ashamed of my grief, helpless to change the disaster that was upon us.

Liam reached out and patted my arm. 'I can see that you love your brother.'

If only he knew how much!

Backing towards the door, he said, 'Remember where I am.'

'I will. Thank you.'

So saying he left the house, and I found myself once more alone with my fears. When I returned to the drawing-room Sir Julius had disappeared and Mama was sitting on the sofa still holding the cloth to her nose. It appeared to have stopped bleeding but when she spoke it was with a clogged, snuffly sound.

'I fear poor Papa is losing his mind.'

'What happened?' I asked, sitting down beside her.

'He came back in such a pass. He was most angry with Clarissa. I have never seen him

237

treat her so before. She in turn was shouting at him, saying that she was in love, saying that she was now married and that he had no authority over her.' She looked at me. 'Whatever has been happening?'

I tried to tell her as if the events were no concern of mine but I could not stop my voice from trembling.

'I can't believe it,' said Mama, indifferent to my anguish. 'I thought that Clarissa was resigned to the marriage with young Cavendish Monroe. Surely a man like Mr Kilbryde could hold no attraction for her?'

How was I to answer? The words came from nowhere. I said, 'You say that my father was wild, that he could win the heart of any woman. Riari is his son, Mama.'

She drew in her breath. 'Well, I wish her well of him. And him of her, not that I imagine they will spend much time together.'

'What do you mean?'

'Papa has forbidden her to see him again. That is why she is locked in her room. She says she is going to him no matter what.'

My heart lurched in the face of Clarissa's passion. I, too, wanted only to flee the house and into Riari's arms. He might not want Clarissa but if she was there then he would still take her. She might bear him a child. The pain surged like a broken tooth.

Mama said, 'Will you not go and see her, try to reason with her. You have met him. You must know that such a match is unacceptable.'

'I don't think she will listen to me. In any case, it is too late now. They are wed and even if it was annulled, Cavendish Monroe would have none of her.'

Mama nodded at the truth of what I said. 'Well, take her some cordial. Try to calm her. And you had better send for Abel to see to the broken window.'

I nodded. 'And you, Mama, are you all right?'

She gave me a watery smile. 'I am well enough, dear. I seem to have failed Papa badly. Perhaps I will do better with the new baby.'

'Nonsense. You have been a good mother, to us both.' I kissed her on the cheek and set forth to do battle with Clarissa.

I knocked at the door but there was no reply. The key was in the lock so I turned it and ventured inside.

'Clarissa, it is I, Karenza.'

'Go away!'

'I have come to help you.'

The room was dark and she was little more than a hump in the bed. I crossed to the window and pulled back the heavy drapes that kept out the light. After a moment Clarissa sat up. Her face was red and swollen with crying and her hair a dishevelled tangle. She looked ugly and it gave me some small comfort. Surely Riari could not want her? I held out the cordial and when she didn't take it, put it down on a table.

I said, 'Papa has decreed that you and Mama and I shall stay here. He is going back to Dublin. I fear we are to be prisoners.'

She pulled the bedcovers around her, tucking her feet under her for warmth. 'What shall I do? I must go to him!' There was something wild about her, as if she was caught up in an emotional hurricane. In the face of her passion I was paralysed.

'Do you love him?' I handed her a dagger to use against me.

'I do. I had no idea that men could be so . . . ' She stretched like a cat and sighed. 'He is so — exciting.'

Her words scalded me. 'Was he the . . . first?'

'None of your business.' She gave another long, sinuous stretch, caught up in her own memories. 'What of you? Are you still a virgin?'

I looked away, not wanting to admit my innocence. Something perverse in my nature made me ask, 'Where do you plan to live with

240

Riari?' Why torture myself like this? I berated myself but somehow even this pain was better than not being able to talk about him.

'In Dublin, naturally.' She began to gain confidence. 'Papa will come round in time. He will make me an allowance. We can move to Dublin and set ourselves up there.'

'Do you think Riari would want to do that?' She did not know my brother at all.

She looked at me in surprise. It had never occurred to her that he might be content with the sort of life he already led. Feeling a certain guilt because I was interfering in things that should not concern me, I said, 'I don't think he would agree to leave Otters Lough. Then there is his mother.'

'Oh her!' She sniffed derisively. 'I'm sure some arrangement can be made for her. She cannot, of course, come with us to Dublin.'

'She's still young. And very beautiful.'

A dizzy mixture of jealousy and hopelessness began to overwhelm me. I was about to ask about Cavendish when I heard the sound of a horse's hooves in the courtyard. Clarissa and I stared at each other then together we rushed for the window. At that same moment someone thundered at the door, a loud, demanding banging. We could see nothing, only hear the altercation.

'I've come for my wife.'

'Get off my land before I shoot you. She will never be yours.'

There was the sound of scuffling and I imagined Riari trying to push his way past and Sir Julius fighting back. A sudden, deafening explosion rent the air as a gun went off in the vicinity. In response, Clarissa shrieked and was already flying down the stairs.

I raced behind, hardly able to bear the thought of what I might find. From halfway down the stairs I could see it all, the bulk of Sir Julius in the doorway, the slender figure of Riari trying to push his way past, the angry waving of a pistol. The air was acrid with the scent of cordite. I did not know who had fired and it appeared that no one had been hurt.

'Riari!' Clarissa squawked his name, moving with remarkable speed, in turn trying to get past her father to reach her husband. Between them Sir Julius was being buffeted but his bulk absorbed the pressure and he stood his ground.

In that moment I saw that other people had appeared, Sir Julius's servants, holding an assortment of firearms.

'That's enough.' Seeing that he had support, Sir Julius moved back allowing Clarissa to clasp my brother passionately about the waist. He stood very still, gazing at his unwelcome father-in-law, ignoring his wife in the way that one pays little attention to the pawing of a dog when more important issues are at stake.

Sir Julius aimed his own pistol at Riari's chest. 'Get out!' His voice was rough as gravel. 'You'll not have her, Kilbryde. From your pathetic house up the valley you can look across here and know that your precious wife is out of reach. She will never leave here unless I say so and that will never be to let her come to you.'

Riari went to move forward but the cocking of muskets, the aiming of pistols drew him back. Suddenly he grinned. 'If that's what you wish, Sir Julius.' He turned and grasped Clarissa, twisting her towards him and proceeded to kiss her long and hard. I watched her melt against him, her hunger roused to boiling point. The sight was cruel, agonizing and I bore it only because Riari seemed detached, a man going through the motions for effect.

Releasing her he pushed her aside. 'Stay here,' he demanded.

'Riari!' She held out her arms to him but he ignored her.

He said, 'Shut her up. Lock her away. It is of little interest to me. The more you try to hold on to her the more she will hate you.

The more you try to come between us the harder she'll fight to be with me, won't you, my love?'

Clarissa looked stricken. She had no idea that she had become a weapon, a pawn to be defended or sacrificed according to the needs of the game being played out by her father and her husband.

In response, Sir Julius grasped her by the arm, pulling her away. 'Get back upstairs.'

'Riari!' She screamed to him for help but he did not even look at her. Bowing, his eyes upon his adversary, my brother backed away.

His lips compressed with contempt, he said, 'Sorry, Wife, but you are not worth dying for,' and with that he turned and left the room. Moments later the sound of his pony grew dimmer as he cantered away towards Otters Lough.

12

Over the next few days Sir Julius began the process of making the house and grounds escape proof. Outside, every gate was tested to ensure that it was locked and every wall scanned so that there were no gaps through which we might slip away. Inside, bolts were fitted to the bedroom doors, bars inserted into the window frames and a series of new servants shipped in from Cork to act as our guards. There was something remote about them. I tried greeting them in Gaelic and English but no one seemed willing to acknowledge me. I don't know what Sir Julius had told them but there seemed to be little likelihood that they would disobey his orders. Slowly it dawned on me that we were truly prisoners.

When he was satisfied, Sir Julius called us all together. We assembled, a small, pathetic group in the drawing-room, waiting for him to pronounce sentence. For once our animosities were tossed aside in the face of our joint predicament.

Sir Julius was dressed in his travelling clothes, his cloak, hat and gauntlets thrown across the back of the settle for when he was ready to leave. Outside, the spring sound of birdsong drifted through the windows, underlining the grim reality of our imprisonment. The thought of his imminent departure was the only light in this otherwise bleak situation.

Fluffing up the lace at his throat, he began. 'You are all three a great disappointment to me. All my life I have tried to do what is best for you but you repay me with treachery.'

I closed my mind to his hypocrisy but Mama began to cry. 'Please, Julius!'

He stopped her with a scowl. 'From now on, this will be your only home. You will all stay here until such time as I decide otherwise.'

'But Papa!' Clarissa, until that moment sitting with her back to him on a sofa, flew up and ran dramatically to him, adopting her little-girl pose, appealing, caressing the arm of his shirt. To my amazement, he shrugged her aside. She began to cry, great howls of anguish — or was it temper? For some minutes the noise of her sobs drowned out all else, then, seeing that he was not going to weaken, she tried again to wheedle her way back into his affections.

'I'm truly sorry. I have been very foolish. I realize that now. It was that man, he made me do such terrible things although I didn't understand. I'll do anything you want, Papa, truly. I can still marry Cavendish. I am under age so without your permission my marriage is surely invalid. Besides, no one knows . . . '

The look her father bestowed on her was one of pure disgust. 'Everyone in Cork knows. Don't play the innocent with me, girl. You were willing enough in your husband's embrace.'

His words turned a knife in my heart. The vision of Clarissa and Riari making love was unbearable but, like a sore tooth I kept returning to probe the source of trouble, flinching with each renewed bout of pain.

Sir Julius continued, 'Besides, do you think I'd suffer the humiliation of the Monroes' rejection? No, my girl. You've made your choice. You'll live and die a spinster.'

Sensing that it was hopeless, Clarissa sniffled forlornly behind her fingers, for once at a loss as to how to get her own way. Mama, ever kind, put a comforting arm around her shoulders.

Sir Julius launched into one of his monologues, bemoaning the loss of opportunity, the ruination of his plans for the linen venture. 'So much work. So much investment in time and planning. We had it all settled, the land to be cleared, the peasants ordered to move away, the prospect of a union with the Monroes and now between you, you have turned to ashes everything that I have worked for. Unless . . . ' He turned in my direction, his brow creased. 'You. I suppose in this extreme situation . . . ' He looked me up and down as if he was thinking of buying me. With a sigh, he said, 'There is so much at stake. If I were to make proper arrangements, renegotiate our contract to his advantage . . . '

I waited for him to finish. His fingers beat a tattoo against his thigh then he nodded to himself. 'Perhaps, just perhaps I could persuade young Monroe to transfer his affections.'

To me? Surely he didn't mean that Cavendish and I should . . . ? I was so astounded that I could only stare at him. Frantically I scrabbled around for some obstacle to such a course but already he had talked himself out of it.

'What's the use? They already know that you ran away from Dublin. Any reputation you might have had is now in tatters.' He fumed quietly to himself. 'No man in his right mind would tie himself to such a disobedient chit of a girl. Besides, why should everything that I have worked for pass to the daughter of a scoundrel like Ashburn?' He turned again to Mama. 'No. It all depends on you now, Madam. Produce me a son and perhaps everything will still be well.'

'But Julius . . .'

His look defied her to do otherwise. 'Anyway,' he signalled that the discussion was at an end — 'I am returning to Dublin today. Pray God that the next time I see you, you will all have learned a lesson.'

As he left the room there was a collective outpouring of breath. 'What are we going to do?' It was Clarissa who asked the question.

'There is nothing that we can do.' Mama, accepting as ever, prepared to sit back and wait.

'There must be a way,' I offered, having no idea what it might be. We all withdrew into our private worlds. It struck me that we all wanted different things. Mama wished only to please her husband so that her goal was now to produce a healthy son. Clarissa — what did she want? To go to Riari? No. I could never believe that. Whatever passion he had aroused in her, when it came to the point, her love of creature comforts would certainly win the day. Surely she would prefer to return to Dublin and take her place in society? That would be better, but she would have to be patient, learn to live out the confinement and hope that her father would forgive her.

Knowing her as I did, this seemed unlikely. I was struck by the inconsistency of her behaviour. One moment she was claiming that Riari was the love of her life, and the next blaming him for her downfall. I guessed that Riari was right in thinking that the more Sir Julius opposed her union the more she was likely to fight for it. As far as true feeling went, never, ever could she be trusted.

A sudden terrible thought struck me. Supposing, just supposing that, like Mama, Clarissa was pregnant? It was too awful. Surely even God, that jealous, punitive god would not torture me in this way? I looked at her, red-eyed, pale and tense. Could these be the early symptoms of pregnancy? I said, 'I am going to the stables.'

'Karenza, please don't do anything foolish.'

I shook my head. 'No, Mama. I am just going to visit Shamrock.'

I wandered across the yard in a cloud of misery. How had I become entangled in this mess? I wanted to get away from here, but where to? I cursed myself for ever having left Otters Lough. With hindsight, I realized that being there with Orla and Riari had been heaven. Why had I not realized that at the time? Why had I not stayed? To go back there, back to paradise was all that I wanted, but even if I managed to do so, it would not be the same place. My half-brother was now married to my stepsister. Nothing could change that.

There was no one at the stables. Even the horses had been turned out to graze so I gazed at the empty loose boxes and wondered what to do. The warm, comforting scent of horse sweat and fresh dung soothed me. I wandered into the harness-room, breathing in the smooth smell of leather. Collars, reins, saddles, stirrup leathers and bridles hung in an orderly fashion. The place was neat and tidy, the walls lined with hooks and shelves. Idly I looked into the bins and buckets that stood about, filled with pieces of harness, nails, hammers, keys . . . I caught my breath. In a wooden box on one of the shelves, thick with cobwebs were at least two dozen keys. My heart began to beat faster. Which locks did they fit? Was it possible that they might belong to the doors set into the boundary walls? I tried to visualise the outer wall. Some of the paths were well used, but there were others where it was overgrown, where nobody went. If I could only find a key to one of those gates then perhaps, just perhaps, I could leave and escape unnoticed!

There was only one thing to do. Carefully I withdrew four or five keys from the box. They were big and heavy and I didn't know where to hide them so I clutched them to me, hoping to reach the perimeter unnoticed. I replaced the box exactly where it had stood, praying that no one would spot the disturbed dust and broken spiders' webs.

Trying to curb my impatience I strolled back across the courtyard, behind the house and down one of the paths then, when I was certain that no one was watching me, I dived into the bushes and pushed my way through to the wall. Turning away from the house I began to walk its length until I came to the first portal. With clumsy fingers I tried all four keys but none of them fitted. I moved on, again and again. Several of the doors were in full view so I passed them by. I had to find one which was hidden. As I walked the third side of the great square that made up the boundary I found what I wanted, a small door set right into the wall, overgrown with ivy and brambles. Ignoring the scratches, I tried all four keys in the old lock but they did not fit. I made up my mind. Little by little I would bring all the keys until I found the one that would open the door. Then, then . . . I felt a sudden sense of elation. Then I would be free to come and go. Then I would fly to my brother's house. I would tell him everything. What had I got to lose? If he could change his religion and marry a girl he did not love, then surely, surely he could love a girl who was closer to him by both blood and affection (his mother excepting) than any other person in the world?

It took me five more days to smuggle out the keys and to find the one that fitted the tiny door. At first, although it fitted easily into the lock, it would not turn and I doubted that it was the right one until I realized that the lock was stiff from lack of use. After some minutes of panic I made my way to the kitchens which were thankfully deserted. There on a shelf in the pantry I managed to find a bowl of lard. Surreptitiously I smuggled it out and took it back to the door, greasing the key and poking more into the lock. Try as I might it still would not give way. I began to panic. Surely soon someone would hear me. This was my only chance. Jiggling the key around in the lock I distributed the lard in all directions and at last miraculously, with a great clunk, the key finally turned. I was jublilant, but only for a moment. The door had not been opened in years and although I pushed my shoulder hard against it, it would not budge. Near to tears with frustration, I scrambled up along the wall to see if there was some obstruction. In so doing I scraped my shin and ripped my skirt but I did not care: I had to find a way to get out.

As I peered over the wall I saw that my efforts were all in vain. Right outside the gate, an ash tree had grown up, flat against the wall and blocking the exit. Even if I succeeded in moving the door at all it could only open a few inches, certainly not enough to let me through. I began to cry with frustration, and the hopelessness of it all. Having emptied my soul I then realized that there was nothing for it but to look for another way out, one equally sheltered but unhampered by anything on the other side. For a wild moment I wondered about simply climbing over the wall but the drop on the other side was much steeper. Even if I did not break a leg or twist an ankle, there would be no way of climbing back in. No, the only thing was to repeat the whole process until I found the right exit.

Every day I went through the routine of taking a few keys and wandering the boundary, gradually eliminating both keys and doors. Just when I was truly beginning to despair, I found another entrance way, identical to the first one and on the opposite boundary wall. If anything it was even more overgrown than the first which was why I had missed it on my earlier sorties. First of all I took the precaution of clambering into the neighbouring bushes so that I could check if there were any external obstacles. There weren't. The gate opened on to a narrow path, half buried in leaves that led through overgrown woods and away into the valley. Once more I went through the greasing process, trying key upon key until I found the one that fitted. Then, on a Thursday morning, two weeks after Sir Julius had left for Dublin, I pushed open the door and gazed out on to the outside world.

* ★ ★ ★

After their initial vigilance, there being nothing of interest to report, the new servants settled down into their own routine. As long as they had seen us at some time during the day they left us to our own devices.

Mama kept largely to her room where she sewed and embroidered garments for the baby. She was now in her seventh month of pregnancy and all still appeared to be well.

Clarissa on the other hand had sunk into a very low state. Having tried bossing and bullying the new servants, when that did not work she, too, retired to her chamber where she spent much of the day in bed. Food did not interest her. She did not bother to wash. Soon she grew wan and distracted as if the spark that was her life was being slowly extinguished. Even I was concerned for her wellbeing. In spite of certain misgivings, I decided to take her into my confidence.

'Clarissa?' I walked into her room without knocking. The air was stale and the curtains drawn across so that everything was bathed in gloom.

'Go away!'

Ignoring her I went to the window and opened the drapes at the same time unlatching the casement and swinging the window outward as far as the bars would permit to allow some fresh air to penetrate the stuffiness.

Turning to her I said, 'I have found a way to leave here. Do you wish me to take a message to . . . your husband?'

She sat up and I was shocked by her pallor. 'You look ill,' I said.

'I am ill. I am with child.'

Inside of me something cried in silent agony. Had the gods been listening? Did they know that this was my worst fear and now they were punishing me for loving my brother? Surely they could not be this cruel? Fighting to hide my pain, I asked, 'Do you wish me to tell him?'

'Why not? Perhaps it will make him come for me.'

At the sight of her misery I held back my

own grief and sank onto the bed. I said, 'Do you really love him? You told your father that you did not.'

'What else could I say? I wanted to find a way to stop Papa from shutting me up here.' She reached out and grabbed my arm with her clawlike hand which had once been so plump and pudgy. 'Go to him. Tell him that his wife awaits him. Tell him that I bear his son.'

I nodded, sucked under by my own anguish. 'Tomorrow. Tomorrow I will do so. Try to rest now, and you must eat. Really you must, for the baby.'

The baby. Riari's baby, growing inside Clarissa. It could not happen. Silently I patted her hand and made my exit.

In the privacy of my own chamber I cried out my hurt, quietly so that no one should hear. In whispered tones I railed against God. In hushed words I offered my soul to anyone in return for giving me Riari's love.

The next morning, exhausted, weary, I rose very early and prepared to make my first exit from the estate. I would have to walk to Otters Lough which was a good three miles. On horse-back it seemed as nothing but on foot it would take time. I was too tired for the journey. I had no plans as to what to do when I got there, other than to pass on the news that broke my heart.

I wanted to see Riari. That was all. I had to see him, to hear his voice, to drink in something of him to sustain me until such time as something, anything happened.

The morning was crisp and bright and spring-like, perfect for a walk. Wearily dressing, I made a point of going to the dining-room. One of the maids was there setting the table. I said, 'It is such a nice morning I am going for a walk in the grounds. I will not wait for breakfast. Please tell everyone that I will be back later.' She nodded her acquiescence, eyeing me curiously. I said, 'I have a headache. The fresh air may cure it.'

Ignoring her wide-eyed stare, I set out, the key concealed inside my bodice. It was large and cold, sticking out prominently. I would not stand up to close inspection.

Once outside in the courtyard I had to fight the desire to run. To a casual observer this must appear like a gentle stroll. I could only hope that no one was designated to follow me. Even if they were, I no longer cared. Seeing Riari, being with him, was all that mattered.

At the point where the path diverged I slipped quickly into the undergrowth and made my way to the boundary wall. In my tense hands the key was cumbersome. Several times I jabbed at the lock before I managed to insert it. As it turned the sound seemed deafening as did the dragging scuff of wood against rough ground as I pushed the door open, but no one came. Shutting it behind me I stopped for a moment to still my pounding blood then set off at a run in the direction of Otters Lough.

Several times on the path I slipped, muddying my skirts, bruising my legs but I kept going. A brisk wind came from nowhere, tugging at my hat, loosening strands of hair so that instead of the cool, dignified girl I wished to appear, I took on a wild, dishevelled look. In spite of myself, tears kept welling in my eyes at the thought of everything that had happened.

'Karenza?' Riari saw me before I saw him. At the sound of his voice, calling my name, my heart threatened to stop.

'Riari!'

He strode across to meet me, putting his arm about my shoulders. It was a warm, fraternal greeting. Somehow I resisted the urge to fling my arms about him. '*Failte.*' He bowed good humouredly. 'How go things at Kilcreggan?'

I couldn't answer because to my shame I began to cry, great heaving sobs, so that every

259

time I tried to speak the words stuck in my throat.

'Hush now, what has happened that is so bad?' Riari's eyes were dark with concern but not with the love I craved.

Between sobs, I said, 'Sir Julius has locked us in.'

To my consternation, he grinned. 'Has he now? Is he afraid that I might steal you all away?'

I didn't answer. All the time we were walking down the valley towards the farmhouse, his arm, strong and brotherly about my shoulders. I struggled to regain control of my pounding heart. 'Where's your mother?'

'Inside.' He looked down at me. 'That's the question you asked the first time you came here. Are you still afraid to be alone with me?'

'No!' In view of my feelings I could not hide the bitterness in my reply. I slowed down. I had to speak with him before we met Orla. I said, 'Your wife is pregnant.'

'Is she now?' He raised one eyebrow and his expression was impossible to interpret.

I forced myself to go on. 'She begs me to ask you to come and fetch her.'

'Am I to assume then that the child is mine?'

'Of course!' Even as I spoke, in my mind's eye I saw her and Cavendish in close embrace. Riari's words came back to me: *No virgin, your sister.* I asked, 'You don't think — ?'

He shrugged. 'Perhaps we shall have to wait the full nine months to find out. Come on.'

He hugged me closer and I felt a sudden surge of elation. First and foremost he was my brother, not Clarissa's husband. The feeling was too good to allow any sympathy for my stepsister. Guiltily, I risked slipping my arm about his waist and in response he hugged me closer. Thus we entered the welcoming warmth of the farmhouse.

Orla gave me a hug then she began to scold. 'You are as bad as your father, the both of you. Why did you not stop him from taking the Richborowe girl? It can only lead to trouble.' I felt a momentary shadow of unease, but the knowledge that she saw us as both alike and that she thought I might have some influence over her son, was too precious not to enjoy. She echoed my thoughts. 'You are two of a kind.'

I dared not stay for long. I recounted all that had happened at Kilcreggan then Riari insisted on walking me back to the estate. 'You'll come again, keep me informed?' he asked, as we drew within sight of the boundary wall.

'Of course.' I hesitated. 'Have you any message for Clarissa?'

'Should I have?'

He turned me to face him. I tried to be fair, to tell him that she was unwell and pining for him. 'I think she loves you,' I finished miserably. 'She is very unhappy.'

He cut across my words. 'Unhappy? She has no idea what the word means. If she thinks she is hurt now then . . .'

I felt afraid. 'Would you deliberately hurt her?'

He seemed to grow colder, more remote. He spoke more to himself than to me. 'I don't know if revenge heals a wound, but whatever happens, it can never wipe out what he did to my family.'

'Sir Julius? What?'

He seemed to come back from a long way away. 'Not now.' He drew in his breath. 'Let me know when he comes back. I might have a surprise for him.'

'What sort of surprise?'

His expression was suddenly elated, throwing me off balance. 'Time will tell, little sister.'

He must have seen the frown on my face for he said, 'What is it? Don't you like to be reminded that we share the same father?'

His closeness, his sudden excitement made

me bold. 'I wish that we didn't.'

He forced me to look at him. 'And why would that be?'

My courage failed me. I couldn't say it. He reached out and placed his hand under my chin. His voice was soft and quiet. 'Could it be that like me you wish we were unrelated? Because if we weren't . . . ' His face was inches away from mine, his eyes clouded and serious. Softly, he repeated, 'Because if we weren't, then . . . ' He did not finish the sentence. Instead, his mouth closed over mine and I was sucked under by a torrent of longing. I knew that I should protest, but I couldn't.

'Riari.' As he stopped, I gazed into his face, the tender smile, the laughter lines about his eyes. 'I love you,' I said.

'I know.'

'What shall we do?'

'Love each other.'

'But we can't . . . '

His look stopped me. 'But we do.' Gently he pushed me away. 'Go now. Come when you can but don't take any risks. One way or the other this will be resolved before too long.'

'You think so?' I thought of Clarissa and Sir Julius, of my pregnant mother, of the fact that we were kin.

'I know so. Now, go.'

In a daze I searched for the key and wrapped in the gift of his unexpected love, I unlocked the door and returned to my prison.

★ ★ ★

How can I describe what I felt at that moment, the heady whirlwind of elation, the wild careering of my soul, carrying me along with an almost exquisite longing to be once more in my brother's company. I did not know when that would be but between now and then I could live over and over again the moment when his lips touched mine, the smell of him, the feel of his hard, restless body pressed urgently against me. I wanted only to be with him, to swallow him up into myself so that no one could ever take him away from me.

'Well?'

The sight of Clarissa caught me completely off guard. I felt my cheeks grow hot with guilt. Surely she must know. I said, 'You are to wait here.'

'Did you tell him that I am with child? Did you tell him that Papa was no longer here?' There was something desperate in her expression.

'I . . . ' I couldn't remember what I might have said.

Clarissa gave a snort and began to pace the room. 'You are useless! I must go to him,' she said. 'I must.'

I bit back any comment, not wishing to be drawn into a discussion that might betray me. I merely said, 'I'm sure he knows what he is doing.'

Did he? Was he not courting disaster in pursuing either of us? The magnitude of his folly struck me. No matter what happened there could be no happy ending for Clarissa or me. If one of us won then the other must surely lose. I said, 'If you'll excuse me I'm tired after the journey. I need to rest.'

But Clarissa was not to be deterred that easily. She said, 'I am going to come with you the next time you go. Once I am there he won't be able to send me away.'

'You can't!'

'Why not?'

I scrabbled around for a reason. I said, 'You would have to climb the wall. There is a huge drop. You might harm the baby. Besides, it is miles away and you would have to go on foot.'

I saw the doubt on her face and quickly repeated, 'I am tired, I need to rest.'

My earlier elation disappeared as quickly as

it had come. Clarissa's determination, her very existence, threatened all my dreams. It did not matter what I wanted, no one was going to let me have Riari. It was against the law, the law of the land, and of God. What would Orla say? What would Mama think? And as for Sir Julius . . . Once again I could not hold back my tears. Crying was becoming an all-too-familiar pastime. In all the world, only Riari could make me happy and yet for the moment he seemed to arouse in me only despair. It made no sense.

I went to my chamber, not wishing to see anyone. Having indulged in the luxury of tears I wiped my eyes and began to make plans. I would go again tomorrow. I would repeat today's visit only this time there would be no holding back. Once Riari had truly made me his then no one, not even God Himself would be able to untie the bond that held us together. Running my hands over my hungry body I vowed before God that by this time tomorrow I would truly be a woman.

13

The next day when I reached Otters Lough it seemed to be deserted. Even the barking dogs brought no one to investigate. After a moment of uncertainty I went to the farmhouse and knocked on the door, opening it when no one replied. To my surprise Orla was sewing by the window.

'Oh! Please excuse me. I didn't think there was anybody here.'

I was shocked by her appearance. For the first time since we had met her hair looked dank and uncombed. Her eyes were dark in a pallid face and she sat very still as if her body had lost some of its vibrant energy.

'I was looking for Riari,' I started.

'Do you know what you are doing?'

'I . . . ' Guiltily I looked at her. Something had happened since yesterday. Somehow she knew about Riari and me. Would she understand, she who had told me that as my father's child I would not be able to help myself when I fell in love?

'I . . . '

Something about my hesitancy seemed to confirm her fears, but when she spoke I realized it was not what I thought. Her voice strangely flat, she said, 'No matter how hard he fights, he cannot win this battle. Your stepfather is too powerful. He will take pleasure in destroying him.' Her eyes grew moist with appeal. 'If you care about Riari then stop encouraging him. He might be angry with you but it could save his life.'

Her words sent a cold chill through me. I didn't know what to say. Did she know then that I was the one to bring Clarissa to him? Did she know about their marriage? About the child? Did she know that it was me whom Riari loved?

In the face of my silence, she said, 'He is cutting peat. You'll find him at the back.'

I wanted to explain things to her, everything, but I didn't know where to begin. Perhaps it was my imagination, or my own guilt, but she seemed disappointed in me. I felt as if I had let her down. After a painful silence, I said, 'I will go and find him then.'

She did not reply and I left the room while she remained seated, surrounded by a cold aura. Outside I breathed easier but the pall of her disapproval hung heavy.

I saw Riari before he heard me. He was bending and cutting, lifting and stacking the peat onto a sled. A warm wind whipped through the valley, tugging at his jerkin, lifting his long black hair. I wanted to be able to absorb him but inside I felt sort of tingly. It was not a pleasant elation, more a sense of foreboding. I forced myself to walk on.

'Good morning.'

He glanced round then continued with what he was doing. After too long he threw the spade aside and stood upright. Still he did not look in my direction. When he spoke his voice was harsh. 'What are you doing here?'

'I . . .'

He turned to face me, his expression hard, angry. He said, 'Did you not hear me when I warned you to take no risks? Do you not think they'll be growing suspicious if you disappear every day?'

'I . . . ' It could not have hurt more if he had slapped my face.

With a sigh of exasperation he picked up the spade. 'You cannot just come and go as you please. This is not one of your grand houses where fine ladies visit to drink chocolate or take afternoon tea. A lot is at stake here and not just for you and me.'

I felt a rush of indignation. 'I'll go then.'

'Don't be foolish. Come along, we'd best go to the house.'

I hesitated. 'Your mother is there. She seemed . . . angry.'

'What do you expect?'

'You've told her about us?'

He looked at me as if I was truly stupid. 'About us? Of course I haven't. Anyway, what is there to tell?'

The haven in which I had stored my love began to crumble away. Miserably, I said, 'I thought . . .'

Again I could see the barely suppressed rage in his eyes. 'What did you think — that I would announce our betrothal?' He looked heavenwards. 'Don't you understand anything? If — if there is ever to be anything between us then it will have to be — discreet, and that can only be after I have resolved the present difficulties.'

'By difficulties do you mean your marriage?' I felt my jealousy erupt.

'I mean the question of who owns my father's land, the question of Sir Julius Richborowe's right to evict the men who work the farms around here for his own ends.'

'He won't. He's changed his mind about the linen venture.'

I wanted to reassure him, to defuse a potentially dangerous situation but he merely spat his contempt. 'That isn't what he told his tenants. They have all had notice to quit.'

I felt sick at the thought that Sir Julius must have changed his mind. For a moment we were both silent then I said, 'Clarissa wanted to come with me but I wouldn't let her.'

'Perhaps you should have done. Perhaps that way we could have provoked her father into coming back.'

My heart missed a beat. 'You want her to come here, to live with you?'

He sighed deeply. 'Want? Can you only see things in terms of what I might want?'

Again his tone hurt me. Trying to keep calm, I asked, 'Does your mother know that Clarissa is with child? Is that why she is angry?'

'No. She does not know. At least not from me. What would be the point in telling her if the brat is not mine?'

'But if you are wed,' I started.

'You think I'm some fool like those English dolts who allow other men to cuckold them, planting seed in their nests for them to raise?' He snorted in disgust. 'I'd die before I raised another man's bastard.'

I couldn't stop myself from blurting out, 'If she came to live with you you'd lie with her. I know you would. I — I thought it was me you loved.'

He swung round so violently that I stepped back. His breath came fast and heavy. 'Here, give me your hand.' Grasping my wrist, he pushed my fingers into his groin, holding them tight against the hard presence of his private parts. I jolted with shock. Never before had I felt a man's cock. I wanted to draw back but to do so would only prove how naïve I was, to show my ignorance about what passed between men and women.

Riari said, 'Feel that? That is nature, basic, lustful. That is what happens to a bull who smells a fertile cow, to a stallion when a mare is in season. Have you not witnessed it a thousand times? It has nothing to do with finer feelings of love, or respect, or any of the virtues you value so greatly.' He sighed, loosening his grip and I let my hand fall to my side but in the palm I could still feel the urgency of him, the intimacy that at the same time excited and frightened me.

He said, 'Offer a love starved man any woman's cunny and he'll use it. You'd better believe me, little sister. It makes no difference to what goes on here.' He grabbed my hand again this time pushing it against his chest where I could feel the gentle thumping of his heart. Suddenly he weakened. 'Oh my poor girl. You are so confused. Will you not believe me when I tell you that I love you? Of course I want to fuck you. What man wouldn't, but you, my bonny girl, are . . . ' He shrugged helplessly, pulling me close and holding me once more like a big brother. Into my hair, he said, 'Men aren't animals. They can say no, but when something is offered to them then nature takes over.'

'Is that why you slept with Clarissa?'

'No. I fucked with your sister because I wanted to make her father suffer.'

'But why? Why hurt her to get back at him?'

He was a long time answering. Starting to walk back to the farmhouse, his arm still about my shoulders, he said, 'I guess it is time you knew.' He swallowed and seemed to brace himself for what he was about to say.

'When I was no more than six or seven years of age, your stepfather came riding over here on one of his visits. My mother was always nervous when he came here but until about that time, James Delany had employed one of his tenants to work here and help her. I wasn't big enough, you see, not big enough to do the heavy work. Anyway, at about that time the man left. I can't remember why. Perhaps I never knew, but from then on there was only my mother and me here.

'One morning Sir Julius came cantering up on a great black hunter. A fine animal it was. I remember hiding behind the cow byre and watching him ride in. I thought how wonderful if must be to have a horse like that.

273

The animal was sort of frothy as if he had been rubbed with soap. I didn't understand then but Sir Julius had ridden him so hard that his chest was heaving up and down like a bellows. When he was about five or six the horse died suddenly from some sort of apoplexy. Your man had ridden him to death.'

There was anger in his eyes, disgust. He took a moment to retrace his tale. 'Anyway, I watched Sir Julius jump down and fling the reins over the horse's neck. The poor animal was too tired to move away. Then himself called out: 'Mistress Kilbryde, I want to see you'.

'My mother was inside the house. She came out and I could see that she was afraid. 'What do you want?' Her voice was grudging, suspicious.

'Sir Julius seemed to find it amusing. 'Come along now', he said. 'Surely you are going to offer a visitor some refreshment?'

'He didn't wait to be invited but went straight into the house. My mother followed behind and I could hear her telling him that she did not want him here, that because of him my father had been killed. It made no sense at the time, but later I realized that it was Sir Julius who told my father's fellow officer about his affair, the same officer whom he challenged to a duel.' He faltered. 'Both men paid with their lives.'

Still the revelations came. I waited, wondering how much more there might be.

Riari said, 'I crept closer to the house to see what was happening. Sir Julius did not know that I was there. Suddenly, without warning, he struck my mother across the face so hard that she fell. In that moment he was upon her, like an animal, tearing her clothes, violating her. I screamed and ran to her defence, but he punched me in the chest and I fell back. I ran at him again but it made no difference. All the time she was tearing at him and screaming while he mouthed filth at her. When he had finished he — he committed other acts I wouldn't even mention, then he placed a sovereign on the table and walked out.'

I saw that his hands were trembling at the long remembered atrocity. Inside I felt sick, sick to be associated with the beast that was my stepfather. I squeezed Riari's arm and he continued, 'After that, James Delany came regularly to see us. He sent more servants to be here day and night until such time as I was big enough to take care of my mother.'

He looked round to gauge my response. 'That, little sister, is why I have no regrets about hurting Sir Julius Richborowe in any way that I can. Do you begin to understand?'

I did, but I felt that I had to warn him. 'Do be careful. In hurting him you might also be hurting your mother — and yourself.'

'And you?' He was calmer now, the Riari of yesterday surfacing once more, tender, loving. He steered me off away from the house and towards the yard. 'Come along. My mother has her own worries. She does not approve of what I have done. She isn't good company right now.'

'Does she blame me for helping you?'

'Perhaps a little, although she knows that nothing could stop me once I made up my mind. I'll get the pony and take you home.'

I did not argue. Somehow I had strayed into uncharted emotional territory and I did not know how to find my own way back, back to the certainties that had until now bounded my life. Riari's story, shocking, brutal, his hatred, so frightening and violent, filled me with fear. I needed time to absorb it all, to decide what to do next.

Riari carried me in front of him on the pony. I tried to capture the feel of his chest rising and falling against my back, the pressure of his arms about me as he held me close. As we rode down the valley, I said, 'My mother told me that Mr Delany was your father. That Otter's Lough belonged to him and he gave it to your mother so that she could support his child.'

He gave a little sniff at the humour of the thing. 'That would be convenient now, wouldn't it, especially for us. That way there would be no bar to our love — excepting that I now have a wife.' He squeezed me against him and I refused to think of Clarissa, revelling in the contact.

He continued, 'I think there's little doubt that James Delany carried a torch for my mother. No doubt he would have married her when my father died, except that he was already betrothed to someone else. When his wife died, my mother had become used to coping alone. She refused his offer of marriage.'

I thought of Mama and the way she had flushed when talking of James Delany. In the face of my father's wildness and his betrayal, had she fallen in love with his quiet and constant friend? If so she had a double reason for hating Orla who had kept both men from her.

Riari interrupted my daydreams, suddenly wheeling the pony off the track and down across the mossy incline. 'I know a short cut,' he said. 'I don't advise you to use it for if you get lost then you could end up in the bog but it saves time.'

I tried to memorize the route, noting

anything that might help me remember the way. If ever I needed to reach him in a hurry then it could be useful. As we drew near to Kilcreggan, Riari said, 'I want to show you something.'

He slipped from the pony, taking me with him and led me to an oak tree growing from the bank. 'You see here?' He bent down and heaved a rock aside, digging amongst the roots. Beneath the stone was a natural hollow. He said, 'As soon as you have news of your stepfather's return, I want you to leave a message here, under the rock. And then I want you to leave the gate in the wall unlocked. Will you do that?'

I nodded, my chest tense at the thought of the showdown to come. Riari said, 'And for safety's sake I want you to stay within the walls. Be sure that I want to see you as much as you wish to be with me, but for the moment we must learn to be patient. One day, God willing, we'll be together as much as we want.'

I couldn't say anything because I didn't trust my voice.

'Here.' Riari raised my face to his. 'Be brave now, little sister. I am relying on you.'

Again I nodded as he kissed me chastely on the cheek. '*Slan agat.*' He remounted the pony and turned him back towards Otters

Lough retracing his steps over the uneven terrain. His words drifted to me on the wind. Perhaps it was my imagination but it sounded like 'Goodbye, my love. Keep me in your heart.'

I will, I thought. Oh, I will! As I locked the gate behind me I repeated: I will keep you so close that whatever happens, nothing and nobody will be able to take you away from me.

★ ★ ★

'Where have you been?' Mama was waiting for me as I went into the house. She sounded suspicious. Wrapped as I was in the magic of Riari's love I was quick to respond.

'Just walking in the woods. I love it among the trees, the flowers and birdsong. You should come with me, Mama, the exercise would do you good.'

It was true. She was growing fat, not just the swelling belly where Sir Julius's child still clung on grimly, but all over. Her ankles and wrists were plump and distended and from the back she looked as if she was padded with soft, silky flesh from her shoulders to her bottom which was as round as the rump of Riari's pony.

The thought of my brother, of what he

wanted me to do was foremost in my mind. I said, 'Mama, has Clarissa told you — that she is with child?'

'She isn't! Oh, what will Sir Julius say?' I could see her scrabbling about in her mind for the implications.

I said, 'If she hasn't told you then please do not say anything. It is up to her to say. She will not be able to keep it hidden forever.'

She nodded her agreement, but I knew that she would not be able to stop herself from writing to Sir Julius with the news. This was what Riari wanted, to bring him back, but almost immediately I was filled with panic at the thought of what might happen.

'Don't tell Sir Julius!' I blurted out.

She shook her head but she wasn't really listening. 'I think I will go and rest,' she said and moved straight away towards the door. Soon she would have her writing materials out and by morning a messenger would be on his way to Dublin with the news.

I went and sat in the drawing-room, gazing from the window in the direction of the valley wherein my mind's eye I could see Riari making his way home. I felt lost, utterly and irretrievably lost. I wanted Sir Julius dead. I wanted Clarissa not to exist. Perhaps she was lying about the child in the hope of binding Riari to her. I drew comfort in the knowledge that he would be neither blackmailed nor bought. It was me he loved.

I wanted to run away from Kilcreggan but now there was really nowhere to go. Orla was angry with me. If she knew the whole truth, how much worse would it be? I could not help how I felt. She had gambled everything on loving Riari's father. I was risking my future because I loved her son. Surely she must see that. Meanwhile I faced up to the unpalatable fact that until such time as Sir Julius returned to Kilcreggan, like Mama and Clarissa, I was once more a prisoner within these walls.

★ ★ ★

Sir Julius arrived in a flurry of dust and ill-temper surrounded by an escort of half-a-dozen surly-looking men. He greeted Mama and me with a look that would put out a fire at ten paces and made directly for the drawing-room where Clarissa was reclining on a *chaise*, seemingly content to gaze endlessly into the distance.

From the hallway we could hear the interplay of voices, one high and one low, muted at first but rising in volume until Clarissa let out a shriek and within seconds she came flying into the hall with a speed that

I would never have believed her capable of.

'I won't do it! I won't!!' She stopped before Mama and me, looking from one to the other for help.

'Do what?' I tried to sound calm, to soothe her.

'Papa wants me to go to London. When the baby is born he wants to farm it out.'

For the first time in my life I was certain that Clarissa was feeling real distress. Whatever she might or might not feel for Riari, her love for her unborn baby seemed genuine. As I sought for something comforting to say, Sir Julius appeared in the doorway.

'Enough nonsense, girl. You'll see in the long term this is the only solution.'

'But Papa, I — '

Ignoring her, he said to my mother, 'As for you, madam, I have decided that once the child is born, you, too, will accompany Clarissa to England.' Before Mama could make any comment, he added, 'If the child is female then you will take it with you. If you provide me with a son then he will remain here in Ireland. I will make the appropriate arrangements for his upbringing.'

'But Julius, you cannot mean — '

'There is nothing to discuss. In every way it will be better if you and my foolish daughter return to the mother country. I shall busy myself with making sufficient funds to support you, but neither of you have a role to play here any longer.'

And you'll need enough money to keep Lady Martin in the manner to which she is accustomed, I thought. For myself I had no intention of going to England. As soon as Riari knew of the plan I was certain that he would rescue me. Hopefully he would take Mama in too. About Clarissa I could not even think except that I did not want her anywhere near us.

I realized that I would miss nothing of my present life. The prospect of days spent at Otters Lough, close to the man I loved, was all that I could ask for.

Both Mama and Clarissa were weeping at the thought of losing their children. Concerned as I was for their grief, my thoughts wandered and I tried to imagine what Sir Julius planned to do with Kilcreggan and the surrounding acres.

I asked, 'Have you abandoned the linen project, Papa?'

He fixed me with his cold eyes. 'And what is it to you, pray?'

'I only wondered, what with Sir Fulton Monroe . . . '

He gave me the benefit of a superior smile, well, more of a smirk, really. 'My dear young lady, I have other friends of influence besides Fulton Monroe. Many more. There is no shortage of men willing to come into the venture. Percy, for instance. He is still very interested indeed.' He paused and stared hard at me. 'Which brings me to your future. You will not be returning to England. If you remember, you have some unfinished business in Dublin.'

I was too stunned to speak. If anything was needed to spur me into action then it was this. While Mama and Clarissa snivelled and Sir Julius pontificated on our failings, I made plans to leave a message for Riari that very night.

I waited until everyone was asleep before leaving the house. Fortunately it was one of those exceptional evenings when the moon is so huge it seems almost like daylight. Having written my note I concealed it in my bodice and crept out into the night, keeping to the edge of the courtyard to avoid being seen.

Once in the woods I hurried to the gate. The lock was now easier to open but in the silence, the noise of the turning mechanism seemed deafening. I did not bother to lock it behind me but ran in the direction of the tree that Riari had shown me, pulling out the boulder.

Even as I did so I knew that my actions

would unleash some terrible consequence. Yet if I did nothing, other events would follow, equally devastating for those affected. I had no doubts now that Sir Julius was still intent on taking back the land from his tenants. Deprived of their holdings they would face starvation. He had to be stopped. As I heaved at the boulder I reasoned that if the local men decided to oppose him then death and destruction would surely follow. It seemed that I, Karenza, held the key that would set events off in one of these directions — do something and a disaster would happen; do nothing and a tragedy would result. The only thing to do was to fall back on my own feelings. Do nothing and Mama might be separated for ever from her baby. Do nothing and I would be shipped off to Dublin to act the courtesan and perhaps never to see Riari again. With trembling hands I pushed the note into the hollow and hurried home.

★ ★ ★

For two long days nothing happened. Sir Julius, having tormented us all in various ways, took himself off to Cork where he no doubt had business to conduct concerning the linen project. Meanwhile, the men who had accompanied him from Dublin kept up a constant presence about the estate. I did not recognize any of them and what their role was no one seemed certain, but they came heavily armed and had the stamp of soldiers about them. I remembered Abel's words at the stable in Dublin so long ago — that Sir Julius always sleeps with a pistol under his pillow when he visits Kilcreggan. If he had felt uneasy before, my stepfather was now seriously expecting trouble.

The men's presence was worrying in another way. Sir Julius had still to resolve his differences with Riari, first about the land and then about the fact that Clarissa was legally his wife. I had no doubt that he would be prepared to kill my brother, for how else was he to extricate himself from these embarrassing situations? I tried to find comfort in the knowledge that Riari was brave, used to defending himself, but then my father had been brave and Sir Julius had negotiated his downfall. Would he plan a surprise attack on Otters Lough or would he lure Riari to Kilcreggan? Either way my brother was in great danger.

Day and night I found myself in a state of readiness, always alert for some unexpected sound, some hint that something was about to happen. I began to feel exhausted. When it finally came, the visit was totally unexpected.

It was a Thursday afternoon. The sun was hot, a spring day that gives the promise of better times to come. Mama and I were in the parlour playing piquet. Mama is not very good at games and I was trying to find a way to let her win but as always, I was beating her.

Sir Julius had been home for about half an hour and he was in the drawing-room, drinking wine and sustaining himself with a plate of bread and bacon. He had not bothered to seek us out since his arrival and I for one hoped that after he had eaten, he would fall asleep. Clarissa as always, was in her chamber.

When I heard the knock at the front door I nearly jumped out of my skin. 'Stay there,' I said to Mama and raced to the parlour door, opening it wide enough to hear what was going on.

As I waited, three men were ushered into the hallway. I took a step forwards. One was Mr James Delany, the second was his brother Liam and the third was my brother.

Sir Julius in stockinged feet, padded from the drawing-room, his mouth still full of ham. He had removed his waistcoat and loosened the top strings of his breeches so that his increasing paunch could spread more comfortably. When he saw the three men he stopped, glancing around him. I followed his line of vision. On a side table in the hallway lay his pistol. He edged casually in that direction.

For what seemed like forever nobody spoke, then Riari said, 'Richborowe, I have come to give you a challenge. My friend Delany here is willing to act as my second and his brother is here to act as physician should he be needed.'

He forced Sir Julius to meet his eye. His voice was low and calm as he said, 'I challenge your right to every acre of this land. I challenge your right to evict the people who farm it. And I challenge your right to hold your daughter against her will.'

At the mention of Clarissa I felt a twinge of jealousy but quickly suppressed it. So much was at stake here. I saw Sir Julius blanch. His eyes flickered as he tried to think of a way out of this. Riari continued, 'I leave it to you to pick the time, and the place and the weapons, but as far as I am concerned, now is as good a time as any.'

My heart was beating so fast that I had to grab the door post for support. My stepfather leaned back against the side table, the pistol within easy reach. He said, 'I do not accept your challenge. You are not a gentleman. You have no status. You cannot challenge me to a duel.'

Riari grinned at the excuse. 'I can and I do. I am the son of a gentleman, in case you have forgot. And I am the husband of your daughter which must put us on an equal footing?'

'Get out!' Sir Julius grabbed for the pistol. What happened next was so fast that it was only afterwards that I could even begin to piece it all together.

Mama, standing behind me, chose that moment to peer right into the hall. There for the first time she clapped her eyes on Mr Delany.

'James!' She called his name urgently and I could see that she was afraid for his safety. James looked in her direction, his attention for the moment distracted.

At that very moment Clarissa appeared on the stairway, tripping down in her haste. 'Riari!' She flew towards her husband as in that same second, Sir Julius let loose with his pistol. The shot was aimed at my brother but it was my stepsister, flying towards him, who caught the full impact of it. I watched in disbelief as Clarissa jerked to a halt then slid slowly to the ground, her eyes wide with surprise, her mouth half open as she formed my brother's name. She placed her hand over the spot where scarlet blood pumped from her chest. Her body began to pulsate, a wild, thrashing that reminded me of the dying moments of a deer Sir Julius had once shot in front of me. With a tiny gasp, a last look of amazement, Clarissa exhaled her final breath and lay still.

Within seconds Liam was at her side, examining the wound, searching for signs of life.

'Get out of here!' James Delany pushed Riari to the door. 'Go, man. There is nothing you can do here.'

Riari gazed down at Clarissa with disbelief. I saw his eyes narrow as anger welled up in him. Looking at Sir Julius, he said, 'Rough justice, Richborowe? You've resolved one of your problems all right. We'll settle our other dispute another time.' He glanced at me, his bleak look warning me to be careful, and taking his friend's advice he strode out into the indecently cheerful sunshine.

Mama, gazing transfixed at Clarissa, gave a little gasp and swooned away. It was James Delany who swept her up and deposited her on a settle in the hallway.

I was too numb to feel anything. Sir Julius still held the pistol, dangling forgotten from his hand. His mouth hung open and he looked at his daughter's body with eyes blackened by shock.

'Come along, man.' Liam led him into the

drawing-room taking the weapon from him as he went. Without asking he poured him a glass of aquavit, holding it to his slack lips. He said, 'Breathe deeply now. There is nothing you can do. It was an accident.'

Sir Julius was like a man in a trance. He seemed unable to take in what had happened. Liam forced him to sit in a chair. 'It was an accident,' he repeated, trying to give my stepfather some comfort. 'She is at peace now. She would have felt nothing.'

'He'll pay for this.' Sir Julius seemed to come back from a long way away. 'He'll hang for what he has done to my daughter!'

I looked at Liam and he shook his head. His expression was sober, his eyes clouded with sadness. 'You need to rest,' he said to my stepfather. 'I will give you something to help you.' I felt reassured by his quiet authority.

Mama had by now come to and James Delany was supporting her while she sipped at a glass of spirits. She sprawled with her head against his shoulder, making little whimpering noises. 'Hush, dear lady. Hush now.'

The horror of what I had just witnessed began to overwhelm me. Liam must have seen my distress for he left Sir Julius and came over to my side. Reassuringly he held me in his arms, his face resting on the crown of my head. 'There now, Miss Ashburn, take heart. There was nothing that you could have done.'

I closed my eyes and snuggled against him, feeling for the first time a sense of safety in a man's arms. I had never known my father. My mother had no brothers and my grandfather was a distant, childhood memory. I cannot recall sitting on his knee or holding his hand or being carried on his shoulder. Riari's touch was dangerously magic, like quicksilver, vivid, darting through me and dispersing before I could ever capture the feeling, whilst Sir Julius, the only other man with whom I had ever spent time was the last person to offer tenderness. Without needing to think about it I knew that Liam, so good and gentle, was the sort of man who would look after anyone in trouble. For the moment I couldn't allow myself to dwell on anything other than his warmth and strength.

Only Clarissa, crumpled and abandoned on the stone pavings in the hallway, was a ghastly reminder of what had just happened — and what was to come.

14

That evening, Liam gave us all a sleeping draught and insisted on staying. Shock lay like a fog over the house, extending to the servants who went about their duties as if on tiptoe, whispering whenever they needed to speak. It seemed as if in some undefined way we had all been condemned to silence. Anything as normal as the human voice felt like a blasphemy in the face of Clarissa's pointless death.

The food the servants laid out for us remained largely untouched, although I noticed Liam surreptitiously grab a few mouthfuls of cold venison and potatoes.

'You should eat,' he murmured in his own defence. 'You need to keep up your strength.' His words conveyed what I already knew, that worse was still to come.

We laid Clarissa, now decently washed and clothed in white satin, on a makeshift bench in the drawing-room, a crucifix clasped in her hands. She looked peeved, as if some unknown person had had the temerity to interrupt her. Guilt weighed heavily upon me and I felt that I owed her an explanation, although there was nothing to say. By my actions I had led her along a path which could only end in tragedy. But then it was not all my fault. Had she not realized that I loved my brother? How could she have been so blind?

'I'm sorry,' I whispered, ill at ease with her wooden emptiness. Did I detect the so familiar sneer in her otherwise immobile features? In the unnatural silence of the room, the ghost stories of our childhood came back to haunt me. Would Clarissa's spirit now be free to roam at will, venting her spite wherever she chose? The same, primeval fear that had enveloped me as a child began to suck me under.

'I'm truly sorry,' I said again, hoping to ward off the worst of her malice. Nodding a miserable farewell to her lifeless form, I tiptoed from the room, steeling myself not to hurry, returning gratefully to the parlour where the others were gathered, seeking safety in their company.

James Delany seemed to have taken control of the immediate arrangements. A carpenter was sent for to make a suitable coffin and James summoned the minister to discuss the funeral. I saw a look pass between him and his brother. Perhaps herein lay the dispute between them. Liam, I am sure, would have preferred the services of a priest. Both looked drained and tired, Liam's face gentle in his grief, his brother's more closed off. They had known my family for a long time.

'We must trust in God,' James said to Sir Julius, who appeared to be in the grip of severe shock.

I found myself wondering: had James embraced the Protestant faith out of belief or for gain? Having done so, did Liam see his brother as betraying their true beliefs? Whatever the reasons, James had certainly chosen a different path in life, and one that had brought him fortune if not fame. In contrast, Liam had eschewed the financial rewards that his profession might offer in return for the satisfaction of helping the poor. I felt a glow of affection for him. Whatever the rights or wrongs of their dispute, I had no way of knowing what had caused it but its contemplation kept my thoughts from the horror of the afternoon.

When the parson arrived, hot and flustered, he offered us a few ineffectual words of comfort. Sir Julius, refusing to retire to bed, sat in an armchair in the drawing-room, gazing vacantly at his dead daughter.

Watching him I don't know what I felt. Culpability certainly, because I had wished Clarissa out of the way and now she was dead. Looking at my stepfather, bowed and grey-faced, I couldn't help but feel compassion for him for he had killed the child he loved. But then, remembering his harshness towards her once she crossed him, I tempered my pity. This was the man who had killed my father, raped Orla, planned to use me as a whore, to abandon my mother and to kill the man I loved. Surely some time soon he would get what he deserved?

Liam persuaded my mother to bed and with James's support she mounted the stairs. She was excessively pale. A damp sheen covered her face and she insisted on holding on to James's hand although I suspect that he would have liked to leave.

Liam warned, 'A shock such as this could bring on an early birth. Perhaps I should prepare Sir Julius?'

I shook my head. I had no words to tell him that my stepfather had little interest in his wife and that the child had a meaning for him only if it should prove to be the heir he had so far been denied. Liam said, 'Then we'll leave him where he is. I've given him a strong sleeping draught. He won't be able to help himself but to sleep it off.'

His words gave me comfort. In the present circumstances Sir Julius was unlikely to do anything foolish, although sooner or later there had to be a backlash. For now I was too shocked to cope with more trouble.

Left alone in the parlour I began to wonder how Riari was faring. Did he blame himself for Clarissa's death? This was certainly not the outcome he had planned. Did he need someone to talk to? At the thought of his loneliness I longed to go to him but concern for my mother meant that my first duty must be to stay where I was. Meanwhile the long hours of darkness closed in.

In spite of the infusion, I slept badly. Worry about Mama, anxiety about Riari, fear for the future dominated my waking moments. In those brief seconds when I drifted into sleep the vision of Clarissa, cold and dead, jerked me back to wakefulness.

Near to daybreak I must have at last escaped into a deep slumber. I have no idea for how long I rested, a few minutes or perhaps an hour, but my sleep was disturbed by an echoing sound permeating the mists in my mind. Reluctantly I opened my eyes, trying to remember what was troubling me. As the memory of yesterday returned, simultaneously I became aware of the sound of horses' hooves, at least half-a-dozen mounts milling around in the courtyard outside. I shot out of bed and rushed to the casement window. There below me Sir Julius and his henchmen were mounted and about to leave.

My heart thundering, I dragged on some outdoor clothes and slipped my feet into the satin slippers that lay beside my bed, racing down the stairs. The first person I came face to face with was Sorcha, the maid.

'Where are they going?'

Her face was pale with anxiety. She shook her head. 'Himself is in a fine state. He says he is going to kill the man who murdered his daughter.'

I stared at her, willing her to tell me that she was mistaken but she continued to shake her head at the appalling prospect.

Racing as fast as I could I crossed the hall and threw the front door open as the riders began to move out of the yard. I ran for the stables, barging past Seamus who was mucking out the boxes. Ignoring him I grabbed Shamrock's bridle from the hook and slipped it over the pony's head, my fingers clumsy in their haste. Without bothering about a saddle I led Shamrock outside and leapt across his back, hitching up my skirts and riding astride, making immediately for the side gate which was still unlocked. As we came out into the open countryside I could see Sir Julius and his band a short distance ahead, clouds of dust flailing about the horses' hooves. Careless of the danger, I pushed Shamrock into a gallop, turning him sharply at the point where Riari had taken his short cut. God willing I would reach Otters Lough before the others.

Fortunately for me there had been several days without rain and although I strayed from the path many times, the spongy ground warned me of the danger before I was drawn into the bog and I managed to regain the track, driving an ever more exhausted Shamrock onwards.

As we scrabbled up the side of the valley I remembered what Riari had said, how my stepfather had ridden his fine black horse to its death. I prayed: dear Shamrock, just this once, put your heart into this ride. So much depends upon it!

As I skirted the last boulders before rejoining the main path I saw that I was too late. The party was already riding into the farmyard ahead of me. There was nothing that I could do but rein in and watch.

Riari, armed with a pitchfork, stood in the yard, facing the intruders. They remained mounted and my brother looked very vulnerable, alone and outnumbered as he was. At the sight of him, his slender body conveying so much strength, his face calm and impregnable, an almost exquisite longing formed under my ribs. I wanted to call to him, to see his cold blue eyes thaw with affection as he realized that I was there, but to do so would be to distract him and he needed all the concentration he could muster.

Without warning, two of Sir Julius's henchmen dismounted and at the same time others rode forward, knocking into my brother. The men on the ground grabbed him by the arms, flinging the pitchfork aside and striking him about the head and back. From his saddle, Sir Julius lashed out with his riding crop. 'Damn you, Kilbryde. I said I would make you pay and now you shall!'

As I started from my hiding place, my stepfather dismounted and strode towards the house while several of the others spread out, surrounding the building. Paralysed with fear, I slid back into hiding, watching as Sir Julius went to the front door of the farmhouse and proceeded to lock it with the key that sat abandoned in the ancient keyhole. I knew that my brother would have little reason to ever bolt his door. Other men circled the building, pulling across the shutters and securing them from the outside. All the while Riari struggled to free himself from his captors.

Once the house was locked up Sir Julius sent one of his men across to the barn. He returned with an armful of hay. In that moment, with cold disbelief I realized what he intended to do. Slowly, deliberately, he took out his tinder box and coaxed a spark against the brittle grass. It flared and smoked and then began to blaze. Raising his pistol he smashed the last remaining unshuttered window into the kitchen and pushed the burning bundle inside then pulled the shutters to.

Orla! Until that moment I hadn't thought about where she might be. Surely she was not inside? The spell was broken and I ran towards the house as Riari, finding some superhuman strength, broke away from his captors and was already ahead of me. Desperately he tugged at the door and finding that the key had been taken, he turned instead to the window through which a cloud of black smoke was billowing. I watched in horror as he forced the shutters open, oblivious to the broken glass and heat, and scrambled his way inside.

'No!' I screamed after him but he did not hear me. In turn I raced to the window intent on following him but the density of the smoke forced me back. Helplessly I turned to Sir Julius.

'There's a woman inside. For pity's sake open the door!' He looked down on me, triumph in his cold, fish-like eyes.

'Save your pity, my dear. That scum deserve everything that they get.'

Desperately I ran from one to the other of his men, looking for compassion but each face was hard and remote.

'Riari!' Again I raced to the window but by now flames had began to curl through the thatch. I no longer cared what happened to me. As I began to haul myself over the window sill, arms grabbed me back.

'Let me go!' I struggled in vain. Two of the henchmen held me in a bull-like grip dragging me away to safety.

In that extreme moment, another sound pervaded the chaos. Suddenly it seemed that the courtyard was filled with men, some on ponies, others on foot. As if from nowhere, dozens of local men emerged from the surrounding woodlands, advancing towards Sir Julius and his band.

Seeing them, my captors released their hold and I took my chance to race to the approaching band. 'For God's sake do something, my brother and his mother are locked inside!'

One or two of them had pistols. The rest were armed with cudgels and pitchforks. There was something unstoppable about their presence. Instead of firing, Sir Julius's supporters began to back away. Only my stepfather turned to shoot.

The men rushed at him and Sir Julius fired wildly, then with an amazing turn of speed he dropped his firearm and began to run, heading for the trees and the path leading down into the valley. One or two of the men gave chase, but the rest turned their attention to the house and began to force open the shutters. As they did so, billows of smoke and flame flared into the air.

'Riari!' The horror of what was happening swept me under. I tried to move forwards but my legs felt paralysed As I opened my mouth no sound came out. My eyes, blinded by the brilliance of the flames grew dim and the ground seemed to vanish beneath me as I was drawn into a merciful oblivion.

* * *

My brother was alive when they brought him out. Dimly I was aware of what was happening, the men carrying him gently and placing him in the shade. Others were forming a human chain passing barrels and buckets of water to quell the still raging blaze.

Moments later someone emerged with Orla in his arms. 'Orla?' My tongue seemed pasted to the roof of my mouth. I struggled towards her but the nearest man shook his, head as he turned me away. 'There's nothing you can do.'

Somehow I managed to crawl to my brother's side. I would never have recognized him. He was black from head to foot, skin, hair, clothing. Only his eyes, red and bloodshot, broke up the uniformity.

'Riari.' I took his hand, seeing too late the charred flesh, and how his skin crinkled like toasted paper. As he opened his mouth the pink of his tongue touched blackened lips. He tried to speak but his breath rasped so painfully that he closed his eyes.

Desperately I looked around for help. 'Quick! We must get him home, to Kilcreggan!'

The men standing in a sombre circle looked away from me. One or two shook their heads in dismay. Nobody spoke the unthinkable, that my brother was dying.

'Riari!' I bent over him, willing him to live, bathing his poor burnt face with my kisses. After an eternity he opened his eyes again. Somehow the corners of his mouth lifted in the semblance of his so familiar smile then, with a gentle exhalation of breath, his head fell back and he drifted into his final sleep.

★ ★ ★

It is only time that has given me the courage to pull back the curtain and look again at that terrible day. Over and over I ask myself: what did I do wrong? What else might I have done to prevent this tragedy that even now wakes me in the night, drenched and cold at the memory.

I recall nothing of the journey back to Kilcreggan. Whether I rode or walked, or whether I was carried I could not say even if my life depended upon it. I only remember the circle of faces staring at me as I stepped into the darkness of the hall.

'Karenza?' Liam's brow creased in disbelief as he came towards me. 'Whatever has happened?'

'Riari. Orla. They're dead.' I asked it almost as a question, unable to believe what I had seen.

A groan from behind Liam turned all eyes. His brother James raised his hands to his face in a vain attempt to silence the cry of pain that rent him. Riari's words came back to me: 'I think there's little doubt that James Delany carried a torch for my mother.' In James's anguished face I saw the truth.

Orla and Riari. I must have been mistaken. They could not be dead. It could never be.

Liam turned briefly and squeezed his brother's arm then came towards me. 'You must come with me, my dear. I know it is hard, but your mother is giving birth. She needs you.'

'I cannot!' I appealed to him and in that moment I think he saw the truth in my eyes — that my love for my brother went far deeper than that of kin.

For a moment he seemed to blink back some pain, then he said firmly, 'Come now, it will help you to be occupied.'

A woman had been brought from the village to help Mama. As I entered the room, she was supported one on each side, by the midwife and by Sorcha. She was groaning, a wild, primeval sound as she writhed like some demented creature in a trap. My throat closed with the agony of it. Please, I prayed, bring her safely out of this.

'Good, madam. Good. One more time now.' The midwife spoke with an authority that would not be denied.

'Mama?'

Her frightened eyes met mine for a moment before the straining started again, ending with a wild, strangled roar.

'Good! Good! See, it's almost here. Push again, dear lady. There! It's nearly over, God be praised!'

For a moment the wonder of the occasion being acted out on the bed blotted out everything else. From the centre of the covers came a muffled, snuffling sound rising to a thin, reedy wail of protest.

'Tis a boy, madam, a fine boy!'

A boy? I had a brother? Another half-brother? I began to cry, flailed by the bitter sweet irony of what had just passed.

'There's no need to be fretting now.' Liam took my arm and I felt an almost childish need to give myself up to him, supported by his adult strength as he gently wiped my tears. 'Hush, sweet girl. Try to be brave, for your mother's sake.' I met his kind, compassionate eyes and nodded.

'See, Karenza. A son at last!' Mama lay back against the pillows, her hair drenched against her face. I could see the relief flood through her. She took the baby in her arms and traced his features with a loving finger. I forced myself to follow her gaze. He had wisps of light-coloured hair. His tiny, pebble of a nose reminded me of my mother's as did the shape of his gently waving fingers.

'Oh, Karenza!' Mama looked up at me with an expression of such joy that I felt sucked under by it. 'Where's Papa?'

For the first time I remembered and looked quickly across at Liam. If my stepfather were to walk in now how would I be able to stay in the same room with the monster who, with such pitiless pleasure, had killed the two people I loved so dearly?

Liam said, 'He's away, dear lady. Lie back now and rest yourself. Your fine fellow here is tired too.' He picked up the child with tender hands and passed him to Sorcha. She held the little one with the confidence of a girl who has had many younger brothers and sisters, rocking him gently.

She gave me a smile. 'Is it not a good day?'

'Aye,' I said, thinking that surely I had been having a nightmare. 'A good day.'

★　★　★

When Sir Julius did not return they sent a search party to look for him. It was quite by chance that one of the jewel-encrusted gauntlets he so favoured should be found half embedded in the morass next to the path between Otters Lough and Kilcreggan. A few yards further on, plastered by mud and trembling with cold and exhaustion, Sir Julius's hunter, Lisburn, had managed to drag himself out of the bog. One of the men led him home, wrapped him in sacking for warmth and fed him a hot mash. Others began to comb the area. It did not take them long to locate my stepfather's body, just beneath the surface of the mud.

When she heard the news, Mama showed a suitably wifely distress but then she is naturally tender and would weep if a sparrow fell outside her window. For me there was only a cold sense of satisfaction. At last, some sort of justice had been done.

'Why? Why?' Mama asked. 'He waited so long for a son and now he will never see him.'

'I don't know, Mama.' Secretly I was doubly glad, not only because Sir Julius deserved his fate, but now the child would not be contaminated by his father's presence.

'What will you call him?' I asked to distract her, looking at my baby brother as he lay across her shoulder, replete, after suckling. She had refused the suggestion of a wet nurse. 'Richard,' she said immediately. 'Richard James.'

I smiled my approval. The baby would give her a new focus in life. Now that she did not have to answer to her husband, already it seemed that she was growing in stature.

The next day, Sir Julius and Clarissa were buried together in the private graveyard next to the chapel at Kilcreggan. Standing in the cemetery, I watched as their coffins were lowered into the vault. They deserved each other. Mama wept copiously as the minister extolled the virtues of the master of the house. I guess he was paid to lie in this way. I swallowed my malice and drew some small comfort in the victory of still being alive. When the ceremony was over, Mama busied herself in planning a suitable memorial.

It was James Delany who arranged for the burial of his life-long friend, Orla Kilbryde, and the young man whom many still believed to be his son. I did not attend the funeral. I could have gone, but to do so would mean admitting to the reality of my brother, to the power of his smile, the music of his voice, the longing he had awakened in me. Risk that, come face to face with his death and I would surely lose the fragile hold I still had on my life. Meanwhile, grief settled upon me like winter, freezing my tears, enveloping me in a sheet of ice that denied me the comfort of light and warmth. I could not feel anything. In some ways it was almost as if Riari had never existed and that the entire episode since my arrival at Kilcreggan had been a dream. As the days passed, I went through the motions of playing music, of riding Shamrock around the estate, picking bunches of newly blossomed spring flowers, floating on the surface of my existence. If I thought anything it was to hope that life might go on like this forever.

Meanwhile, Mama and the baby flour-ished. Sir Julius had had the foresight to write into his Will that in the event of his leaving a legitimate son, then the child should take precedence over all other claimants to the estate. Mr Toby Burlington, Sir Julius's lawyer, came from Dublin to read the Will. For me there was nothing. The generous arrangements he had made for Clarissa would be absorbed back into the estate.

As he finished the reading, Mr Burlington declared himself content that Mama should be the child's guardian until he came of age. Watching him in his golden wig, I remembered that day in Dublin when he had counselled caution as my brother chained himself to the railings outside, warning his client against rash acts of folly. I was suddenly certain that he, too, had not liked my stepfather. I felt a tiny glow of triumph.

With a third of the estate as her widow's portion and the rest in her trust until Richard James attained his twenty-first birthday, Mama was suddenly both rich and powerful. When the business was concluded she requested that all her affairs should be transferred from her husband's lawyer into the hands of Mr James Delany. I smiled at her transparency. In that way she would have many opportunities to see him. I guessed that whatever his feelings for Mama, the prospect of such a lucrative business would make him an attentive lawyer and with this, Mama could weave whatever fantasies she chose into their professional relationship.

After the funerals, Liam returned to Dublin. He came to see us before his departure, bringing flowers for Mama and a rocking horse for the baby, hiding his embarrassment with a smile. 'A little premature I know, but one day he will be big enough to ride it.'

'It is lovely.' I looked at the fine carving, the tooled leather of the tiny saddle and bridle.

Liam nodded. 'It was mine as a child. I have no use for it now.'

'Will you not one day have children of your own?' I remembered the girl at the concert.

He shook his head. 'I doubt a woman would choose to share me with the poor of Dublin.'

'Nonsense.' For the first time since the tragedies I found myself thinking of someone other than myself. Without needing to think about it I knew that Liam had enough love to give to many people. I said, 'I am sure that there are dozens of women who would be proud to share your life.'

He looked unconvinced, merely saying, 'Then, of course, it also needs to be someone with whom I, too, would wish to share my life.'

We were both silent, looking from the window across the newly awakening valley. My own life was still trapped in its winter chill but the first thaw was beginning to take place. Outside, nature was weaving her eternal pattern of spring across the landscape.

Liam broke into my reverie. 'Karenza, why do you not come back to the city? In staying here you are condemning yourself to loneliness and isolation. I feel that for some reason you are blaming yourself. You cannot hide away for ever.' I was struck by his perception, his words echoing the very feelings that I could not voice.

'Perhaps, some day. It is up to Mama.'

With a rueful grin he took his leave, holding my hands in his, instilling some unfamiliar warmth into my emptiness. 'Goodbye my dear. Do not forget your friends.'

I did not reply but a tinge of sadness threatened my security when he had gone.

As the weeks passed I continued my daily round, holding always on to the knot beneath my ribs that tied my emotions firmly inside. All the time the thought nagged that just three miles away lay the deserted, ruined farmhouse where my brother and his mother had passed their days. Try as I might to deny it, I had left my heart there. Without it I could not function. It was no good hiding from the truth. One day I would need to go there, to face the emptiness and claim it back. Every day Otters Lough beckoned to me and yet I was afraid.

I don't know at exactly what point things changed. As I was riding alone one warm spring afternoon I found myself taking the path that led to the head of the valley. My heart began to pound but I could not turn back. As I drew near I felt almost blinded by my turmoil but still I rode on into the deserted farmyard. In a daze I slid from Shamrock's back, not bothering to tie him up. Ahead of me the shell of the farmhouse beckoned to me from its poor, blackened windows.

Not only was there no human within the four, partly disintegrating walls, but the very animals, the smallest birds seemed to have fled the devastation. As I gazed around I knew there was nothing there.

'Riari, where are you?' I wandered about, forcing myself to go inside where the ravaged timbers flaked and twisted in their last agony. I stood very still, listening, but there was nothing, no echoes from the past, no whispering souls calling to me. Somewhere I had lost my brother. If I was ever to find him again, it would not be here.

Going back outside I wandered through

the arch towards the stables. With shock I saw a horse tied up in the yard. Quickly I gazed down into the orchard behind the house. There, standing beside two solitary graves, was James Delany.

I didn't know what to do. I could not bear to share my solitude with him and I dare not intrude upon his privacy. As I watched he bowed his head in the direction of the graves and turned back towards the house. In that moment he saw me.

'Karenza!'

My eyes were transfixed on the two simple mounds of earth out there in the orchard. He was there. Riari was there, beneath the soil, gone from me forever. I began to cry. A great tidal wave of hurt burst from me, my sobbing so raw that I could hardly breathe.

'There, my dear girl. There now.'

James enclosed me in his arms, rocking me, uttering fatherly words of comfort. When at last the pain began to recede I forced myself to look at him. His eyes too were wet with crying.

'I loved her,' he said simply. 'All my life I loved her.'

I nodded. From somewhere I found the strength to ask, 'And Riari, could he have been your son?'

The second it took him to answer seemed

to last forever. What if he told me that what Mama had claimed was true? What if Riari and I had not after all been related by ties of blood but had been free to marry, to have a life together? How would I bear his loss?

'No. Orla never loved me.'

'She loved my father?'

'She did. There was no one else for her.'

I nodded my head. I said, 'I loved him. I was in love with my brother.'

'I know.' He squeezed my shoulder, pressing me against him again. 'It's over now. Let him go.'

I was too exhausted to argue. As we rode back along the track my inward-looking thoughts were disturbed by a sound to our left. Peering into the bushes that coated the upper reaches of the valley I saw a movement, gentle, silent, hardly more than a shadow. I reined Shamrock in and waited. Beside me, James frowned, searching the bushes.

'Look!'

I followed the direction of his pointing finger and suddenly from the gap between the bushes, a stag emerged. I could not take my eyes from his pale polished coat, almost ashen in the afternoon sun. A white deer!

I caught my breath. Had I not led Clarissa to look for non-existent white deer? Could this beautiful creature that regarded me with

316

round dark eyes, be real — or was it something beyond nature — the essence of the man I had loved so forlornly? Moments later a second animal, a hind stepped timidly into the sunlight.

I looked at James and saw the pleasure in his eyes. 'Are they real?' I whispered. As Shamrock began to paw the ground the stag snorted, then swinging away it fled into the distance, the hind following close on his heels. In my heart, a profound sense of joy took hold. I was in no doubt that I had just said goodbye to my brother.

In silence James and I rode on. At the entrance to the estate we parted company. We both needed time to absorb what we had seen.

When I got home, I said to Mama, 'Who decides what happens to the land in the valley?'

She raised a questioning eyebrow. 'Why, I do, I suppose. Why do you ask?'

I looked away. 'Then will you command that no deer is to be killed there?'

'If you wish, dear?' She waited for an explanation but I had none to give.

As we sipped hot chocolate I felt a strange sense of peace. I had seen my brother. I knew it. Knowing that he was out there filled me with peace. As long as the deer remained, so would his spirit.

As I finished my chocolate I thought, now that Orla and Clarissa are dead, there is nobody left to guard Riari's memory. In a strange way he has become mine in a way he had never been before. I who had loved him, but could never have possessed him here on earth, was now the sole keeper of his place in this life. The knowledge brought with it its own comfort.

* * *

Word reached us that an epidemic of fever was rampaging through the squalid jumble of habitations around Oxmantown on the borders of Dublin. The lying-in hospital was nearing completion so that Liam's services were needed twice over. I felt suddenly ill at ease. Surely with so much illness he must be in danger? A physician of all people would be in peril from the very diseases he sought to cure. It was a shocking realization. With mixed feelings I knew that I was vulnerable again to the harm that might befall the living.

A few days later James Delany came to visit us.

'Have you decided what you intend to do?' he asked Mama. 'If you will be staying here then the house in Dublin needs to be closed up.'

'Shall we return to Dublin?' Mama looked to me for my opinion. I had no thoughts on the matter. Until this moment it had not mattered greatly where we were.

'Is that what you would like?' I countered. Inside I felt the merest stirring of interest.

She considered my question. 'Perhaps we should go back. There are so many interesting things happening in Dublin.'

I was fascinated by the change in her. Here was a woman beginning to be aware of her own needs, of the interest she would arouse as a wealthy widow. Besides, James Delany spent most of his time there.

'What of you, Karenza? Perhaps it is time that you started to plan your future.' James looked kindly at me.

'Perhaps it is.'

For no reason in particular, he said, 'Liam is planning another fund raising concert for the hospital next month.'

'Is he?'

'He is.'

He raised an eyebrow the merest fraction and I had the feeling that I was giving myself up to the fates.

★ ★ ★

319

Six months later I married Liam Delany. Our courtship was brief and glorious and before long I found myself fully occupied in helping to raise money for the new hospital. Apart from the pleasure of the all too brief times spent in Liam's company there was barely a moment to think of anything outside of Dublin and the need to help the poor.

When Liam asked Mama for permission to marry me she expressed delight, but then her brow creased. 'I fear there will be some difficulty over religion. Is not Liam a Catholic, whereas you have been firmly raised within the bounds of the Church of England. I don't see how . . . '

For the first time in a long while I thought about Riari. His voice came back to me like half-forgotten music in my ear. Once he had said, 'I will do anything, even swear allegiance to that fat king of yours if it means having what I want.'

In that moment I had no doubts at all about what I wanted. Aloud, I said, 'Mama, I am going to be a doctor's wife. God isn't going to worry what path I choose as long as I am doing something worthwhile.'

'Well, if you think it will be all right.'

'I know it will.'

At the prospect of my new life, a peace I had not known since childhood settled upon me. I thought to myself, if my father could change his religion to marry the woman he loved then surely his daughter can do the same? In that moment I knew that I had all the blessing I could need, my father's, Orla's — and the tender, affectionate approval of Riari, my brother.

THE END

We do hope that you have enjoyed reading
this large print book.

Did you know that all of our titles
are available for purchase?

We publish a wide range of high quality
large print books including:
Romances, Mysteries, Classics
General Fiction
Non Fiction and Westerns

Special interest titles available in
large print are:
The Little Oxford Dictionary
Music Book
Song Book
Hymn Book
Service Book

Also available from us courtesy of Oxford
University Press:
Young Readers' Dictionary
(large print edition)
Young Readers' Thesaurus
(large print edition)

For further information or a free
brochure, please contact us at:
Ulverscroft Large Print Books Ltd.,
The Green, Bradgate Road, Anstey,
Leicester, LE7 7FU, England.
Tel: **(00 44) 0116 236 4325**
Fax: **(00 44) 0116 234 0205**

DEAD FISH

Ruth Carrington

Dr Geoffrey Quinn arrives home to find his children missing, the charred remains of his wife's body in the boiler and Chief Superintendent Manning waiting to arrest him for her murder. Alison Hope, attractive and determined, is briefed to defend him. Quinn claims he is innocent, but Alison is not so sure. The background becomes increasingly murky as she penetrates a wealthy and ruthless circle who cannot risk their secrets — sexual perversion, drugs, blackmail, illegal arms dealing and major fraud — coming to light. Can Alison unravel the mystery in time to save Quinn?

MY FATHER'S HOUSE

Kathleen Conlon

'Your father has another woman'. Nine-year-old Anna Blake is only mildly surprised when a schoolfriend lets drop this piece of information. And when her father finally leaves home to live with Olivia in Hampstead, that place becomes, for Anna, the epitome of sinful glamour. But Hampstead, though welcoming, is not home. So Anna, now in her teens, sets out to find a place where she can really belong. At first she thinks love may be the answer, and certainly Jonathon — and Raymond — and Jake, have a devastating effect on her life. But can anyone really supply what she needs?

GHOSTLY MURDERS

P. C. Doherty

When Chaucer's Canterbury pilgrims pass a deserted village, the sight of its decaying church provokes the poor Priest to tears. When they take shelter, he tells a tale of ancient evil, greed, devilish murder and chilling hauntings . . . There was once a young man, Philip Trumpington, who was appointed parish priest of a pleasant village with an old church, built many centuries earlier. However, Philip soon discovers that the church and presbytery are haunted. A great and ancient evil pervades, which must be brought into the light, resolved and reparation made. But the price is great . . .

BLOODTIDE

Bill Knox

When the Fishery Protection cruiser MARLIN was ordered to the Port Ard area off the north-west Scottish coast, Chief Officer Webb Carrick soon discovered that an old shipmate of Captain Shannon had been killed in a strange accident before they arrived. A drowned frogman, a reticent Russian officer and a dare-devil young fisherman were only a few of the ingredients to come together as Carrick tried to discover the truth. The key to it all was as deadly as it was unexpected.

WISE VIRGIN

Manda Mcgrath

Sisters Jean and Ailsa Leslie live on a small farm in the Scottish Grampians. Andrew Esplin, the local blacksmith, keeps a brotherly eye on the girls, loving Ailsa, the younger sister, from afar. Ailsa is in love with Stewart Morrison, who is working in Greenock. Jean is engaged to Alan Drummond, who has gone to Australia, intending to send for her when his prospects are good. But Jean shocks everyone when she elopes with Dunton from the big house . . .

BEYOND THE NURSERY WINDOW

Ruth Plant

Ruth Plant tells of her youth in a country vicarage in Staffordshire early in this century, a story she began in her earlier book NANNY AND I. Together with the occasional dip back into childhood memories of a nursery kingdom where Nanny reigned supreme, she ventures forth into a world of schooldays and visits to relatives, the exciting world of London and the theatre, the wonders of Bath and the beauties of the Lake District. She travels to Oberammergau, and sees Hitler on a visit there. On the threshold of life the future seems bright and war far away.